P9-DYY-098

"Don't touch me."

"Is there anything wrong with that? Lynn, I want us to be that close."

"Don't push me." She hated what she'd just said, and yet she had to. "I've been on my own for so long. Changing what I am isn't easy."

"I've been alone a long time, too," Gabe whispered, "but I'm willing to let that change."

Lynn turned back toward him. She refused to let last night dominate her. "We're different people. We come from different backgrounds."

"That's a problem only if you let it be."

The thought surfaced while she was in the shower. There was something she had to do for herself. And for Gabe. He wanted them to be more than they now were. She didn't know if that was possible, but there was one step she could take....

ABOUT THE AUTHOR

Vella Munn claims she has only one pseudonym—Mom. Originally from California, she now resides in Oregon with her husband and two sons. Before turning to writing full-time, Vella penned more than fifty ariticles and a nonfictional book. She has also worked as a reporter and a social worker.

Books by Vella Munn

HARLEQUIN AMERICAN ROMANCE
42–SUMMER SEASON
72–RIVER RAPTURE
96–THE HEART'S REWARD
115–WANDERLUST

HARLEQUIN INTRIGUE
6–TOUCH A WILD HEART

These books may be available at your local bookseller.

Don't miss any of our special offers. Write to us at the following address for information on our newest releases.

Harlequin Reader Service
901 Fuhrmann Blvd., P.O. Box 1397, Buffalo, NY 14240
Canadian address: P.O. Box 2800, Postal Station A,
5170 Yonge St., Willowdale, Ont. M2N 6J3

Black Magic
VELLA MUNN

Harlequin Books

TORONTO • NEW YORK • LONDON
AMSTERDAM • PARIS • SYDNEY • HAMBURG
STOCKHOLM • ATHENS • TOKYO • MILAN

Published August 1986

First printing June 1986

ISBN 0-373-16164-6

Chapter One

Lynn Tresca's Mazda came within a half inch of scraping bottom as she eased off the Denver city street and onto the construction site. There was a trailer bearing the name Updike Contracting, trucks weighted down with pipes and lumber and other construction materials, and stakes with ribbons tied to them sticking up at odd angles, giving credit to what she'd heard about a shopping center opening here in a little over a year. But Lynn hadn't come here for a tour of the acreage.

She was here because some kid named Kirt had been found on the site and the contractor wanted him hauled away.

Well, Lynn thought as she rolled up her windows against the dust billowing over from a massive earth mover, that's the way Friday afternoons usually went. The standing joke in the office was that if a juvenile officer wanted to be tied up for the weekend, all he or she had to do was answer the phone after 4:00 P.M. Unfortunately, Lynn had drawn the short straw fifteen minutes ago.

Lynn reached for a pair of tennis shoes and exchanged high-heeled sandals for comfortable walking shoes. After a year of working for the Boulder County juvenile department, she knew enough to be prepared for anything.

Her tan slacks would be ready for the washing machine the minute after she got out of her car, but that wouldn't be a first.

As she was looking around for someone who looked as if he knew what he was doing, her eyes again lit on the contractor's trailer. Updike Construction. There had to be more than one Updike in the county. Surely this one wouldn't be related to Judge Updike. That was more than she could handle today, or any other day.

She was stepping through packed gravel to the trailer when someone standing by a massive truck piled with long iron bars waved at her. Lynn changed direction, stepping gingerly, because small pieces of gravel were already working their way into her shoes. She nodded at the man with a dirty T-shirt pulled over his impressive belly but didn't try to match her voice against the roar and whine of machinery.

"You with the police?" the big man asked once she was close enough to be yelled at. "I told the boss he should have the kid arrested."

That sounds like an Updike, Lynn thought. She quickly buried the thought. She didn't know how the man could think that a five-foot-two-inch woman in a nylon blouse that gave away her slight build was a policewoman. "Are you the one who called?" she asked, careful not to get close enough to test the effectiveness of the man's deodorant.

"Not me. The boss. I sat on the kid when he tried to run. He's in the trailer now. Don't you have handcuffs?"

Lynn stifled a laugh. The man had definitely been watching too much TV. "If we need the police, we'll call them. Right now I want to find out what's going on."

"What's going on is some damn kid's been sneaking around the equipment. Stealing tools for all we know.

Someone's always coming here and taking off with things. The boss's getting damn tired of it.''

Lynn couldn't blame the boss for that. She'd been conned by enough kids to know what it felt like to be taken. But if they were dealing with a juvenile, different rules were in effect. They couldn't simply take this Kirt kid and throw him in jail.

"They're in the trailer?" Lynn asked.

"The kid is. We locked him in there. Gabe's got some pipes he has to send back. Always happens on a Friday. If a delivery gets screwed up, it always happens on Friday."

At least we have one thing in common, Lynn thought as she took off in the direction the man indicated. From what she could make out through the dust, there were four or five men standing around a flatbed truck loaded with pipe. She winced when the men stopped talking to turn and look at her. Obviously women in outfits that belonged in offices were a rarity out here. *Well, don't blame me,* Lynn thought. *I was supposed to spend the day in counseling sessions.*

"Cast iron," the one man wearing something other than a T-shirt said. "It's right here in the invoice. Cast iron. I'd like to know what idiot thought he could get away with brass. Take it back." He turned toward Lynn. "What do you want?"

This was the boss. Lynn could reach out and touch that simple fact. "Don't yell at me, mister," she warned the bearded man with hands that looked big enough to unload the pipes single-handed. "I don't have anything to do with your delivery problems."

"If you're not part of the solution, then you're part of the problem," the man pointed out. "Look, if you're with the paper—"

"I'm not here to take pictures. Do I look like I'm here to take pictures?" The decision whether to laugh or swear at the man was a toss-up. "I'm from the juvenile department."

The man uttered a curse and rammed a massive fist against his forehead. "You know karate? That's what it's going to take to get that kid out of here. Why the hell didn't they send a man?"

Lynn was ready for the question. "Because they were down to scraping the bottom of the barrel. Will you lighten up on the criticism and tell me what's going on?"

"What's going on is I'm going to be lucky if I'm out of here by midnight, and then they send—you."

"You want I should call a SWAT team?" Lynn challenged. It seemed as if everyone at the construction site was arrest-happy. "I repeat, what's going on?" Lynn waited for anger to roll through her, but the emotion didn't come.

"You got me, lady." For the first time, Lynn caught the glimpse of something that might be called a softening around the man's mouth. "He'd hot-wired the rig and was trying to get it out of four-wheel drive. I haul him out of the truck, and he takes off running like a scared rabbit. It takes three of us to corner him and throw him in the trailer. Then I figure I don't want the cops here, since the kid looks pretty scared. I called you people because that's the only thing I could think of. Now you know as much as I do." The man took a deep breath, as if the explanation constituted the most words he'd strung together in a long time.

"I'd like to talk to him." Lynn was still aware that the other men were watching her, but she no longer cared what they might be thinking. The man she was talking to had a way of dominating a conversation, even the very air around him. He wasn't a tall man, probably a little under six feet, but he was built like someone who had physically wrestled his way to ownership of his own business.

"Good luck," he said. "What I got from him wasn't the most civilized conversation I've had this week. I suppose you'd like me to go with you."

Lynn debated. She didn't need a bodyguard, but she was curious about how the man would handle himself in a situation that didn't call for brawn. "It's up to you. I'll need a key to the trailer, won't I?"

The man dug into the pocket of badly faded skintight jeans and pulled out a key. He started to hand it to her but stopped with his hand in midmovement.

"Hold on a second. I better come along with you."

Lynn shrugged. She should be bent out of shape by that, but getting out of here and salvaging what was left of Friday was more important than an argument about women being good for more than throwing what was left of his jeans into the washer. She stepped back while the man glanced at the stack of papers trapped in his left hand. She was close enough to recognize them as order forms, but as happened when she wasn't concentrating, the numbers after the dollar sign in the columns made little sense. After a couple of seconds she stopped staring and let her eyes roam over her surroundings.

Now that the newness of the construction site was starting to wear off, she saw that the acreage was swarming with men. They were operating equipment, spreading granite, stacking supplies and taking measurements with instruments on tripods, all of which involved a million details she couldn't pretend to understand.

And this Gabe Updike was responsible for everything that was taking place. It wasn't bad for a man who probably wasn't much over thirty, although with a dark brown beard running from one ear to the other, his age was hard to pin down.

"You ready?"

Lynn blinked but gave no other indication that her mind had been wandering. "Anytime. How did you find out the boy's name? It doesn't sound as if he was interested in carrying on a conversation."

"He wasn't." Gabe actually grinned this time. One front tooth was chipped. "What words did take place between us weren't of the conversational variety. It says Kirt on the back of his shirt."

"So either that's his name or he stole the shirt, too."

Gabe's grin widened. "I didn't think of that. Why don't we go meet this character. You know—" Gabe paused as if thinking over what he was about to say "—I have to hand it to him. I didn't know how to hot-wire at his age."

"A budding mechanic. You never know when you're going to need a skill like that." Gabe's comment made Lynn think she might get out of here without first hearing a lecture about today's generation of teenagers.

"I'm still surprised you didn't call the police," she said. "Our department basically deals with kids on probation."

"Yeah. I figured I wasn't doing it by the book, but maybe it'll turn out for the best."

Gabe unlocked the door to the compact trailer and quickly stepped inside. Lynn followed behind him, gritting her teeth against the single high step leading into the trailer and forced her 112 pounds up and in. Despite the late October day it was hot and sticky inside. Smells that were a mix of sweat, paint, glue, turpentine and tar closed around her. How anyone could stay inside for longer than a minute was a mystery. If Kirt wasn't unconscious from the smell, he was probably so sick that he wouldn't present much of a problem.

A tall kid with dangling arms and long legs that would fit his large frame once he'd put on about thirty more pounds was standing in the middle of the cluttered trailer interior

His fingers were knotted into fists, his legs spread defiantly. What Lynn zeroed in on was that his eyes darted around instead of focusing on either her or Gabe.

Lynn stepped forward and took control of the situation. Even if she knew how such things were done, this wasn't the time to play to the male ego. She thought of telling the boy that he was in a heap of trouble, but that sounded a little too corny. "You want to explain what you're doing here?" she asked conversationally. From experience that went deeper, more personal than her time on the job, she never once took her eyes off the boy's face.

"What the hell do you care?" Kirt shot back. His words would have made more of an impact if his voice hadn't turned soprano at the end.

Lynn ignored the warning growl from Gabe. "You're right. I don't care," she said in a voice with all emotion stripped from it. "I'm not crazy about being called out here this afternoon. It's been a long week, and all I'm interested in doing is going home. Look, why don't you do both of us a favor and apologize to the man."

"What for?" Kirt squeaked again.

Lynn shrugged. The conversation wasn't the most stimulating she'd had this week, but since she was stuck here, she might as well make the most of it. "It seems like the thing to do," she pointed out. "Mr. Updike admits that you did a pretty good job of starting his truck despite not having keys. However, since that happens to be his truck, it does present a problem."

"Yeah?" Kirt's eyes flashed toward the bearded man and then back again. "What kind of problem?"

"Attempted robbery. Trespassing. Maybe assault. What's your name?"

"I don't have to tell you nothing."

"Anything. You don't have to tell me anything." Lynn's mouth twitched. "You're right. You don't have to. But you do have to go with me, and in case you don't know where we're going, I'll tell you. Someone as smart as you must know what juve is."

"I'm not going nowhere with you."

Lynn sighed. "The correct way to say that is, 'I'm not going anywhere with you.' But don't bother memorizing that, because it isn't true. You do have to go with me, because I represent authority."

"You can't make me." Kirt unclinched and clinched his fingers but didn't move.

Lynn pointed to a phone in the trailer. "Do you want to take a guess at how long it would take the police to show up? Of course, if I do have to call them, we can add a couple more charges to what a judge is going to be looking at. Let me give you a piece of advice. The youth center is not where you want to go."

"The center? Hey! I haven't been in no trouble before."

Again, Lynn sighed her practiced sigh. "Repeat after me. 'I haven't been in any trouble before.' Don't they teach you anything in school?" She shook her head at what she was saying. "I'm asking you to make a decision. Do you want to come with me like a civilized human being and save yourself a lot of trouble, or shall we try for all the marbles?"

When Kirt unwrapped his fingers this time, they stayed loose. His eyes were still chasing an errant pattern around his surroundings. "Why do I have to see a judge?" he asked. "I didn't hurt anything."

For the first time, the contractor entered the conversation. "You don't want to have to face a judge. Believe me, that's the last thing you want to do. Listen to the lady. She's trying to give you a way out."

Lynn wondered at Gabe Updike's comment about facing a judge, but she had to concentrate on the teenager in the room. "I can be on your side, Kirt, or I can make you wish I were dead. Which is it going to be?"

The boy made a stab at straightening his dirty, torn shirt. "You aren't going to call my folks, are you? I mean, my dad's got a terrible temper. He'll beat me if he finds out." Kirt glanced at Lynn and then looked away quickly. "I can't let my dad find out."

Lynn felt Gabe's eyes on her, but she was more concerned with the message she was getting from Kirt. She had to give Kirt credit for thinking on his feet, but it wasn't washing. "Bull."

"Bull?" Once again, Kirt tried to make eye contact and failed.

"You heard me." Lynn could take anger, hostility, even hate from the kids she came in contact with. What she wouldn't accept was a lie. "Your father doesn't use you for a punching bag, and we both know it. Come on, Kirt. What did you want with the truck?"

"What?"

"I said—" Lynn sighed impatiently "—what did you want with the truck?"

"I don't know." Kirt shrugged. "Honest. I don't know."

"I believe that." Lynn allowed herself a faint laugh as she exchanged glances with the contractor. "It just seemed to be the thing to do at the time. That's what you're saying, isn't it?"

"Yeah. I guess."

"That's stupid." Lynn took a step forward. "That is really stupid. Why the hell didn't you think? Forget it." She waved her hand in Kirt's direction. "Well? What are we going to do with you?"

"We could chalk the whole thing up to experience," Gabe offered.

Lynn turned toward him. "You think so?" she asked, aware that Gabe was standing closer to Kirt than he was to her. Maybe the man was thinking about protecting her.

"He didn't hurt anything."

Without being obvious about it, Lynn kept her eye on Kirt. It saddened but didn't surprise her to see the calculating look reach the boy's face. She waited, wondering if Kirt would tip his hand. "I didn't mean any harm, mister," Kirt said. "I just, well, I'm not going to be old enough for a license for another year, and even then it won't do any good. My folks don't have the money to buy me wheels."

"You could get a job," Lynn pointed out, but she didn't think Kirt was listening.

"Is there a standard procedure for this?" Gabe asked. "If I don't press charges, they can't do anything to him, can they?"

"Why wouldn't you want to press charges?" Lynn asked. She didn't want to have to say what was coming next. The contractor seemed to be a man with his antenna tuned to the emotions of others. But part of her job was to make sure kids teetering on the brink of trouble didn't tumble in the wrong direction. "He trespassed on posted property. If you hadn't come along, you might have found your truck in a ditch or wrapped around a tree somewhere. If he were an adult, you wouldn't be so quick to turn the other way, would you? The cops would be here, not me."

"That's just the point." Any hint that they were on the same wavelength was wiped from Gabe's voice. "We're talking about a kid."

"We're talking about the law being broken."

"Okay, okay," Gabe said impatiently. "So what happens now?"

Lynn quickly sifted through her options. She could, if she insisted on being hard-nosed, haul Kirt off to juve, where he'd spend the night and probably the next day locked alone in a small room, thinking that the world had turned against him. But Lynn had a feeling that being locked up wasn't what Kirt needed. She knew that too much time spent trapped with one's own thoughts could be flirting with insanity.

Probation was the easiest way of keeping an eye on the long-limbed fifteen-year-old until he'd been forced to face the ramifications of his impulsive act. "Let's go have a talk with your folks, Kirt," she said in a stern tone she'd practiced to the point of perfection.

Although Lynn was concentrating on Kirt's reaction, she didn't miss the tightening of Gabe's facial muscles. "What about his father?" the contractor asked. "I can't believe he made up that business about a temper."

Lynn sighed but didn't make the mistake of telling Gabe that he didn't know what he was talking about. "What about it, Kirt?" Lynn challenged. "That business about your father? He doesn't even kick the family dog, does he?"

Kirt dropped his eyes. "My dad lives in Colorado Springs. I won't see him for another three weeks."

Gabe stared at Lynn. "How did you know that?"

"I didn't," Lynn admitted. "I mean, I don't know where his father lives. But I've been burned enough times that I'm starting to catch on. Come on, Kirt. Let's go see your mother."

A docile teenager folded his long legs into the front seat of the Mazda and stared silently out the now-dust-caked window. Lynn got behind the wheel, started the car and ran the windshield wipers until she could at least see where she was going. She was reaching for the shift when Gabe leaned

in the open window and touched her lightly on the left
shoulder.

"How did you know?"

How did I know what? Lynn thought about asking, but
for a stretch of time that had no true definition, she concentrated on nothing except that massive hand on her
shoulder. His hands had fascinated her from the moment
she met him. There was more to them than calluses and
short nails and broad knuckles. "I'm sorry," Lynn said
somewhat lamely. "What are you talking about?"

"How did you know he was lying about his father?" The
big hand hadn't left her shoulder.

Lynn swallowed and looked up into eyes pulled into slits
against the late-afternoon sun. "No eye contact," she
whispered. "He didn't look me in the eye."

"And that's how you knew he was lying?"

"Mr. Updike, I've been taught by some of the best cons
in the business. I usually know when a kid isn't telling the
truth."

Gabe straightened up, the movement breaking the physical contact between them. "That would be important in
your business. Knowing when someone is trying to put
something by you, I mean."

"Unfortunately, yes. I'll be getting in touch with you if
he has to appear in front of the juvenile judge. Unfortunately, I'll have to write up a case report."

"Okay." Gabe nodded slowly. "This is a first for me. I
mean, sure, I've been ripped off before. It happens in this
business. But I've never caught a kid red-handed before."
Gabe paused. "You handled things better than I did." He
glanced over at the stony-faced teenager. "You didn't have
to sit on him."

Lynn laughed. "I've had to do that."

Gabe started to turn away as Lynn slid her Mazda into gear; then he turned back. "What's your name?"

"Lynn Tresca. Would you like my card?"

"Tresca? That sounds—are you sure we haven't met before?"

"I don't know."

"The name is familiar. I'm sure I've heard it before."

It took Lynn a moment to catch her breath. "Maybe. Well, look, I'd better let you get back to work."

"Thanks for nothing. I'd much rather—I hope you don't get saddled with too much overtime, Ms Tresca."

Lynn guided her car over the loose ground until she bounced onto the main road. Why she felt this panic every time she met someone who might make the connection with her past was an emotion she kept to herself. Gabe Updike wasn't that much older than she was. If he'd grown up in Denver, it was possible that their paths had once crossed.

It doesn't matter, Lynn told herself after getting Kirt's address. *I'll probably never see him again.* The thought caught and wouldn't let go.

"Hey," Kirt interrupted. "You just turned left. I told you right."

"Oh." Lynn looked out in confusion. She should know her way around the city with her eyes closed. As she pulled over, waited for traffic to pass and then got going in the right direction, she was grateful that the boy next to her didn't know that at one point she'd lived only a few blocks from here.

The need to concentrate on where she was driving left Lynn with no room to think about the man she'd left behind. Right now Kirt thought she was a savvy lady, for he hadn't been able to pull the wool over her eyes. She'd blow it if she made a wrong turn again.

Kirt's mother was home, which meant that Lynn was able to get the conversation over with and herself back on the road again in less than a half hour. From what Lynn was able to learn during the short conversation, the mother wasn't the one in control of the home situation. Kirt wasn't a rebel; he was simply a kid without direction. Because it was obvious that the mother wouldn't be putting more controls on her son's life, Lynn made the decision to set the wheels in motion that would place Kirt on probation.

However, that meant paperwork for her. Lynn was gritting her teeth as she drove back to the building that housed the county's juvenile department staff. She would like nothing better than to be able to dictate her report into a tape recorder instead of laboring over the tedious, for her, task of completing forms. However, adequate clerical help was an unfulfilled dream of the department.

Lynn used her key to let herself into the now-deserted office and quickly switched on enough lights to chase away the darkness, which felt like bars closing around her.

She hurried through her tasks, ignoring a couple of phone messages and a new case she'd been assigned. Taking time to read would mean spending more time alone in a deserted building. It was irrational to feel this way; she was too old to be scared of her shadow.

But the fear remained. It would probably always remain.

There was no way she could escape the memory of locked doors and darkness. Her only solution was to grab her belongings and bolt from the building before her emotions blew out of control.

Lynn breathed easier once she was back in her car and the radio was blaring a current rock hit. She hadn't turned on the radio while Kirt was in the car because she couldn't concentrate on that and finding his house at the same time, but now she felt relaxed enough to surrender to the hard sounds filling the car's interior. It wasn't that she particularly liked the sound, but it gave her something to think about.

At least it did until she drew a parallel between the grinding sounds of an instrument she couldn't identify and the sounds the earth-moving equipment made earlier.

Gabe Updike was such a part of the world he'd surrounded himself with that it was impossible to separate the one from the other. He might swear at a wrong delivery and have to fight the urge to crumple endless invoices, but he was part and parcel of his machinery, his men, even the dirt and dust and tar. Gabe Updike was born to construction; she'd seen that in his hands. She could no more picture him dressed in a suit and seated behind a desk than she could see herself sitting comfortably in a dark room. It was as if the man had found that rarity—his niche in life.

When she reached home, she was still thinking about the unexpected gentleness in those big hands. Lynn lived in an apartment complex surrounding an inner courtyard. Although she could admit that she lived here because she needed sounds and light around her, she seldom joined the casual groupings among the mostly single residents.

Lynn nodded at the man who lived in the apartment above hers, but she didn't stop to talk. He'd been trying to work his way into an invitation to her place since he moved in, but his talk of singles bars, swinging weekends and a credit-card life left her cold. Instead, Lynn hurried inside and locked the door behind her. Automatically, she reached for the light switch and put an end to the dark. Her next move was to turn on the TV but when the picture showed an evening game show, she headed toward the kitchen.

As she kicked off her shoes, Lynn glanced at the mail she'd brought in with her. Two bills, an ad from an auto-parts store and a postcard from her sister, who was in New

York for a conference that had something to do with the stock market. Lynn ran her free hand through the bangs that gave a feminine touch to her short haircut and studied the picture of the Statue of Liberty before turning it over to read Brandy's message.

"Having a ball. Lots of time to play tourist between workshops. Talked to the folks. They've bought a new car. Am thinking of dropping by to see them on my way home. Can you believe it? They've been in the same place for better than two years now. That's a record, isn't it?"

That Brandy knew that their parents had bought a new car, while Lynn didn't, was no surprise. Although she now considered Brandy her friend, Lynn seldom communicated with her two older brothers or her parents. Sometimes, when she was in a particularly reflective mood, Lynn acknowledged the pain that went with that relationship. But she couldn't change history. Lynn was the family's black sheep.

Lynn thought about dropping Brandy a note to tell her what she'd been up to but dismissed the thought as soon as it surfaced. Lynn could count on the fingers of one hand the number of letters she'd penned.

A half hour later, Lynn was sitting in front of the TV eating a dinner that resembled breakfast. The first time the phone rang, Lynn mistook it for a sound from the TV. The second time, she left her plate on the arm of her chair and hurried into the kitchen.

"Lynn Tresca?"

"Yes." If this was someone trying to sell her something—"

"It's Gabe Updike. I was going to call earlier, but I'm still at the site. I hope I haven't disturbed you."

"Is something wrong?" He had remembered her name.

"Other than a minor matter of a nonfunctioning fork-lift, nothing. I just was thinking—well, I wanted to make sure you got home all right."

That's nice. Very nice. "Yes," she said, careful to keep her tone light. "Kirt was a model passenger. He took it as a point in his favor that he knew how to hot-wire. He wondered if that might lead to some kind of job."

"You knew how to handle him. I thought we had a caged bear on our hands, but when you started talking to him, he turned into a teddy bear."

Lynn had the feeling Gabe was fishing for things to say, but she didn't mind. She liked the sound of his voice. "I'm going to ask to have him put on probation," she explained. It was rare that she revealed anything of what went on behind the scenes in juvenile work, but the deep tones coming from Gabe's voice made it easy for her to keep the conversation going. "I don't see much control coming from his mother."

"Why do you do it?"

"What?" Lynn didn't think she'd missed anything in the conversation, but she couldn't be sure.

"Why are you a juvenile officer?"

Lynn had been asked that before, but there wasn't an easy answer. "It beats being a contractor. I'm home, while you're still burning the midnight oil."

Gabe's chuckle seemed to eat up the distance between them. "Good answer. Well, I guess I'd better get back to work. I just wanted—I'm glad you're home."

"I'm glad you called." Lynn wrapped her free arm around her shoulder, hugging herself.

"Tresca..." Gabe spoke her name slowly. "I know I've heard it before."

I hope not. Oh, I hope not!

Chapter Two

Gabe Updike hung up the phone, but it was more than a minute before he forced his battered office chair into an upright position and rose to his feet. The trailer had been so gloomy a few minutes ago. Now, with her voice still clinging to his thoughts, the gray had gone out of his surroundings. She was probably laughing at him, if she wasn't mad because he'd implied that maybe she couldn't take care of herself. That wasn't the way men were supposed to talk to today's women. They were supposed to—what the hell was the right thing to do, anyway?

Lynn Tresca.

For the second time today the name tugged at him. It was a logical enough name for a slight woman with an almost boyish figure and soft, short light brown hair and big hazel eyes. And yet there was that intangible something about her that was out of the ordinary, that took her out of any mold he'd ever seen.

Someday he'd have to ask her for an honest answer to the question of why she did what she did for a living.

What was he thinking about? Gabe shut off the lights and prepared to lock the trailer that doubled as an office and storage shed. Now that there wasn't a kid trying to hot-wire his truck, he had no reason to get in touch with the woman again.

Gabe's leather work boots were silent on the packed gravel as he walked toward his dust-carpeted truck. A couple of temporary spotlights gave definition to the site, but the corners remained in the dark, giving Gabe a sense of having been dropped into a small island in the middle of an endless black ocean. A thought that bespoke of a touch of the philosopher broke through concerns over jumbled delivery orders and broken-down forklifts. This might have been a little like what Columbus and his men experienced when they set sail on an ocean that was supposed to end with a drop-off into hell.

Only the world surrounding Gabe Updike was a far cry from hell. This was his. What he'd fought for and was going to create with his strength and intelligence and instinct.

Then maybe the judge would admit a simple fact about his oldest son. Success came in many different forms, not just the ones his old man deemed worthy.

Sure he will, Gabe taunted as he hoisted himself into the truck. *Like hell he will.*

Gabe had given up trying to figure out why he was considered a failure. Oh, he knew it had to do with the judge's fixation on certain standards of power. Gabe didn't wear a white collar and tie. When he spoke, his words didn't wind up on the front page of the paper or in a legal stenographer's records. Because he quietly wrestled his living with his scarred hands, he couldn't, according to the judge, be considered a success.

He wasn't Brook Updike.

The thought of his younger brother brought a twitch to the corner of his mouth. Brook had been able to accomplish something Gabe couldn't. The kid, as Gabe insisted on calling a twenty-five year-old who threw for three thousand yards last year, completed 60.6 percent of his passes and could stand in a pocket longer than a sane man should, had won their father's respect despite the fact that Brook wore black mesh with white numbers on his body like some 1920s convict.

Gabe reached over to snap open his glove compartment. Inside was the envelope bearing a ticket to Sunday's game with the Broncos. Gabe hadn't been able to see Brook play yet this season, and nothing, by God, was going to keep him out of the stadium Sunday. He wouldn't have the chance to talk to Brook until after the game, but the kid had promised to drop by the house before the team plane left. Gabe was looking forward to seeing the kid with the centerfold body and Frankenstein knees.

As Gabe pulled into the driveway, which was long overdue for a layer of asphalt, he admitted that the best part of the weekend would be over once the judge stepped foot on his property. If the neighborhood had been zoned exclusively residential, Gabe would have been taken to court by his neighbors long ago. But fortunately for his line of work he was surrounded by a mixed bag of residents on his street that included a retired man who painted cars in his garage, a leftover from the hippie generation who collected scrap iron and three young male housemates who owned more cars than they could ever get running at one time.

But it wasn't the kind of place to which a man should bring a woman with a fragile body and strong eyes. Damn! He had to be punchy from lack of sleep to be thinking that way.

Gabe was ready for the hot breath on his legs as he stepped out of the truck. "Hey, stupid," he said conversationally. "It's me. The guy who feeds you."

Ninety-five pounds of short gray hair with an oversized head backed away from Gabe's legs. The rumbling growl ceased. In the five years Gabe had lived with Ranger, he'd never heard any other sound come from the dog's throat. "How's it going?" He leaned over to dig his fingers through the matt of fur to the soft flesh behind the dog's ear. "Scare off any Avon ladies today?"

Ranger padded silently beside Gabe as they made their way up the dark walk to the front door. Ranger was another reason why Gabe stayed where he was. The mutt, who reminded Gabe of a country-and-western song about a junkyard dog, was content to stay on the property, but any attempt to fence him or keep him inside the house turned Ranger into a frantic caged animal. Gabe needed Ranger to guard the thousands of dollars of equipment and building materials surrounding the house. Ranger needed his turf. It was as simple as that.

His old man hated Ranger. And the emotion was returned.

"You're a good judge of people," Gabe told the dog as Ranger devoured his dinner. "I hate to tell you, but you know who is going to be here this weekend? Brook, too. You remember Brook? I hope he takes a shower after the game. Otherwise he's going to smell worse than you do."

Later that evening Gabe showered and climbed into bed. He acknowledged the bone-deep feeling dragging him down and he rolled over on his stomach, more than ready to let go of the day. His last thought was of direct eyes and soft wavy hair styled by a towel and blow dryer. If she had time, maybe she'd like to go to the game with him. No. He only had one ticket. Besides, after saying hello, what would he talk to her about?

On Sunday morning Gabe spent an hour making a halfhearted attempt to turn the house from a bachelor's pad into something his mother would be able to bring a white wool suit into. When the clock said it was time to leave for

Mile High Stadium, he picked up a pile of newspapers to dump in a spare bedroom. A headline caught his eye and he stopped his hand.

There. He'd found a way to make contact with Lynn Tresca again.

"You be nice to Brook," he told Ranger. "The kid moves pretty good for a quarterback. He'll drop-kick you across the street."

Four hours later Gabe was pulling back into the driveway, his younger brother next to him. Brook was dominating the conversation with talk about contracts and free agents and some endorsements he was looking into. Gabe ran interference with Ranger, who found Brook fascinating to sniff but no challenge to control of his turf. "You've still got him," Brook observed. "Hasn't he bitten anyone yet?"

"He tried to take a hunk out of the judge a couple of times, but our old man doesn't get out here much. I wish you didn't have to leave tonight."

"Me, too." Brook accepted the beer his brother handed him and swallowed deeply. "God, that's fantastic. I took a couple of hits that are going to need to be anesthetized. Speaking of the judge, how long do you think it's going to take them to get rid of that couple they brought with them? The woman looked bored out of her mind."

"That happens to be the mayor and his wife. When a judge's son is quarterbacking a pro team, the man isn't going to bring just anyone to watch."

Brook lowered himself into a Naugahyde couch that was starting to crack along the seams. "Funny, isn't it," he said softly. "We used to be so in awe of him. I figured I'd never learn what he wanted out of us. Or what we'd have to do to get his approval. Now I'm the one with the silver spoon. You know, he even asks for my autograph."

Gabe pulled on his beer, his eyes on his brother. Brook looked as if he'd aged three years in the months since he'd seen him last, and yet there was an air of confidence in the way the kid held himself that couldn't be denied. Gabe used to wonder how someone could become a slave to a sport to the exclusion of everything else, but he couldn't argue the point that, for Brook, it had turned out to be a damn good investment. Even the judge was impressed. "Do you give it to him? Your autograph, I mean?"

"Yeah." Brook shrugged and then winced. He rubbed his shoulder. "I always wanted his approval, more than you did. Now that I've got it, I'm still feeding into his hands."

Gabe thought about that. Brook still might be "the kid," but he had damn good insight about the forces that shaped their family. Brook was the fair-haired son because he was a public figure, a national hero. The judge knew that Brook was carrying his own ticket in life. There were those endorsements, investments and business opportunities that would come his way once his knees gave out on him.

Brook, whether he wanted the role or not, was the son who had made it. Gabe? Gabe was the black sheep.

"Funny thing," Brook was saying. "All the time we were growing up, the judge kept pounding away about how he expected us to settle down, get married and join the country club. Now, although he won't come out and say it, he loves reading about the women in my life. You know, if I was really making it as much as the press says I do, I'd never have time to earn a living. What about you?" Brook lowered his beer. "You're making good money now. Isn't it about time you looked for someone?"

"Maybe." Gabe held on to the thought for a moment. "But what woman would put up with this?" He pointed toward a stack of oak paneling that he intended on putting up someday.

"The judge still after you about this place?" Brook asked as the sound of their father's car shattered the brothers' time together.

"Of course." Gabe rose to his feet. "I don't measure up." He glanced at his hands, which looked as old as Brook's knees. "No white collar."

LYNN SHOOK HER HEAD and rolled her eyes in Chuck Rubin's direction as the two were leaving their supervisor's office. She waited until they were back at their desks before speaking to her co-worker. "I thought it was another one of those plans that were never going to get off the drawing board," she admitted. "Who got the Chamber of Commerce to back this one?"

"My guess is some business thought it would make good PR for them."

"I hope it works," Lynn said. "I can't believe some of the companies that have signed up to hire our kids. I can just see Cat with her dangling earrings and miniskirts fitting in one of the dress shops. Most of our kids are functionally illiterate. What are they going to be able to do in an office?"

"We're about to find out. Didn't you see the article on it in the Sunday paper? It was pretty comprehensive."

Lynn shook her head. Even now she seldom read for pleasure, but this wasn't the time to remind Chuck of that. He wouldn't be aware of what had made a major impact on her life if he hadn't been worried about one of his own children's progress in school. Lynn had warned him not to let things slide. "Fight for him" was what she said. "He needs you on his side." Now Chuck was the one person in the office who knew of the years when it felt as if there were no one on her side.

Lynn had resigned herself to a morning of paperwork and was staring at a directive from the current juvenile-court

judge, her hands clamped over her ears so she could concentrate, when she realized that Chuck was trying to get her
to pick up the telephone.

Her hazy hello was answered by a greeting she recognized instantly. Lynn closed her eyes, losing herself in the
sound of a voice that had stayed with her all weekend.

"I asked to talk to you," Gabe was saying, "because—
well, because I thought you could answer my questions. I
saw that article about the work-placement program your
department is starting."

Lynn tried to explain that she probably knew no more
about it than Gabe did, but he didn't give her a chance. Instead, he launched into a discussion of the work he thought
teenagers could do on the construction site. Finally, Lynn
was able to break in.

"I think you should be talking to my supervisor," she said
reluctantly. "He's been involved in this a lot longer than I
have. I'll transfer you."

Only when Gabe was no longer on the line did she realize
that she felt hollow inside. She hung up the receiver and
stared blankly in Chuck's direction.

"Irate customer?" Chuck asked.

"No, no, a major building contractor interested in the
new program." She hugged the contractor's identity to herself. Lynn's mood lasted for another half hour. Because she
couldn't dismiss the vibration of Gabe's voice inside her, she
found it next to impossible to make sense out of what she
was trying to read; it didn't matter. A masculine tone hum-
ming its way through her senses was more important.

It wasn't until her supervisor called her into his office that
she was forced to deal with the reality of what seeing Gabe
Updike meant to her.

"I don't know how you made such a positive impression," William Speel said before she'd had time to sit down.

"But Mr. Updike said he wouldn't have thought to become involved in the work program if he hadn't admired the way you handled that situation on Friday."

"Luck," Lynn admitted. "Some of our kids, like Buck, would have mopped the floor with me."

"Be that as it may, Mr. Updike is willing to cooperate with whatever work experiences the agency feels our kids will benefit from. Updike Contracting is a major local employer. He has space for apprentices. I know manual-labor jobs aren't the best way to train teenagers to enter the work market, but some of our kids aren't capable of doing anything except manual labor. At least not unless we can get them back in school."

Lynn was aware of what William had left unsaid. His hope, like hers, was that the kids they placed with Updike Contracting would learn that they were in dead-end jobs. Unless they were willing to gamble on their backs lasting for the next forty years, they'd have to trade an immediate paycheck for an education. "Do you think Mr. Updike is aware of how we view this?" she asked.

"Indeed. In fact, he brought up that very point himself. You know—" William paused "—I'm surprised he isn't a lawyer. That's what his father wanted for him."

Lynn forgot to breathe. "His father?"

"Judge Updike. That's going to cause some problems, I'm afraid. The judge wasn't in favor of the work-experience program. He said we weren't in a position to adequately administer it or handle any legal problems. Fortunately—" William winked "—the good judge isn't hearing juvenile cases now."

Lynn barely heard what her supervisor was saying. Her mind had hung up on a simple fact. Gabe Updike's father was Judge Updike.

Like father, like son.

"Mr. Updike wants to work exclusively with you. He says he has faith in your judgment."

"Why me? I mean, I don't know that much about the program." Lynn swallowed. "Can't you work with him?"

"And get between a single woman and a man in a like condition? No way, Lynn. It so happens that my wife would love to see you married. She'd never forgive me if I hampered any promising relationship."

Lynn frowned but said nothing. She was aware of the matchmaking her supervisor's wife had been pushing but couldn't tell the woman that getting her life on track after years of feeling like the only one swimming upstream was all she felt she could handle now.

"I really don't think I can work with him, William," she tried again. "You know what my caseload looks like. When would I find the time?"

"You'll find the time. You have for everything else I've dumped on you. In fact—" the supervisor consulted a note on his desk "—Mr. Updike offered to buy you dinner in return for an in-depth discussion this evening. He's expecting you around seven at that new steak house near City park."

Lynn left without speaking. She couldn't turn down the dinner invitation without opening herself to questions, and much as she respected William, she couldn't open up to him the way she had with Chuck. The judge's position as a board member of the Department of Institutions ensured his position as one of her several bosses. If Lynn wanted to keep her job, she would continue to keep her mouth shut.

The day raced by as Mondays usually did. As a result of last week's court action, Lynn now had three more juveniles to supervise. By 5:00 P.M. she felt as if she'd been drawn through a knothole backward. If it hadn't been for one small, undeniable fact, Lynn would have tried to beg out of her meeting with Gabe and gone home to collapse. What kept her from falling asleep on her couch was the memory of those powerful, impressive hands and a solid body topped by dusky, deep-set eyes that despite his beard managed to dominate his face.

Lynn closed her eyes against a tide of emotion she couldn't put a name to and buried herself in paperwork for another hour. Long before she had to leave the office to meet Gabe, she pushed aside folders and forms and went into the restroom to salvage what was left of her makeup. She found lipstick in the bottom of her purse and fluffed her hair with a blunt-tipped brush, but the hint of eye shadow she'd dabbed on in the morning had rubbed off, and she had nothing to replace it with. She was no more pleased with her outfit, which was nearly a carbon copy of the one he'd seen her in on Friday.

"What does it matter?" she asked her reflection. "This is a business dinner, isn't it?"

Needing the answer to that was what took Lynn out of the restroom and into her car. She tried to drive slowly so she wouldn't show up too early, but it was only quarter to seven when she pulled into the parking lot. Two stalls to the right was the huge pickup bearing the words Updike Contracting.

Lynn sat listening to the sports report on the radio for another five minutes. Since local sports didn't concern her and she had only a freshman knowledge of what the Denver Broncos were up to, she couldn't tell herself she was really interested in the local professional football team. However, listening killed five minutes.

At length, Lynn got out and locked her car. She walked slowly toward the front door of the restaurant. As she reached for the heavy glass handle, she felt the door moving toward her. Lynn took a breath and looked up into dark eyes and an even darker beard. "I saw you drive up," Gabe was saying. "What took you so long?"

"I was listening to a sports wrap-up." Lynn wondered if there'd been too long a pause before her answer. He smelled nice, much nicer than he had the other day. That he'd had a shower before meeting her settled gently in the back of her mind. She was glad she hadn't gone home. She took a minute to look at him, seeing nothing of the judge in the son.

"You a sports fan?" Gabe placed an arm around her shoulder and drew her away from the entry hall. He steered her past a group of elderly people and placed them at the end of the line, waiting to place orders. "I know it isn't the Ritz," Gabe explained, "but some of my men have been here and swear by it. Besides, I'm not one for the Ritz. Do you follow football?"

Because Gabe was waiting for an answer, Lynn set aside her reaction to his easy dismissal of elegant eating establishments. "Some," she said, stretching the truth. "It's hard not to in a city with a pro team."

"You a betting person? You wouldn't like to put a little wager on where the Broncos will stand at the end of the season?"

Lynn had the sneaky suspicion that Gabe was testing her. "I don't believe in betting," she said, sidestepping the issue.

Gabe placed a finger over her lips. "That kind of talk could get you tarred and feathered in this town."

Because Lynn had to struggle against the impulse to touch his finger with her tongue, she remained silent. It was only when he finally removed his hand that she was able to concentrate on what he was saying.

"Their big problem is in not having enough pass protection. Getting sacked every time he turns around is bound to make any quarterback gun-shy."

"Oh," Lynn said, knowing how stupid she sounded.

"Don't worry." Gabe leaned toward her, his soft, deep voice insulating Lynn from the activity around them. "I promise not to talk football all night. It's just that football savvy is a requirement for the Updike family."

"Oh," Lynn said again. Despite Gabe's comforting strength, she felt herself drawing away from mention of the family name.

"You don't know, do you?" Gabe was asking. "I figured you were a phony. Now I've caught you at it."

"Phony?" Lynn stiffened at the accusation.

"You're no more a football fan than I'm an interior decorator." His smile blunted the effect of his words. "Don't worry about it, Lynn. I'll explain things, in detail, another time. What do you want to eat?"

Lynn's eyes fell on the salad bar. "That looks good."

"If you're a rabbit. You aren't on a diet, are you?" He threw her a look of dismay.

"I like salads," she repeated. "You got something against that, mister?"

Gabe leaned over her, arms folded across his considerable chest. "When I'm footing the bill for a feed, I expect the woman to soak me for more than rabbit food."

It took more effort than it should have for Lynn to resist the need to bend away from Gabe, but she was determined to continue the game they'd started. "You got it, fella. Porterhouse. About two pounds. And dessert. They got baked Alaska?"

"You eat all that and I'll have to carry you out of here."

Lynn was about to point out that if she ate all that he wouldn't be able to lift her, but the costumed woman behind the cash register was waiting for her to place her order. Lynn glanced at the menu behind the cash register and named the first item that straightened itself out for her. She only nodded when Gabe added a trip to the salad bar to her selection. Her palms were sweating as she waited for Gabe to place his order, which made it impossible for her to decipher the other items on the menu.

It's happened before, she reminded herself. *It'll happen again.*

Lynn let Gabe steer her over to the salad bar, but once they were there, her stomach took over, making it easy for her to heap her plate with fresh vegetables.

"You aren't one of those health-food nuts, are you?" Gabe asked as she was topping off the overflowing plate with avocado dressing.

"I'm hungry," she admitted. "I missed lunch."

"They work you too hard." Gabe nodded at an empty window table and waited until they were seated. "Take my advice. If you want to loaf your way through life, you should become your own boss."

Lynn smiled. "Like you? How many hours a week do you work?"

Gabe shook his head and picked up his fork to attack his own salad. "You don't want to ruin my appetite, do you? If you promise not to talk shop, I won't, either."

Lynn sampled a cucumber slice. She couldn't taste a thing. Only the senses of sight and sound were working. "That's going to be rather hard to do, considering that's why we're seeing each other tonight. You wanted to know about the work program, remember?"

"Is that what we're here for, Lynn Tresca?"

"What do you need to know?" Lynn managed to ask as Gabe's question sunk in. "Are you interested in the money angle, in your liability?"

"I'm interested in you." Gabe seemed fascinated by the task of mixing dressing through his salad. "Go on," he said softly. "Tell me what liability I'd have."

As Lynn outlined the program, she realized that her voice had taken on a robotlike tone. She was saying all the right things, for she'd been determined to have the answers, but she was no more interested in what she was saying than if the conversation had been about pass protection. She wanted Gabe to look up and settle his eyes on her, but when he did, her voice faltered, and she wasn't sure whether she'd finished her sentence.

His eyes were nothing like his father's. Where the judge could slice a delinquent to ribbons with a slashing stare, Gabe's eyes were curious and giving and questioning, with the unsettling ability to reach deeper inside her than she thought possible.

When their waitress brought the main course, Lynn dug in with a devotion to food that shocked her. She'd become aware that she'd have to slow down eating or finish before Gabe when he asked the question she wasn't ready for.

"Why did you become a juvenile officer?"

Lynn looked up, her eyes as blank as her mind felt. "Why?"

"I mean," Gabe continued, "it sounds noble and all that. There have to be rewards, but I'm guessing there's a lot of frustration in the job."

Although Lynn had never heard anyone outside the field pinpoint that central issue so directly, hearing it from Gabe didn't surprise her. To succeed the way he had called for viewing life through clear eyes. "Yes," she answered softly, her eyes not wavering from his probing stare. "There are days like that. Sometimes I feel as if I've been thrown in front of a train without brakes. For example, today I talked to a girl who's determined to get married next week. She's sixteen and thinks that's the answer to everything she's ever wanted. I don't know if she heard a word I said. But, Gabe, if we don't try, if someone doesn't try, too many kids wind up on the outside of life, looking in.''

''Why does it have to be you?'' Gabe had stopped pretending interest in his meal, a fact Lynn couldn't dismiss.

''I'm not sure,'' she hedged, even though she knew all too well why it had to be she. ''Maybe I like the challenge. The fringe benefits aren't bad, and I get out of the office a lot.''

''I think it's more than that.'' Although Gabe wasn't touching her, she felt a bond there. ''I don't think you became a juvenile officer because you're a starry-eyed do-gooder believing you'll be able to change the world. I also don't believe that business about fringe benefits.''

''You know an awful lot about a field you've never been part of,'' Lynn said softly.

''I know about butting my head against a brick wall. Isn't that what it feels like sometimes?''

''Not always. But I don't expect miracles. Success is measured in a kid deciding to stay in school, not by setting his sights on becoming a brain surgeon.''

''But what if the kid's so hostile he's not going to listen to anyone who represents the establishment?''

''My job is to stay with that kid until he's exhausted all his defenses. Under that protective shell is a heart and mind as vulnerable as everyone else's. Gabe, there isn't a human alive who won't respond to signals that someone believes he has value and worth.''

''And you believe you know how to give those signals.'' This time the contact Gabe was making went a step further. He took Lynn's fingers and swallowed her hand in his work-tempered paw.

Lynn's eyes were drawn to her wrist, which was all she could see of her hand. ''Gabe, I needed those signals myself once. I want to give what I didn't get.''

''It hurt, didn't it?''

Lynn felt the depth and breadth of what Gabe was saying deep in her core. That made it all but impossible to give him the answer he was waiting for. "It was a long time ago," was the best she could manage.

"I don't think so." Gabe squeezed her hand briefly. "The scars are still there."

Yes, they are, Lynn acknowledged. But she couldn't say that. If she did, she'd have to tell this compassionate man that his father was responsible for many of the scars.

Chapter Three

Lynn admitted to herself that there was no need for her to accompany her supervisor and the three teenaged boys out to the construction site two days later. Just the same, she went.

Mostly it was the lingering memory of the way Gabe had held her hand when he walked her back to her car after they'd finished dinner. "I don't want to let you go," he'd whispered when she tried to open the Mazda's door. "And it has nothing to do with getting some kids with strong backs to work for me."

She hadn't said anything then; even now she wasn't sure she'd have the courage to tell him what she was feeling, but maybe seeing him in his scuffed boots and dusty jeans would put things into perspective and make sense of something she'd never experienced before. "I don't want you to let me go," had been the thought that stayed with her while she drove home.

Lynn glanced over at the well-built sixteen-year-old sitting next to her. When she first met Rob Wilks, he'd just been found guilty of assault and was a whisper away from being sent to the state training school. He didn't care. At least that's what the kid had told the juvenile-court judge, the police who handcuffed him and Lynn. But Lynn was slowly working her way through the protective layers Rob had built around himself.

He did care. About his little sister and shooting pool and someday having the money to go skiing. And other things he hadn't mentioned yet. When Lynn reached the site, William's car, with the other two boys, was just pulling up. She stopped the car and turned toward her silent passenger. "Ready to enter the lion's den?"

Rob shrugged. "I'm not going to be anyone's mule."

"Is that what's bothering you?" she asked. "Because you're big, you think this guy's going to work you into the ground?"

"It figures. He wouldn't happen to be related to Judge Updike, would he?"

"I'm afraid so," Lynn admitted. "Look, the judge wasn't involved with your case, so what do you care?"

"I know that guy's reputation. This isn't going to work, Ms Tresca. Believe me, it isn't going to work."

"It probably isn't." Lynn leaned against the car's backrest as if she had all the time in the world to talk. "We probably ought to throw in the towel right now."

Rob obviously wasn't expecting that response. "So what else can I do?"

"Go back to school."

"To hell with that! They don't have any more use for me than I have for them. Let's get this over with."

Lynn's reaction to getting out of the car was slightly more positive than the sixteen-year-old's, but when she saw Gabe walking toward them, she almost turned tail. He could do things to her she didn't understand. Each step she was taking was so new.

Gabe stuck out his hand and introduced himself to Rob. Lynn admitted that having only his shoulder to look at as Gabe faced the teenager made things simpler. "I see she dragged you out here,'' Gabe was saying. ''What do you figure I'll want out of you?''

Rob shrugged. ''Beats me,'' he muttered.

''Beats me, too. Do you drive? Legally, I mean?''

''I've got a car. Or at least I did until I couldn't keep up the insurance payments. That's why I need to work.''

''Don't we all?'' Gabe shook his head sympathetically. ''I need someone to run errands. How's that for a thrill a minute?''

''That's what I'm going to do? Run errands? I thought— Who runs the machinery?''

''I'm afraid I can't let you do that.'' Grinning, Gabe glanced in Lynn's direction. ''My insurance company would come unglued. However, if you'd like to work on a little muscle development, that's no problem.''

Rob turned on Lynn. ''See. That's what I told you. Look, I'm no mule.''

Gabe's second glance told Lynn that he considered the teenager as stubborn as any mule, but his words betrayed none of that. ''That's what I thought when I got into this business. I was the boss, the brains of the show. I was going to watch everyone else work. However, it goes with the territory. It takes sweat to get things accomplished. End of lecture. Come on. We'd better join the others.''

A half hour later, Gabe had finished outlining what he expected of the boys and had told them when and how much they'd be paid. Lynn gave him a nod of approval when he didn't say a word about the consequences should they wind up with any of his tools in their possession.

When Gabe opened things up for questions, the first one took Lynn by surprise. ''Do you know Brook Updike?''

''Yeah.'' A slow smile took control of Gabe's face. He winked at Lynn before going on. ''What do you know about Brook Updike?''

"Are you kidding, man? All-American. Drafted in the second round four years ago and now starting quarterback." The boy's voice rose. "He'll take them to the Superbowl this year."

"Unless his knees go out on him again."

"No way," the boy objected. "Those two surgeries were minor ones. His knees are like new."

"Three surgeries," Gabe corrected. "And the last one laid him up for two months after the season was over. There isn't much left to cut."

The boy was unimpressed. "That's not what they're saying," he said, pressing home his point. "Man, oh, man, does he have the hands. Biggest hands in the business."

Gabe glanced down at his own hands. "Yeah. The hands are good, but don't make him into a superhero. When he goes down, he hurts just like the rest of us. Now, any more questions about what you'll be doing here?"

Gabe waited until the others were out of earshot. He had his head turned toward her, his voice betraying a lack of confidence she hadn't expected. "How did I do? I hope I covered everything."

"You did fine," Lynn acknowledged. He'd just given her a part of the private man; she appreciated that. "You treated them like employees, not convicts."

"I tried. I went over my spiel twice on my way here. I hope this works out."

"I hope it does, too," Lynn admitted. "Who is Brook Updike?"

"Brook Updike is a professional quarterback."

Lynn rolled her eyes. "I gathered that from the conversation. What I mean is, who is he to you?"

"My brother."

Lynn concentrated more on the emotion that went with the words than the words themselves. She sensed both pride and the complicated relationship that exists between siblings. "You must be proud of him."

"Most of the time. Occasionally I get hung up on the memory of the kid brother who dumped the blame for a half-dozen broken windows on me. My parents would say that it couldn't be Brook; he was just a little kid. The rat! Lynn, I'm glad you came here today."

Unprepared for the quick change in the conversation, Lynn could only say, "Oh."

"Aren't you going to ask why I'm glad to see you here?"

"All right," she said softly, slowly. "Why?"

"I'm not sure." Gabe laughed at his own reply but then turned serious again. "I don't know how to explain this, but when I'm with you, things feel different. I think that's worth exploring."

I feel something, too, Lynn thought. "Is this feeling dangerous? I'm not going to be shocked if I touch you, am I?"

"I doubt it." Gabe laughed again. "The only people who consider me dangerous are my competitors."

Feeling brave, Lynn touched the coarse hairs on Gabe's muscled forearm. "Nope. No current." But she wasn't sure that was true.

"That's a relief. I'd hate to singe your fingers." Gabe paused just long enough for Lynn to wonder what he was thinking. "Do you know what time I went to work this morning? Five o'clock. That's the third or fourth time this month. I was looking forward to seeing you and the kids, because at least it would be a change of pace."

"You're not going to get any sympathy out of me," Lynn returned. "You don't have to put up with commuters that way. Try bumper-to-bumper traffic every morning and see what that does for your blood pressure."

Gabe patted her on the top of her head. "Poor kid. All right. If you could do anything you wanted to today, what would it be?"

"I don't know. Sleep in, maybe," was the best she could come up with. "I don't believe in wishful thinking."

"I think it's time you did. Everyone needs a little fantasy." Gabe touched her cheek with gentle fingers that belied his strength. "I wonder—do you like ghost towns?"

Lynn thought about her need to surround herself with sound and light but found herself nodding. The man might be capable of helping her experience many things she never had, never dreamed of. "I don't know. Actually, I've never been to one."

"You're kidding?" He looked almost, but not quite, shocked. "How are you ever going to learn anything about Billy the Kid or the Lone Ranger? I'm an expert on those things, and I didn't graduate from college. I did a lot of hiking around the state in my younger years," he was explaining. "It was my way of getting away from pressure. Unfortunately, that was before I got into the construction business and it became my mistress. You know, there are a couple of places I'd like to share with you. No Cisco Kid, but maybe the ghost of an old miner or two."

Lynn's world warmed at Gabe's offer. He could make her forget the quiet alarm that sounded when she heard his name. "We could try that," she ventured. "You don't suppose we'll find any lost treasure, do you? I don't know if I have the right kind of boots."

A shadow touched Gabe's face. "I don't have time anymore for a decent hike. We'll have to do this by car. But I think you'll like it."

"I know I will." Lynn didn't know she was going to take hold of Gabe's hand until she felt his rough skin rubbing against her palm. She wanted to bring his calluses up to her cheek and soften them with her lips. "On Saturday?"

"Yes, early. There's so much I want to show you."

Gabe watched her walk over to where the teenagers were gathered, but instead of returning to the trailer, he kept his eyes on the slight figure that was shorter than the boys she supervised. There was an unconscious grace in the way she carried herself. He understood that her body was something she took for granted, as if more important things filled her mind. He'd never taken anyone with him during his hikes into the mountain country outside Denver. Part of it was because hiking was his way of getting away from the tourists who descended on his state; part of it was simply because Gabe was at ease in his own company. He'd never expect others to understand that. Maybe, though, Lynn Tresca would. Saturday. The day couldn't come soon enough.

Lynn made it through the rest of the week, with Gabe's invitation giving her days definition and making it possible for her to forsake her constant nightly TV viewing, listening to music on an FM station while she read, actually read, a short history of Colorado. On Friday night she picked out jeans, tennis shoes and a flannel shirt to wear the next day, and spent half the night wondering why Gabe Updike could keep her from sleeping even when he wasn't around.

The next morning she had just prepared a thermos of coffee when her doorbell rang. Lynn let her visitor in. He was like an oak or a rock in his rugged outfit, a man capable of turning naked earth into concrete and steel. Or he might even come up with a few grains of gold for them to bring back.

"I didn't tell you what to wear," Gabe said, pointing to his own flannel shirt, "but we look like twins."

Lynn came closer to stare up into his eyes. She touched his beard. "I don't think so."

"No. I don't think so, either." He leaned toward her, the length of time he took to touch her giving her more than enough time to draw back.

Lynn stayed where she was. She knew he was going to put his hands on her. Their weight on her shoulders reinforced what she already knew. They were the center and substance of what the man was.

"I made sandwiches," she said. "I have to warn you, though. Cooking is not my long suit. I can't promise anything."

"Well, thanks for providing lunch, anyway. What did you pack?"

"Ham and Swiss cheese. Oranges, not apples." Standing so close to Gabe, she realized he smelled of soap and warm flannel.

"Good choice. We'll need the moisture." He hadn't stopped looking at her. "Lynn, I think we'd better leave."

Lynn heard a voice that had to be hers, but she wasn't sure where it was coming from. "Why?"

"Because . . . this is going to take all day. I want us back on the road before it gets dark."

That made sense. "Should I have made more sandwiches?"

"No, we'll live off the land, ma'am." Gabe pushed an imaginary Stetson back on his head. "Rattlesnake stew. Berries. Skunk salad." He snapped his fingers. "I forgot old Betsy."

With one hand Lynn picked up the thermos. She used the other to complete the pretense of blowing smoke from the barrel of a hand gun. "That's all right. I've got my six-shooter."

"I didn't expect to find you living in a place like this," Gabe said as he waited for Lynn to lock the door.

"What did you expect?"

"I'm not sure. I've never known anyone who lived in one of these swinging-singles places. You don't strike me as the type."

Lynn realized that he wanted her to deny that she was a member of the singles set. That was easy to do. She said something about the rent being in line with what she could afford and the complex being near work. "It gets pretty noisy here on the weekends, though," she finished up lamely.

"I couldn't stand that." Gabe frowned. "My place looks like a storage yard, but at least I have elbow room."

Lynn settled into her side of Gabe's pickup. She was impressed by how high off the ground the oversized tires placed the cab. "My complex has a heated swimming pool and a sauna," she said, hoping he wouldn't ask her how often she used the facilities. "Maybe I should have brought a camera along today."

That wasn't the last time Lynn regretted having no way of recording the day. Despite the need for substantial clothing in the early-morning chill, Lynn could smell the day's promise. Soon the sun would warm the earth and chase away the fragile whispers of morning fog. Gabe headed west out of town on Highway 70, but when they reached the small town of Dillon, he turned off, found a country road Lynn didn't know existed and drove slowly through the rising mountains. A few miles farther he abandoned the paved road for a dirt road that called for shifting into four-wheel drive.

"When I first started hiking, I took trails to fire lookout posts, and dropped in on the men manning the forest service towers," he explained. "They were so happy to have company that they put up with my tourist-type questions. Later I came across the year-round glaciers and snowfields the tourists never see. I have a collection of pressed wild-flowers you wouldn't believe."

Warmed by the thought of Gabe holding fragile blossoms between his leathered fingers, Lynn looked up at mountain peeks still topped with snow and snuggled down inside her flannel shirt. She was gripping the door handle to keep from being bounced about but felt no desire to tell Gabe to go in any direction except farther into the mountains. Here, the silence she usually avoided felt right. She was safe with Gabe beside her. She hadn't felt that way around a man before. "I never had the chance to collect wildflowers," she admitted.

"Deprived childhood?" Gabe winked at her. "I don't know how they let you grow up without a wildflower collection."

Lynn backed away from the term "deprived childhood" and allowed herself to be distracted as Gabe talked about fireweed, fairy trumpets, redwood lilies and, later in the summer, Indian paintbrush. She wondered how a man who made his living with heavy machinery knew that the Alpine forget-me-nots had two-foot roots in order to reach what little moisture existed above the timberline.

"We lived in northern California when I was eight or nine," Lynn explained. "One day my sister and I decided to see how many dandelions we could find. What we came back with was a case of poison oak that landed both of us in the hospital. Fortunately, that was my first and last experience with a hospital."

Gabe waited until they'd bounced over a cattle guard. "I wish my track record was that good. At least I haven't been in a hospital as much as Brook has."

Lynn fell silent as Gabe filled her in on a little more of his and Brook's childhood. Beneath the tale of scrapes and skirmishes she sensed an undercurrent of emotional and financial stability. And competitiveness. It was still morning when Gabe guided the truck down the last hill and came to a stop a few hundred feet before a weathered collection of buildings the world had forgotten.

"That's part of what I wanted to show you," Gabe said as he was getting out of the pickup. Until today he hadn't wanted to bring anyone here, because this area was, for him, a world preserved, a place for a man who needed time with his private thoughts. Even if he seldom came here, he could think about it when the pressure of business threatened to reduce him to a frazzle, like the raveled ends of a cheap rope. Now he was bringing a woman, this woman, into his island of sanity. How she would react meant a great deal to him. "This place doesn't exist on most maps," he explained. "It's called St. John."

Lynn recognized what had once been a barn and the remaining half of a farmhouse. Weathered wooden fencing ran around half of the area but died out without accomplishing its mission. "Does anyone ever come here?" she asked, her voice no louder than a whisper. The area seemed to have a life and personality of its own, one that wouldn't welcome loud voices. Gabe belonged here, but she wasn't so sure about herself.

"A few ranchers. Maybe some tourists. But I've never run into anyone else here." Gabe was whispering, too. "I like to believe it's mine when I need it."

Lynn moved close to Gabe. "Not completely yours," she said as fingers from the past seemed to reach out and touch her. "I don't think about the history of the state when I'm in the city, but it exists here." She paused a minute to give her thoughts time to jell. "It's as if the past and present are all part of the same experience." The solitude, the wind, the crystalline sky—all were things she had to share. This corner of the world was theirs, at least for today. "Thank you."

Gabe rested his arm on Lynn's shoulder. "For what?"

"For bringing me here. For sharing this. I wasn't sure at first, but now I'm glad I came."

Gabe acknowledged the lift in his heart. She did understand. "You're welcome, Ms Tresca." He turned her toward him. "Don't make any judgments yet. Give these old settlements time to grow on you. Tell me what you think when the day's over."

Lynn stepped forward into Gabe's embrace. It seemed so natural that she was barely aware of having moved. His arms across her back cut down the wind's impact; she closed her eyes to block out the distraction of an incredible view. "Billy the Kid wouldn't dare come here. Only hero types and miners allowed." She drew out her breath. "Denver seems a million miles away."

"We're the only ones here." She felt his breath on her cheek, his mouth coming closer. "No telephones. No... anything."

His lips were sweeter, more alive, than she'd imagined them. It might have been because she'd had this morning in which to learn more about what made his world go around. It might be that their surroundings had charged her senses. Whichever the answer was, Lynn was content to savor these moments set aside in their lives. She loved the feel of flannel over his muscles, the tiny vibration of his heart against her breasts. But mostly she loved the experience of their first kiss.

Gabe's hands slowly worked their way down Lynn's back; her every conscious thought went with the journey. Their lips were still pressed together, his beard adding warmth to her cheeks, but it was the feel of his fingers reaching under the loose hem of her shirt and touching her bare waist that brought her breath to a halt. She was melting. The sharp corners of personality necessary for her job were being sanded away.

Although they were miles from any other humans, Lynn never entertained the thought that Gabe might take advantage of that fact. He was asking her to mark the boundaries of their relationship. He would go no farther than she dictated.

How far that might eventually be Lynn couldn't answer. All she knew was that the joining had begun. Her world went no farther than Gabe. She parted her mouth slightly, but only to help her breathe. Gabe touched her lips with the tip of his tongue and then retreated. It was Lynn's turn. She felt both brave and newborn, a novice at something other women might take in stride. The inside of his lips were incredibly soft; her tongue told her that. They served as the perfect contrast for his hard external competence. There were two sides to the man, both of them capable of capturing so much of her.

It took courage she didn't know she had, but Lynn forced herself away from Gabe's strength. She understood too little about the emotions touching her; she needed more time to feel her way slowly. She opened her eyes and looked up at him, wondering if she'd have to say anything or if her eyes carried enough of her confusion.

Silently, Gabe took her hand and led the way down the slope to the abandoned farm. They poked their heads in the hole where there'd once been a window and pushed open what remained of a front door. "Anyone home?" Gabe called out. His voice echoed.

"They're probably out rounding up the cattle," Lynn offered. No furniture remained, and parts of the wooden flooring were so rotten that she didn't dare step on it. Lynn let go of Gabe's hand and dropped to her knees. When she stood up, she was holding a square nail. "I think I'll keep it as a souvenir," she explained as she put it in her pocket. "I've never seen one of those outside a museum."

"I found a few arrowheads over that hill," Gabe said once they were back outside. He pointed in the opposite direction from where they'd come. "Makes one wonder how well the settlers and Indians got along."

"Maybe that's why the settlers left." Lynn started in the direction of the hill and then came back for Gabe. "You might as well reconcile yourself to a hike," she pressed. "I might not get out here again. I intend on making the most of it."

"You'll be here again," Gabe said. "I've just begun showing you things."

For the next hour Gabe and Lynn scrambled over rocks and around brush, hunting for arrowheads. Although they didn't find any, Lynn picked up a rock that looked like one. Gabe said she'd be back; she believed him.

"We'd better leave," Gabe finally said. "We're going to run out of time and daylight if we don't."

She didn't want to leave. There hadn't been enough time to examine their surroundings and discover what of Gabe existed here. What made it important to him. But Gabe hadn't accomplished everything he wanted to today.

They were back in the truck, heading toward the main road, before Gabe broke what was, surprisingly, an easy silence. "Sometimes," he started slowly, "I'd like to chuck what I do and buy a farm near Hereford."

Lynn had slid next to Gabe on the high seat but managed to bring her thoughts around to what he was saying. "Hereford? There's nothing out there. Nothing except dry fields. And heat."

"And a chance to prove myself the way I've never had to before. Lynn, have you ever wanted a challenge no one expects you to meet?" Gabe put his right arm around her shoulder, his left hand fighting the ruts that threatened to throw the truck off course. "I felt that way when I started in the construction business, but sometimes even that isn't enough. I'd like to be one of the few not to buckle under to the sun, winds, winter blizzards. I want to be there when the rain finally comes."

The goal Gabe wanted to set for himself revealed even more about the man. "I know about those kinds of challenges," she whispered, her words more for herself than for him. "I've met a few of them. Buckled under a few times, too." She could sense Gabe looking at her, but she wasn't able to meet his eyes. There was so much he didn't know about her. She wasn't sure either of them was ready for that.

"I hope someday you'll tell me what you mean," he said softly.

I hope I can, she thought. Then aloud she said, "Why a dry-land farm? You'd be so dependent on water. The struggle would never end."

"I don't know. Maybe you're right. It doesn't matter when no one cares, does it?"

Lynn reacted to the loneliness she heard in Gabe's voice. She didn't know what was behind the emotion, and because he respected her privacy, she had to do the same for him. However, she could give him something of herself. She leaned away slightly and ran her left hand up the side of Gabe's neck, burying it in the thick mat of beard trailing over his jaw. For more than a minute they traveled like that, her simple contact making words unnecessary. Then Gabe took her hand in his and held it in front of him. He glanced over at her other hand. "You're left-handed."

"How did you guess?"

"The nails on your left hand are shorter. Is it hard, being left-handed, I mean?"

Yes, but not in any way you'd understand. "I can't borrow anyone's golf clubs. On the other hand, no one tries to use my special scissors."

The subject changed to other things as Gabe reentered the freeway. During the time it took to reach the junction that lead to Aspen, they talked about politics and history and Colorado winters. His destination, however, wasn't the famous ski resort but Independence Pass to the southeast. "This is another one of my discoveries," he explained as once again he had to resort to four-wheel drive. "It's an old mining town."

"Does anyone live here?" Lynn asked.

"Not permanently and certainly not in the winter. I thought about planting my flag on it, like mountain climbers do, but decided that was being a little too possessive. This town has belonged to the elements for more years than I've lived. I wouldn't want to try to change that."

When Lynn saw the small collection of wooden buildings carved out of rough cut logs in the middle of a small tree-dotted valley, surrounded by barren mountain peaks she agreed. Modern man should treasure what was left of the past, she believed, and not try to change it. It moved her to know that Gabe had the sensitivity to feel that way also. She left the truck and started poking into what was left of the structures, turning her head into the wind as if she could catch the echoes of words spoken by miners over a hundred years ago. The thought that words could remain in the wind forever intrigued her.

"It isn't much like the TV stereotype, is it?" she asked, as she ran her hand over a weathered log wall. "Somehow I can't picture gunslingers riding into town or a brave marshal sending them packing. I don't think there was much time to worry about the struggle between good or evil; just staying alive was the goal."

Gabe joined her. "I doubt if there was any formal law and order here," he observed. "The men were too busy trying not to starve and mining for gold to have time to get into trouble."

"Only men?" Lynn said teasingly. She didn't want the mood to stay somber. "I wonder which one of these buildings was the tavern. Can't you almost see the dance-hall girls in their bright costumes."

Gabe placed his arm around Lynn's waist, pretending to make out the scene that her imagination was supplying. "The costumes are kind of sad. Faded and patched," he said softly. "And whoever they are, they aren't girls anymore." Gabe pointed toward the harsh landscape around them. "Land like this could kill a man or a woman before they reached forty. I don't think many girls came to live here."

As Lynn looked about, she had to agree that it was hard to imagine anyone fighting to wrestle a living from the unyielding land that now claimed what little trace humans had left behind. She tried to picture herself forsaking her noisy apartment complex for life in this awesome solitude. A few days ago the mental image would have darkened before it could begin to form.

But today Gabe Updike was beside her. Her need for bright lights and human contact—other than this special human being—had diminished. She didn't fully understand the change, but she was starting to. It had to do with the man who owned a construction company and who found beauty in weathered wood. "There's elegance here," she said from within the circle of Gabe's arms. "A certain grace. I feel as if I could really get in touch with myself here. There's nothing to get between me and my thoughts."

"That's why I wanted to bring you here." Gabe turned her toward him, his eyes demanding her total attention. He felt inwardly shaken. She was saying the words he'd been waiting for all day and maybe much longer than that.

"Thank you," Lynn said, but she didn't dare say anything more. Being with Gabe, in this nakedly beautiful place, was affecting her on a deeper level than she thought possible. Other than for Gabe's presence, there were no distractions, no other demands on her emotions. She felt caught between the past and present, not caring which age would ultimately claim her.

Lynn reached forward to place a kiss on Gabe's mouth. As she stood on tiptoe to cement the contact, her fingers dug into his shoulders. Something was happening between them. The question of what that something was now and what it might become later would keep her awake tonight, but for the present she was content to blend her emotions and her thoughts with his.

Her fingers had found the open neckline of his shirt. Despite the press of his body against hers, she managed to work her fingers inside his shirt to the thick, soft wall of hair covering his chest. His skin was soft, but beneath it she could feel the strength of bone and muscle.

Lynn became aware of the quickened pace of her own breathing. Her mouth was slightly parted to bring enough air into her lungs. Gabe's lips were on her cheek, moving along the side of her face, dipping lower to her neck and toying with the line of her collarbone. Lynn clung to him, not knowing how much longer she could trust her knees to stay locked in place.

When Gabe's lips reached her shirt's open neckline and found her throat, her nostrils flared in response. From somewhere that seemed to have no point of origin Lynn became aware of a sound—a voice. "Lynn? I don't think we're ready for this."

It was Gabe's voice. He was saying something she had to respond to. The answer she gave came with difficulty. "I don't think we are, either."

He groaned and held her close for a moment. "I'm going to take you home now."

"Do we have to leave?" she managed to say, but then answered her own question. "Yes, I know we do. But Gabe, I would like to come back here with you again, please."

"Do you mean it?"

"I'll be leaving a little of myself behind," she said by way of explanation. "I've never felt like this before."

"You've never felt attachment for a place?"

Lynn shook her head. "I moved around so much when I was younger. First with my parents and then...I was trying to hold myself together, not putting down roots...." Lynn's voice trailed off.

Gabe sensed that she wanted to tell him more but was either afraid or didn't know how to start. Maybe, when today was behind them, it would be Lynn and not he who would benefit the most from the trip they'd taken. Over the years he'd learned that people can hide from themselves while caught up in the daily treadmill of their lives. It was only when they took themselves off that treadmill that they listened to the sounds inside their heads. He'd learned something about coming to peace with himself in the ghost town; maybe it was time for the same thing to happen to Lynn.

Lynn said a silent goodbye to the generation of men and women who had built and then abandoned the old mining town, but as she sat inside the silent truck, watching Gabe's hands on the steering wheel, she realized she'd been using these thoughts about the past to distract herself from her own emotions.

"Are you going to have to work overtime because of the time you took off today?" Lynn asked, after a silence that had continued for the twenty minutes it took to drive five miles through the mountains.

"If I do, it's worth it. Lynn, I want to ask you something." Gabe glanced in her direction, but only momentarily, because driving was a full-time job. "Is there anyone in your life?"

Lynn thought about the few relationships she'd had since graduating from college. "No," she answered honestly. "Not really. I've been too busy to get involved with anyone. I had a partial scholarship, but I had to work to go to college. Between getting an education and learning the ropes with the juvenile department, there hasn't been time for much else."

"But what about before college and now? There had to be... relationships."

"Not the kind you mean. I've been a square peg in a round hole for a lot of years."

"Why?"

"Why am I a square peg?" Lynn took a deep breath to give herself time to think. She fingered the square nail in her pocket. "It's a complicated question demanding a complicated answer. Gabe, it's been a beautiful day. I don't want anything to ruin it."

"In other words, don't pry."

"For now, please," Lynn managed to reply. She hated drawing this protective shield around herself, but she'd done it for so long that the habit was deeply ingrained. "I hope you understand."

"No I don't. Not really." Gabe glanced at her again before returning to the task of driving. "But I don't have any choice." He sighed. "We all have parts of ourselves we keep boarded up, don't we?"

"Yes." Lynn leaned over and brushed her lips across the back of Gabe's hand which was wrapped around the steering wheel. "You're including yourself in that statement, aren't you?"

"Do you think I'd let you corner the market on private thoughts? If you're going to have secrets, then so am I. It's like kids who won't share their ice-cream cones, isn't it?"

Lynn shook her head, trapped within herself. "There's nothing I'd like better than to be able to put my thoughts in the same category as an ice-cream cone. And wouldn't it be nice if we could turn up the heat and all our problems would melt. Gabe, we really are on a heavy subject. It's too nice a day for that." To change the mood, Lynn pulled out of her pocket the rock she had picked up earlier. "I still say I found an arrowhead. You just don't want to admit I had better luck than you did."

Gabe laughed and started to tell her about a hiking trip that ended with him on crutches, but as she concentrated on the sound of his voice echoing within the cab of the truck, she sent him a silent thank-you for safely drawing them away from topics neither of them was ready to discuss.

When Gabe dropped her off outside the apartment complex, she accepted his gentle kiss before wrapping her hands around one of his. "It isn't enough to say thank you for a perfect day. What comes after perfect? I feel as if I've been in a time warp. It's as if there are two worlds existing at the same time. Do you think that's possible?"

"I'd like to think so. It would be nice if we could move forward or back in time at will."

There wasn't any reason for her to stay in the truck. The day was over; it was time for her to leave him. "When will I see you again?" she asked boldly.

"How about tomorrow. No, wait a minute, not tomorrow. I'm expected to show my face at some carnival my folks are holding." As if reading her mind, he continued. "It's nothing any sane person would do if he had a choice. I refuse to impose it on you. I'll call Monday."

Lynn nodded and got out of the truck. She didn't turn around when she heard the big motor gaining strength. Another time, with another man, she might have been cynical about the promise of "I'll call you," but she knew Gabe meant it. They were on the same wavelength. That hadn't happened to her before with a man.

Later Lynn tried to interest herself in some dinner, but she was halfway through eating her hamburger before she realized she had forgotten to season it. She couldn't concentrate on food or cleaning her apartment or listening to TV or joining the party above her. There was only one reason for her restless mood. She wanted to be with Gabe.

You're doing crazy things to me, she told the image of him she carried inside her head. *I wonder if you know that?*

She jumped when the phone rang. When she answered it, she realized that the voice on the other end of the line was the only one she wanted to hear.

"Lynn? I've been looking through some of my old high school annuals. Now I remember."

Chapter Four

Lynn closed her eyes and took a short, quick breath. She knew Gabe was waiting for her to reply, but he would have to wait a little longer. From the moment she had learned who Gabe was, she knew that eventually he would be saying the words he'd just uttered. But she wasn't ready for them. He hadn't given her enough warning.

"Lynn? Are you still there?"

"Yes." She took another breath but still felt bloodless. "Why were you looking through your annual?"

"Curiosity. It's been nagging at me all day, where I knew you before. I finally decided we must have gone to school together. You were a freshman when I was in my senior year."

She couldn't fault him for that. And yet there was so little about the teenage Lynn she wanted to remember. "What did you learn?" The question was so hard, so damn hard, to get out.

Although there were miles between them, Gabe sensed the tension in Lynn. He understood the reason behind her mood. If his memory was clear, hers must be a cutting edge. He had to move slowly or she might bolt. If she withdrew now, he wasn't sure how long it would take for him to bring her back. Or if he ever could. "That your hair looks darker now than it was back then."

"Oh. Anything else?"

She was brave. She could have tried to change the subject, but she wasn't doing that. She could also be waiting for him to say something she couldn't forgive. "That your mouth is softer now. You're aging well."

"I'm not sure that's a compliment." He heard her forced laugh and hated the attempt she was making. "You wouldn't like it if I told you your hairline is receding."

"We weren't talking about me, Lynn."

A long pause. "I know. What else do you remember?"

If Gabe hadn't been surrounded by the memory of a perfect day, he might have accepted her frightened challenge. He didn't want to hurt Lynn or risk driving her from him. "Not much," he lied. "Like most kids, I was pretty self-centered in those days. I was much more interested in what was happening to me than the people around me."

"In other words, I don't stand out in your memory."

"I can't say that you do. Sorry."

"I don't believe you, Gabe."

Despite the harsh sound of the slammed receiver, it was a moment before Gabe realized that Lynn had actually hung up on him. Not that he blamed her. The image of the angry, trapped girl staring back at him from the pages of the old yearbook wasn't one that would fade from the mind of anyone who'd gone to school with her. He'd backed away from his memories and lied. She'd caught him at it.

What demons possessed Lynn back then Gabe could only guess at. What he did remember was walking down the hall toward the school office one day at the moment Lynn exploded from the office, the principal and a male teacher in pursuit. When a yell from the principal prompted Gabe to use his body as a barrier between her freedom and the authority figures, Lynn had whirled back toward the two men, her fists knotted, face deadly white. To this day, Lynn's words still rang in Gabe's head. "I'm not stupid! I am not stupid!"

"Ah, Lynn," Gabe muttered. "What was wrong? Was it all that hard for you?" He should be getting in his car and going over to see her, but he didn't. Lynn had had years of trying to escape her childhood. She might hate him for dragging it back out in the open again.

And yet there was so much he needed to understand. There were other memories—the day in the school library when she hurled a book against the wall, the icy silence and a cordlike body when she was called on in class, whole weeks when she wasn't in school at all.

"I'm not stupid," she'd said. The words had been a plea, a desperate prayer. Ten years ago Gabe had been embarrassed to be part of that scene; today he wanted to wrap Lynn in his arms and say the words no one had been able to say to her back then. She wasn't stupid. Not now and not then, either.

He had to know what had happened. He remembered gossip to the effect that Lynn Tresca hadn't been able to keep up in school. A pity, some of the jocks said. A girl ripe for the plucking but so screwed up that no guy could get close to her. There'd even been talk about her parents kicking her out and her becoming a ward of the state. And then . . . she wasn't around anymore.

"Lynn, it's behind you. Let it die." But Gabe knew it wouldn't die. He was a link to her past. That's why she had hung up on him.

Gabe picked up the phone again and redialed her number. He wasn't going to let the two of them end like this. She picked up the phone on the fourth ring but for a moment said nothing. Gabe broke the silence. "I lied. I remember you, and who you were."

"Tell me something, Gabe." Her voice was hard but brittle, as if it might break at any time. "I was good for a lot of laughs with your friends, wasn't I?"

"Not laughs, Lynn. Please believe that." Damn. He should be with her, holding her, instead of existing as a disembodied voice. "We didn't understand you. No one knew how to approach you."

"Neither did the teachers." She laughed, but her voice cracked. He wondered if she was crying. "They could hardly wait to get rid of me. Did you and I have any classes together? Did you get to watch me make a fool of myself?"

He could have said yes and taken his chances, but Gabe knew how close he was to losing her. He had to try something else. "I don't think we had any classes together. If I remember, I was a senior the year you were there, and you were a couple of years behind me. But we met. Do you remember trying to run away from the principal one day? There was a boy standing in the hall who wouldn't let you go. I was that boy. I didn't have much choice," he tried to explain. "The principal was yelling for me to stop you. Lynn, I remember the look on your face. I don't think I've ever seen anyone look that desperate."

"Desperate?" The word came out as a deflated whisper. "I swore; I did so much swearing in those days. I'd think you'd remember the foul-mouthed, wild person."

"That, too," Gabe admitted reluctantly. "But that day you were standing alone in the hall with those men coming after you. I remember that you looked like a trapped animal, with the hunters closing in."

There was a sob in Lynn's voice when she spoke. "I felt like that a lot of the time. Gabe, I was considered the class fool. I hated who I was."

"You aren't that person anymore. And Lynn, despite what you might have thought, you weren't the class fool. There were a lot of kids who weren't on the honor roll." She wasn't hanging up on him. Gabe wanted to believe that it was because they'd in some way bonded earlier in the day. He knew he was tied to her by forces he couldn't understand or deny. "You're an intelligent, competent woman."

"Thank you for saying that." Lynn took a shaky breath before going on. "It hasn't been easy."

"Lynn? Tell me if it's none of my business, but I'd like to know what happened. What the problem was."

"I—I don't know if I want to do that. Gabe, I've worked so damn hard to put my childhood behind me."

"We can't separate ourselves from the past. Not completely," he said gently. He still regretted not being with her, but at least he was listening to her voice and not the sound of a slammed receiver. Every second he kept her on the line meant something. "Things fester inside unless we let them out."

"I'm not sure I can let it out."

"Try. With me." Gabe took a moment to erase the intensity from his voice. There was still a danger of pushing her too far. "You aren't that desperate girl anymore. I think we can talk about her without bringing her back to life. I'd like to know more about who you were and why. And how you got your act together."

"Maybe someday."

The tentative promise was all Gabe had to go on. Although they talked for another five minutes, Lynn carefully steered the conversation toward other topics, and Gabe didn't try to stop her. He was a little shaky himself. Before hanging up, he promised to get in touch with her after the mandatory visit with his parents but left the occasion of their next meeting up to her. He wasn't going to push her no matter how much he wanted to understand the complex woman known as Lynn Tresca.

The next day, less than two minutes after arriving at his parents' house for dinner, Gabe understood the true meaning behind their seemingly casual invitation. It was as he expected. His parents were attacking on two fronts.

The first was in the form of one Alyce Burk, an attorney specializing in business contracts and satisfying her sexual rights, not necessarily in that order. The other was another in a long line of power struggles aimed at getting Gabe to knuckle under to the judge's need to see his eldest son obtain a university degree.

Alyce, as the judge explained it, was on her way to becoming a law partner in one of the city's most prestigious firms. She'd been married once but had long ago shed herself of the man who couldn't reconcile himself to the fact that a woman's career could mean as much to her as catering to her man. The latter fact Gabe learned from Alyce as they sipped before-dinner drinks. "My ex was, shall we say, Neanderthal," she said. "He never could understand that cooking a meal for him wasn't the only thing on my mind. Actually, that was pretty funny, since he was a better cook than I'd ever care to be."

Gabe could see where the poor man had been misled. Five or six years ago, before Alyce had taken on the look of a circling vulture, she'd probably been a beautiful woman. Gabe guessed that it took constant dieting to keep her hipbones sticking out the way they did, to say nothing of a hefty salary to keep her in silk suits. Other than the fact that Alyce was a woman and Gabe a man, Gabe didn't see how his parents could have thought the two of them would have anything in common. Alyce's nails were done weekly by a manicurist; Gabe had grease imbedded in his calluses. Perhaps, Gabe admitted, his parents hoped that Alyce was capable of filing the rough edges off their son.

Like hell. Granted, he was interested in the flicker of thigh showing under the off-white skirt, and there was no denying the message when Alyce licked her lips. But Gabe wasn't interested in the messages she was sending out. And he didn't give a damn about picking up on Alyce's offer to help him find tax loopholes for his construction company, and he wasn't about to satisfy her thinly veiled curiosity about the bottom line in his checkbook.

"She has one of the sharpest minds I've seen in a long time," the judge said while Gabe's mother was taking Alyce on a tour of the Updikes' ornate tri-level home. "She's nobody's fool. You could do worse."

"Let me do my own picking, Judge," Gabe said absently. He'd been warding off his father's matchmaking for so many years that he could now do it with half a mind. "She wouldn't set foot in my place, and you know it."

"You could move." The judge was staring into the depths of his crystal whiskey glass. "I don't—"

"You don't know how I can stand living in a dump. If you recall, I believe we've been over this before." Gabe turned his whiskey glass around in his fingers, feeling not the expensive design but a weight that could be hurtled through a window if he didn't keep himself in check.

"It's a disgrace! My God, Gabe, you're too damn old to be playing around with your life the way you are. I knew it was a mistake to let you drop out of college after your sophomore year." The judge met Gabe's eyes with a look designed to cut the younger man in half. "Brook graduated years ago."

Gabe opened his mouth to tell his father that he had no interest in finishing college but didn't bother speaking. This topic, like too many others, had been ground into the dirt before. Feeling detached from everything except his desire to see Lynn Tresca again, he waited for the judge to speak.

"I've been talking to Carter over at the university." The judge paused. "He understands your position, Gabe, but he says there's no disgrace in older men coming back to college these days. You'll get credit for the courses you've taken plus some life-experience credits. Carter says he doesn't see why you can't begin your master's studies in about a year."

"Do you think I can live in the dorm?"

"Don't be sarcastic!" Despite the women elsewhere in the house, the judge didn't attempt to keep his voice down. "I'm about fed up with this life-style of yours, Gabe. You'd think you'd have outgrown this fascination with machinery. And that beard. You know how much I hate it. Go back to college. I'll pay the tuition, whatever it takes to get you back on track."

"Until I get on your track, you mean," Gabe said through clenched teeth. No matter how many times he told himself he wasn't going to let himself be sucked into this conversation, the judge always managed to have his way. "In the first place, I wouldn't take a dime from you, and you know it. I can support myself and at least twenty other men. You may not have noticed, but I've been supporting myself for a number of years. In the second place . . ." He paused until he was sure he had the judge's attention. "I have no intention of getting some damn degree you can parade around. I don't need it. I don't want it. Just like I don't want that woman you're trying to throw at me."

"You're a fool, Gabe."

"Then I'll probably always be a fool," Gabe said as he rose to his feet. "It's hell having a son who insists on living his own life, isn't it?"

Although Gabe tried to distract himself during dinner, there was still a bitter taste in his mouth when he slipped out of the house without responding to the cool hand Alyce let linger on his thigh. He honestly wanted to make peace with his father. But unless the judge acknowledged that his eldest had the right to follow his own road map, they would never be on the same wavelength. Let the judge keep his standards of success; Gabe wasn't going to sacrifice himself to meet those standards.

As he drove home, Gabe wondered what the judge would think of a woman who spent her days working with juvenile delinquents instead of corporate mergers.

At the moment when Gabe turned into his driveway and whistled to Ranger, Lynn replaced the phone receiver without completing her call. It was barely eight o'clock, surely too early for Gabe to be back from a Sunday dinner with his parents. Lynn tried to imagine what the judge's house looked like, but because she'd never been in a home at the end of a block-long driveway, she couldn't bring any images to life. What she could concentrate on was a soft full beard with dark flecks around the outer corners, shoulders broad enough to carry the weight of his own business and eyes that didn't ask any more than they were willing to give.

Eyes like that couldn't be dismissed.

Lynn returned to the telephone, her hand drawn to the instrument. He'd said he would call, but that was before their last conversation. She'd told him that someday, maybe, she'd tell him about her early years. Lynn wasn't sure whether she'd made that decision yet. All she knew was that she needed to hear the sound of Gabe's voice.

She was almost ready to hang up when he finally answered. "Lynn?" was the first word he spoke.

He wanted me to call, she thought. "Are you psychic?" she teased, because her other thoughts were too intense to be revealed over the phone. "I wasn't sure you'd be back yet."

"I just got in. Is everything all right?"

"Yes, of course. I ... how was your dinner?"

"The same as always. I don't remember what Mom served. Roasted something. Did you call just to ask what I had to eat?"

"No, of course not." Lynn stopped. She wasn't sure why she'd called, only that her living room seemed larger and brighter now. "Was your brother there?" Dumb question. She should have something better to say.

"Brook is in California. Fortunately, he was spared tonight's ritual. The judge had dragged some woman over to meet me."

Lynn wondered if Gabe had said that in order to gauge her reaction, but then she decided that it wasn't his style. He was simply stating the facts. "What was she like?"

"Like no one you'd ever want to meet. What would you think if I went back to college? I walked out one day halfway through a philosophy class that I knew I'd never have any use for."

"What?" Lynn was thrown off balance. "Are you thinking—"

"Of course not," Gabe interrupted. "However, I haven't been able to convince my father of that. Tell me, does it bother you that you have more education than I do?"

That was the last thing Lynn expected to be asked. "I never thought about it. Of course not."

"Good. Maybe I should send you to talk to my old man. And while you're at it, tell him that my beard's my own business. No, forget it. Debate's another course I didn't have much use for. When are you free?"

Lynn surrendered to the happy glow of warmth spreading through her. Gabe had said what she'd been wanting to hear. "Anytime," she started to say, and then forced herself to stop. Things were going so fast already. Maybe she was supposed to be putting on some kind of brakes. "I have to work tomorrow."

"Me, too."

He was making her say it. "After work, then?" she asked. "I don't know. Maybe you don't like my pushing you." Should she have waited for him to call her? That was still the traditional way.

"You aren't pushing me, Lynn. I was going to call you as soon as I'd fed Ranger. If you want to talk to me, just pick up the phone."

But what was she going to talk about? Lynn asked herself. They could talk about a million subjects, but there were certain bases that had to be touched eventually. The only barrier was the one inside her. But she'd never told anyone about the pain of her early years. So much was being asked of her. "Central Park? Could we meet there?" Gabe named a time and then put an end to the conversation by pointing out that Ranger was going to start eating a tire if he wasn't fed. Lynn tried to imagine what Gabe's dog looked like. Unless Ranger was a German shepherd or a husky, she couldn't picture any dog that would match what she already knew of the man. Certainly Ranger wouldn't be a ball of fluff curled up on a couch.

By quitting time on Monday, Lynn was so nervous that she had to go back to her desk twice to pick up things she'd left behind. She waited until she was in her car to check her appearance and then used her rearview mirror to replenish the lipstick she'd put on in the morning. She ran strangely numb fingers through her hair but gave up trying to tame it when a lock at her crown refused to join the rest of the curls. Her hands were shaking slightly, and her stomach felt as if a football game were being played inside her.

It wasn't right to feel this way about meeting a man. Something was wrong.

Maybe she felt this way because seeing him was more important than anything she'd done in a very long time. "He has you all turned around," Lynn told the wide-eyed reflection in the rearview mirror. "This isn't any worse than taking a college exam. You survived those. You'll survive this."

Still, Lynn wasn't so sure when she parked her car and walked over to the picnic table in Central Park where she was going to wait for Gabe. She climbed up and seated herself on the table, using the bench as a footrest. In the past she simply wouldn't have allowed herself to get so close to someone with the power to throw her off balance. However, this wasn't the past. Lynn couldn't live with choosing only the safe route anymore. Not after having spent that wonderfully intimate day with him.

She was watching a couple of toddlers arguing over which one should get to climb a tree first when she heard her name being called. For a moment the echo of Gabe's voice hung in the air. She had to grip the table she was sitting on to keep from jumping to her feet and letting her nerves get the best of her.

"Have you been waiting long?" Gabe asked as he came up to her. He was still wearing the faded jeans and dusty T-shirt that was his usual uniform.

"Not long," she said, smiling to reassure him that she didn't mind what he wore as long as he was here. He made a sharp contrast with the businessmen who were strolling about the park to escape their offices and the high-schoolers and college students who were burning off energy in games of touch football. He was, Lynn understood, a man who should never try to be anything but what he wanted to be. "I envy you," she said. "You're tanned, while I look as if I've been stuck in a cooler." Her voice had a casual everyday tone, but her heartbeat was rapid.

"You aren't that pale." Gabe sat down beside her on the wooden table. Although they weren't close enough to be touching, Lynn could sense something of him reaching out toward her.

She didn't shy away from the emotional contact. "I wasn't sure you'd be out here this soon. Did I take you away from something you should be doing?"

"Nothing that's as important as being here with you." Then, as if he were uncomfortable with what he'd said, Gabe quickly switched topics. "The boys you sent me are working out better than I thought they would. Remember the big kid who came with you? He's smart. He sees what needs to be done and does it without being told. My men are watching them pretty close to make sure they don't goof off or get themselves into dangerous situations, but for the most part I'm pleased."

"I'm glad." Lynn wrapped her hands around her upper arms and hugged herself tightly. A breeze was playing with the little boys around the tree. Some of it was reaching her. "I've talked to a couple of them. They're enthusiastic. It's the most money any of them have ever earned. Of course," she said, smilingly, "it might not last. They could get bored."

"Everyone gets bored if he does the same thing all the time. That's why I'm trying to work them into a variety of tasks. I just want them to know that they can come to me if they have any complaints."

"I'll remind them of that," Lynn offered. "But they might be shy about coming to the boss."

It was Gabe's turn to smile. "I haven't noticed that. Now that they know my brother's a rich jock, they're hanging around me hoping some of his aura will rub off."

Although she wasn't cold, Lynn rubbed her hands up and down her bare arms. Her thoughts were on the difference

between her slender build and Gabe's powerful competence. "Did you ever play football?"

"Yes, in high school. I was a guard. All-state." Gabe was
watching her hands' slow, rhythmic movement. "I was offered a football scholarship, but I turned it down."

"You did? What did your family think?"

"That was the first true clash my father and I had. It set
the stage for our relationship since then."

"I'm sorry." Lynn reached out and touched Gabe's arm.
"I didn't mean to pry."

Gabe turned slightly and looked into Lynn's eyes. His
smile seemed forced. "Don't apologize. I've made my peace
with my father. Or at least I no longer try to juggle trying to
please him with what I need for myself. I just wish he felt the
same way."

Lynn went back to nervously rubbing her arms. "Relationships with parents can be so complicated," she said, her
voice no more than a whisper. "When we aren't what they
expect, it colors everything."

"You weren't what your parents wanted."

Although Gabe was making a statement and not asking a
question, Lynn didn't try to deny what he was saying. He
had, maybe, traveled the same road she had. "I wasn't even
what I myself wanted to be," she said. "I can admit that
now, but it wasn't so easy at sixteen."

"Are you going to tell me about it?"

"I'm not sure." She wished she were braver.

"Lynn?" Gabe took the hand closest to him, putting a
stop to her nervous gesture. He laced his larger fingers
through hers, bringing warmth to their cool tips. "You're
talking to someone who remembers what you were like on
the outside when you were growing up. I'd like to know
what it was like on the inside. I think I deserve that."

"Damn you, Gabe," Lynn whispered. "No one's ever asked that before."

Gabe's arm went around Lynn's shoulder. He didn't speak until she was nestled against his ribs. "Yes, I'm asking. Look, what I saw was a juvenile delinquent, someone who drove her teachers crazy. I think that you probably felt even more crazy than they did."

"You're right." He understood; he cared. He would understand so much more if only she could get the words out.

"You felt as if you were going crazy?" Gabe prompted her. "Why? What was going on inside your head?"

"That's what I didn't know." Lynn's laugh was so bitter that she hated the sound of it. But because Gabe was holding her, she found the courage to take the next step. She could, she believed, spend the rest of her life molded against him. "I had no idea what was wrong with me. That's what was so hard. I—I understood what the teachers were saying when they lectured, but when I had to read or write, I couldn't make things come out right. It was taking me two years to accomplish what others did in one, and even then I wasn't sure things would stick."

Gabe sighed but didn't say anything. Lynn could sense his eyes on her, but she couldn't lift her eyes from their study of an ant trying to climb from the picnic seat to her shoes. The ant was safe. She couldn't be sure about anything else. "I thought maybe I was going crazy. I was failing. Drowning. There wasn't anyone there to pull me out."

"You couldn't read in high school?"

Because she needed to know if there was condemnation in what Gabe was asking, she dragged her eyes away from the ant and found his. "Just about." Her words were clipped and wary. She was on the edge, courting either destruction or salvation. "I couldn't read well enough to get through a comic book."

"Why?"

"You don't let up, do you?" Lynn challenged. She could have pulled away from him, but she didn't. She needed his warmth and strength too much. She felt like the fragile spring that comes after a Colorado winter. "I was lazy; I didn't care—at least that's what the teachers and my parents told me."

"Damn it, Lynn. You aren't stupid, and I can't believe you didn't care. Where did the system fail you?"

He was siding with her. Lynn had expected as much, but hearing it meant more than she thought it would. She'd taken herself to the edge; he was pulling her back. "The system didn't fail me," she said softly. She rested against Gabe's side again and let his strength support her. "At least no one saw it that way in those days. They had certain methods for teaching and I didn't respond to those methods."

His lips were moving against her hair. "Why?"

For a moment Lynn lost her train of thought. It would be much easier it he weren't touching her in that intimate way, and yet she needed the physical contact. She didn't know if she would ever not need it. "Have you ever heard of dyslexia?" There. The word was out.

"Dyslexia? No." Gabe's right arm had been at his side, but now he touched her cheek with a gentle hand. "Tell me about it."

Tell him. How easy that was, now that she finally understood what had been wrong. The only thing lacking from the explanation was the years of anguished frustration before the label had been pasted on her. "It's a learning disability. It's inherited, although it didn't show up in my parents. Maybe it went further back," she said simply. "It means that by the time an image travels from my eyes to my brain it gets garbled." To demonstrate, she rotated her wrist in several directions.

"Is there a short circuit somewhere?"

"Not exactly." Lynn could laugh at Gabe's confusion. "For example I would look at a letter *d* on the blackboard, but by the time the image of the *d* reached my brain, it might become a *b* or a *p* or a *q*. There was never any consistency. I couldn't tell anyone what was happening because I didn't know what was wrong. I thought it was like that with everyone."

"And reading was hard because your brain was receiving confused signals. It was as simple as that?" Gabe asked.

"As simple?" Lynn spat out the words. "You call a wasted education simple! I'm sorry," she relented. Anger had no place in her feelings today. "I know what you mean. It's just that dyslexia has shaped my entire life. There's nothing simple about that."

"I didn't mean to make light of it. I know you must have gone through hell in high school. I was there for a little while, remember. But you're on track now. You graduated from college."

Lynn waited until Gabe's warmth had once again seeped deep inside her before starting to speak. "All those years of feeling as if there was something wrong with me. Gabe, I felt as if I was the only one out of step. Sure, there were other kids who were struggling, but I couldn't talk to them about how I felt. I hated going to school because I knew I was going to make a fool of myself. I wanted to be able to read for enjoyment, to write, to understand math. Damn! I wanted what everyone else took for granted."

"Ah, Lynn, it was hell, wasn't it?"

All she could do was nod. Gabe's voice carried some of the pain she'd felt for so long. She hadn't heard that from another person before. Knowing that he was able to absorb her emotions touched her more deeply than she thought possible.

"Take your time," he was saying. Once again, he brushed her cheek with his work-hardened fingertips. A sensation like a spark of raw lightning traveled through Lynn's body, but she fought it off. Later she might surrender to what his touch was doing to her, but for now she had a story to finish.

"It doesn't seem so bad now," she said. "I have some success in my life these days. I still can't take reading for granted, and I don't trust myself with math, because the numbers get transposed, but I'm supporting myself. And—" she smiled a little "—I know what kids are talking about when they say they hate school. The kids I deal with tell me I'm the first one they've met who doesn't lecture about the value of an education. I'd like to; I just know that approach isn't going to help."

"This dyslexia—how did you find out you had it?" Gabe asked.

Lynn didn't answer right away. Gabe's question could take them close to something she wasn't ready to talk about yet. She took the hand that Gabe had been resting on her cheek and held on to it. She knew she was gripping him tightly but couldn't help herself. "After I dropped out of high school, I was sent to a place for juvenile delinquents. I was tested there. They were set up to zero in on learning disabilities. The schools were, too, I guess, but I never stayed at one of them long enough because we were always moving."

Gabe was staring at Lynn's white knuckles as she gripped his hand, but he didn't try to stop her from bruising him. "You don't look like a juvenile delinquent now," he said with forced lightness. "They must have done quite a make-over."

"They taught me how to master reading. It took different techniques such as writing the words in the air and endless repetition, but it finally sank in."

"It sounds as if it was a good school."

The juvenile center had been closer to a prison than a school, but Lynn wasn't going to get into that. She wanted to turn the conversation away from her period of being institutionalized because Gabe might put two and two together. This moment was crystal glass; she wasn't going to drop it.

"It solved some but not all of my problems." Lynn took a deep breath and focused on Gabe's hand. Her fingers had left white indentations on the back of his hand. "When I was twelve, I started running away from home. We moved around a lot because of my dad's job. He was a dynamite expert who worked on bridges, dams, tunnels. I've gone to school in at least a dozen states. Despite that, my brothers and sister were able to fit in and keep up with school. My folks didn't know what to do with me."

"I think that's my line," Gabe said with a laugh. "See how much we have in common."

Lynn thought about that for a moment. "Too bad I didn't know that back when we were in high school. I could have used someone like you running interference for me."

"Yeah." Gabe expanded his chest boastfully. "I would have told everyone to lay off, that you'd get your act together if they'd just leave you alone."

"That's just the problem." Lynn no longer felt overwhelmed by what she was saying. She wasn't sure whether it was because she was coming to the end of her story or because Gabe's playful gesture had lightened the tone of their conversation. "They couldn't leave me alone. By the time I was in high school, I knew I was in trouble. The teachers couldn't contain me. Neither could my parents."

"It must be a relief to them to know that you've been able to put that behind you," Gabe said as Lynn again settled against him.

They could have been walking as they talked. Central Park was a beautiful place. She should have asked if he wanted to do something other than sit on a wooden table. But it felt so right to be making this kind of contact while she searched for the words she had to say. "It isn't as simple as that," she whispered. "Some bridges are harder to span than others. Sometimes... sometimes I think it's the years I spent in foster homes. There's so much distance between me and my parents."

"I'm sorry to hear that." Gabe took Lynn's middle finger between his lips. She felt his breath on her flesh.

"It's all right," she managed to say. The energy that had charged through her earlier was back full force with his touch. She didn't want to talk anymore. "I—I'm used to it."

"I don't think we ever get used to being estranged from our parents. Can't you talk to them?"

Lynn had no idea how Gabe could keep on concentrating on what he was saying. Her mind was no more than splintered fragments simply because his lips had been on her finger a moment ago. "I don't think so." She fought off the real need to run her fingers along his temple until she could feel his life force pulsing through the strong vein there. She tried to place her hand back in her lap but wound up touching his arm instead.

Gabe slid off the picnic table and then turned around to pull Lynn down with him. He enclosed her hand in his and started to walk back toward the parking area. "This has been quite an afternoon, hasn't it? You've been through the wringer. I think—" he paused "—it's time for other things. I want to take you to my place."

Chapter Five

Gabe drove with one arm around Lynn. Although he'd been touching her much of the time that they were sitting on the picnic table, he hadn't gotten enough of feeling her next to him. He'd sensed her shrinking within herself as she began her story and then took heart as her breathing became deeper and more regular. His hand still ached from where her fingers had dug into him. He wished he knew what was behind the gesture, but any more personal revelations would have to wait until she was ready to confide in him again. Although he tried to remember what she'd been talking about when her hand had suddenly clamped down on his, he couldn't concentrate on anything except the slight, warm body curled next to him.

She was so damn trusting of him. He hadn't expected that; he wasn't sure he was worthy of her trust.

Taking her to his place might be a mistake. And yet it would give them an opportunity to be alone, and he didn't want to share her with anyone. "Are you hungry?" he asked.

"Hungry? No, my stomach's all tied up in knots. I'm sorry. You must be starved."

"My stomach can wait. It's used to crazy schedules," he said as he forced himself to concentrate on traffic flow and stoplights. "Are you going to be all right? You aren't used to talking about your dyslexia, are you?"

"I don't know why it's so hard." She shook her head as if trying to break free of her own prejudice. "After all, I've heard the word enough in the past few years. Thank God I'm dyslexic. At least I'm not all those other things I thought I was when I was growing up. And I'm not stupid."

"You were never that." Gabe didn't know he was going to kiss Lynn until he glanced her way and saw that she was looking at him and her mouth looked so vulnerable. He covered her vulnerability as best he could, with a quick kiss to let her know that it was all right to expose her every emotion to him. He'd never felt like anyone's protector before, but now Gabe sensed a little of what a man must feel when a child places a small hand in his.

Gabe almost forgot to turn his attention back to the job of driving. It was a good thing they were almost to his house. Now it was his turn to be on edge. There weren't many women who could look at his place without making some comment about its rugged, if practical, appearance. In the past he'd gauged a woman's reaction to his home as if the house and yard were an extension of himself. He didn't feel any different this time, but now he wanted the house and what it represented of him to be accepted by Lynn Tresca.

Lynn didn't say anything. She had straightened up and was leaning forward a little, her eyes taking in the sight of the well-used equipment, the weathered exterior of the house, the brown, almost nonexistent lawn, and the massive dog standing silent on the walkway.

Gabe cut the engine and opened his door. Lynn slid past the steering wheel and got out on his side also. For a moment she stood with her legs slightly spread, as if waiting for the house and its surroundings to come over and touch her.

When she finally started toward the house, with the dog standing in the way, she didn't cling to his side. Gabe admired her for that.

Ranger came forward with his head and tail held high. He didn't bare his teeth, but neither did he wag his tail. That was the dog's way with anyone except his master, but most people were taken aback by the big animal's cool demeanor. They were used to dogs who either snarled or exploded with joy, not one capable of making judgments.

Lynn stepped ahead of Gabe and held her hand out slightly, her head cocked at an angle. "Cautious, aren't you?" she asked softly. "That's good. No one's going to pull anything over on you, are they?"

Ranger took the last few steps that brought him and Lynn within reach. Lynn let the dog touch his nose to the back of her hand; she didn't try to pat him or establish the usual human/dog relationship. She continued speaking in whispered tones. "I don't know much about dogs, big boy. You're going to have to show me what you want me to do. I think we could get along, but if you don't want that, I'll respect your space."

Slowly, almost shyly, Ranger butted his nose against Lynn's hand and then slid his massive head under her relaxed fingers. It was the first time Gabe had ever seen the dog allow anyone but himself to touch his ears. "He understands," Gabe said, a note of awe in his voice. "He accepts you."

"I take that as a compliment." Lynn was running her fingers along the base of Ranger's ears. "I like your friend."

"That's what he is, all right," Gabe admitted as he steered Lynn past Ranger and toward the stairs leading to his front porch. "There's a definite relationship, but it's not the usual one with dogs. He'll never be my pet."

Lynn didn't speak until they were inside. Once again, she was standing with her feet slightly spread. The corners of her mouth were upturned, but she gave no indication of what she was thinking. Gabe busied himself by opening the front drapes and unfolding the paper he'd brought in. He waited for her to speak.

"It's a man's place. Gabe, this house is you."

She was reading the house as clearly as she'd read Ranger. Gabe had intended to leave her alone while he searched the kitchen for something cool for them to drink, but instead he was placing his arms around her and pushing his hands gently into the small of her back. What he was feeling was both physical and emotional. He had little control over either sensation. "I'm not much on housekeeping," he whispered, his lips inches from hers.

"It doesn't matter. But—" she looked pained "—it needs work. Don't you want to do things to it?"

"Someday." Gabe shrugged. "When I have the time."

"When it becomes important, don't you mean?" Lynn's eyes didn't leave his. "It isn't a home yet."

"That didn't take long for you to decide." If it had been anyone else, he would have taken offense at what she was saying.

"I'm just telling you what my reaction is. It's your place. Gabe?"

He didn't need to hear the rest of what she was going to say. She was asking where they were headed. He wanted to give her an answer without words. As he kissed her, Lynn's lips were soft but strong, pliant, yet taking as much as they gave. He pulled her against him, drinking in her smell and loving the way she fit against his thighs and chest. Her arms went easily around his neck. She tipped her head back so their kiss wouldn't have to end. Gabe could feel her breathing deepen and matched her quicker rhythm.

Gabe sensed quicksilver in his veins. The first time he'd turned a blueprint into a building, he'd known he had found what he wanted to do with his life. He was being touched in the same way tonight, with a sense of rightness.

Sweet wonder flowed through Lynn. She hadn't given much thought about what going to Gabe's house could lead to, but she was glad they were alone. She wanted to use this time to discover what he thought and felt and believed about a million things. "It was a lifetime ago. The first time we met," she whispered.

"We were two different people then. Just children." Gabe touched her lips so lightly that she might have imagined the contact. "Back then I had no idea what I was going to do with myself."

She arched her back and gazed into Gabe's eyes. "You turned out well," she managed to say before shyness overcame her. She didn't want to say anything that would embarrass him. With her arms still around Gabe's neck, Lynn buried her head against his chest, feeling his strength.

She felt Gabe's lips brushing against the top of her head. He'd used the same gesture in the park. Knowing that he was capable of that much tenderness caught in her throat and made her giddy. She pressed her head more tightly against his chest until she heard the muffled hammering of his heart. His arms were around her shoulders, holding her close and safe, igniting her at the same time.

"You said you didn't know much about dogs." Gabe's voice sounded as if it hadn't been used in years. "Didn't you ever own one?"

Lynn blinked away tears she wasn't ready to explain and answered as best she could. "I remember a puppy my father brought home when I was five or six. I played with him all the time, but he was run over after we'd had him about a year. Then we got another dog. Buff. Did you have pets as a child?''

Instead of replying, Gabe took her face between his hands and tipped it upward. His lips were waiting. Lynn closed her eyes in an attempt to merge herself with him, to know his thoughts and feel his emotions. His fingers on her jaw were gentle but firm. He didn't want to let go. Not that she would fight him. She couldn't. Lynn wanted nothing more than to be in Gabe's arms, her lips pressed against his. He smelled male, alive, warm—a precious blend of scents that stirred something deep inside her and also frightened her.

"I've been trying to get my landlord to let me have a little dog, maybe a toy poodle," Lynn said when their kiss ended. She didn't know what, if anything, people said during moments like this. Rattling on seemed easier than saying nothing. "One of my co-workers has offered me a puppy when his dog has her litter. But I don't know. I don't want to leave a puppy alone all day."

"Then get an older dog." Gabe chuckled. "We could let Ranger interview the prospects."

Gabe's voice surrounded Lynn, and buried itself within her. She spoke but paid little attention to what she was saying. "I trust his judgment. Whatever he decides is fine with me."

"I'm glad you trust my dog. I hope you feel the same about me."

Lynn had been careful not to press herself too tightly against Gabe, but now she couldn't remember the reasons for her caution. It wasn't just his mind and intellect that she was interested in but his whole being. She felt terrified and brave, shy and courageous all at the same time, as if teetering on the brink of an uncharted adventure. As her hips sought contact with his, she became aware of a warmth building throughout her body.

Gabe groaned but didn't try to pull away. Instead, he held her so close that the boundaries between them blurred and began to merge. Lynn held on to the sensation with new-found strength. She'd never felt this joined with someone before. There was no guarantee the feeling would ever come again.

"Lynn?" Gabe groaned. "Do you know what we're doing?"

"No," she answered honestly, achingly aware that he was robbing her of his lips.

"You're asking a hell of a lot of me."

His plea broke through the fog surrounding Lynn. He was right. They were in dangerous territory. She was letting go, asking him to provide the controls she was unable or un-willing to maintain. She forced her eyes to focus on his. "I'm sorry," she whispered. "I—what do you want me to do?"

"What I want is to make love to you, but not unless that's what you want, too. I'm—I've never said it like that be-fore." Gabe paused. "Whatever you want is what I want."

Gabe's simple integrity told Lynn what she needed to know. He hadn't brought her here simply because he didn't want to spend the night alone. She believed that now, at least, no other woman could take her place. "I think that's what I want, too," she answered, shocked by how easy it was to say the words. "I—I want to spend the night with you." She was shaking, but tonight was for taking risks, for giving and taking and learning from the experience. He wasn't promising anything, but she didn't expect him to. He was too honest for that.

"You have to be sure. It wouldn't be right if it was any other way."

He was wise, so terribly wise. Lynn couldn't remember ever being this honest with another human being, and yet it

felt as natural as breathing to bare her soul to this man.
"I'm sure." She laughed a little. "I'm scared, but I'm sure."

"Ah, Lynn, what have I gotten hold of?" Gabe didn't
reveal any more of what he was thinking; instead he rewarded Lynn with a kiss that reached far deeper than any
she'd ever experienced. Forgotten was the quick, hot college romance that had burned itself out almost as soon as it
began. Despite the power she sensed in him, Gabe kept the
kiss gentle. It was a caress, a treasure, something to savor,
perhaps, for the rest of her life. In return, Lynn gave what
she could of herself. The warmth that had touched her a
moment before flamed brightly and threatened to consume
her. Lynn fought to control her response. She didn't try to
deny that she wanted Gabe. What she wanted was to pro-
long the emotion, to explore its valleys and hills. They were
like two people caught in the flood of a river. The current
could run slow and deep if they wanted that. Lynn did. She
believed that Gabe did, too.

Gabe had gone back to holding her against him, but as
their kiss continued and deepened, his hands slid slowly
from her back to her waist. When his fingers found the swell
of her buttocks, Lynn moved restlessly. The touch was intimate but not nearly as intimate as what was to come. She
needed this contact and everything it foreshadowed. Lynn
forced herself to relax the pressure her fingers were creating
on the back of Gabe's neck. He wasn't going to leave her.
They were locked in a magic space undisturbed by time.

Made bold by his hands, Lynn started her own exploration. His shoulders felt like blocks of granite, his arms capable of transporting her to another room or another world.
It was his waist that her fingers finally settled on. She shyly
touched the top of his hipbones, awed by the life-style that
stripped his body of any excess fat. It was a little awkward
keeping her lips pressed against his while her fingers inched

around to discover the fine, strong line of his backbone, but because she needed to sample all of him, she kept her back arched. She was standing on tiptoe, her calves taut with effort.

"Do you have any idea how good you feel?" Gabe whispered as he took a breath. "I've wanted to do this for so long."

Lynn had to be honest. It was the only thing she could be. "I've wanted it, too. Gabe, you're a good listener. You made things so much easier for me."

"I don't often play father confessor. In fact, you're my first customer. It felt good. Just like this feels good."

She didn't argue when Gabe twisted her around in his arms and pressed her back against his chest. She no longer tried to stand on tiptoe, but her back was arching with a will of its own, pressing her spinal column and hips against him.

She didn't move away when his hands found her breasts, but she wasn't sure she was still breathing. His exploration took so long that Lynn wondered at her ability to stand still, to let her arms hang at her side despite her trembling. Gabe unbuttoned her blouse with slow, dancing movements, pausing as each barrier fell away. When he finally pushed the simple cotton blouse off her shoulders, Lynn gave up the struggle to keep her breathing regular and drew in a drugged, ragged breath. There were flames throughout her body, flames that could be controlled only by feeling his body tight against hers. Yet she allowed his hands' search to continue.

He was running his sandpaper fingers over the swell of her breast above her bra. The first response was recorded in her nipples. It caused them to spring to new life. Lynn took another ragged breath when the first finger inched under her bra. She leaned heavily against him, her head thrown back, lips slightly parted. He was telling her that she was desirable. She could only thank him with her body, a body now beyond her control.

Gabe managed to release the bra fastening, and he slipped the straps off her shoulders so slowly that Lynn was in an agony of desire before he finished. Naked from the waist up, Lynn could only stand in willing surrender as Gabe explored her upper body.

She knew that he liked what he found without having to ask. His touch was loving and gentle. When he lifted her in his arms and strode into his bedroom, she clung to him, knowing that no words were necessary. They'd been two separate individuals when they entered his house. They would no longer be separate by the time the night was over.

Gabe stretched Lynn out on his unmade bed, but she was unaware of the uneven bedding under her aroused body. She lifted her hips to assist him in removing her skirt but shyly averted her eyes as her panty hose and panties followed. She knew he was studying her naked body, but she simply wasn't brave enough to read his reaction.

Lynn thought about sitting up and helping Gabe to undress, but cowardice, or perhaps weakness, overcame her. Unable to control her body's faint trembling she watched as he dropped his clothes to the floor. He was more magnificent than she expected, with a trail of dark hair nearly touching his navel. He was deeply tanned from the waist up, proof that he appreciated Colorado summers. He was ready for her. He was hers. Nothing was hidden any longer.

Smiling with what Lynn sensed was a shyness of his own, Gabe lowered himself beside her and kicked at a tangle of coverlet. "If I'd known this was going to happen, I would have made my bed," he whispered against her ear.

Lynn turned toward him, a moth drawn toward the warmth and life of his breath. Now that he was beside her, she no longer felt hesitant. He was offering her his body and she meant to savor the gift. "I don't care. It's you. It even smells like you."

"You smell like—" Gabe buried his face in her hair "—like shampoo."

Lynn laughed. She couldn't remember why she'd been so shy before. Being with Gabe tonight was right—the most perfect thing she'd ever done. "I don't believe that's the most romantic thing a man has ever said to a woman. You're supposed to say I remind you of wildflowers or something." She reached out, feeling the soft mat of hair defining his stomach.

Gabe sucked in his breath and drew her against him, trapping her hand between them. "Next time. I'll say that the next time."

There's going to be a next time, Lynn thought as Gabe covered her body with his. *There's going to be a next time,* flickered through her mind as their bodies united. After that there was no thinking. Lynn knew nothing except the feel of Gabe's lips on her mouth, down the side of her neck, tasting her breasts. After that came the exquisite explosion.

She had no idea how long they clung together after they'd both been satisfied. It might have been hours; it might have been minutes. It didn't matter. Lynn Tresca had never before felt as if she belonged anywhere, with anyone.

"I take it you don't do this every night?" Gabe suddenly asked.

Lynn easily gave him the answer she knew he was seeking. "I don't like the concept of a one-night stand. That cheapens something that should be special. Getting close to someone else, I think, takes an act of courage."

"For you it does." Gabe brought his lips to her throat for a moment before continuing. "You're wonderful to make love with, Lynn, and I think that's because you don't take the act lightly."

"I don't." Lynn left the rest unsaid. Gabe would have to fill in the blanks. They lay together in companionable silence for a while; then Lynn opened her eyes and took note of Gabe's bedroom for the first time. "What's wrong with that wall?" she asked. "It isn't painted."

"Observant, aren't you? I had to replace the wall because of some old storm damage. I just haven't gotten around to putting up paneling." He groaned and stretched luxuriously, flexing his muscles. "Do you want to talk about paneling or eat?"

"Eat. I'll cook if you want, but it's not my favorite thing to do."

"You watch; I'll cook."

To her surprise, Gabe served not canned soup or a TV dinner but ham and sweet potatoes cooked in a microwave along with the fruit salad she made. Lynn was dressed in one of Gabe's T-shirts. It hung in limp folds over her shoulders and clung to her breasts but came down over her hips just far enough for decency. She could have put her blouse and skirt back on after her shower, but when Gabe handed her his T-shirt, she knew it was the only thing she wanted to wear.

"I'll wash the dishes in the morning," Gabe said after they were finished eating. They'd hardly spoken since making love, but there was a comfortable quality to the silence. Lynn liked knowing there was no need to fill the room with a barrage of words.

Lynn had been wandering around the living room constantly aware of the way Gabe's eyes followed the movement of her bare legs. Although she wasn't sure she'd ever feel brave enough to tell him, she liked knowing she was capable of holding his attention. "How long have you lived here?" she asked as she took note of the books on a shelf in the corner of the oversized room that was devoted to his desk and computer.

"Five years. It was practically given to me by a man who couldn't pay his bill after I did some work for him." Gabe joined her, draping his arm easily over her shoulders. "My dad wanted me to take the man to court, but I considered it an ethical form of barter. I received payment for my services."

Lynn stared up at the fifteen-foot ceiling. The room was perhaps twenty by thirty feet, while the rest of the house was traditional in size. "What was this room originally? I can't believe it was always a living room."

"It wasn't. I understand that the building was once a small store. The family lived in the rest of the house and operated their business from this room." He pointed toward his massive oak desk, its scarred surface buried under invoices and blueprints. "This was where the cash register sat."

"What did it look like when you moved in?" Lynn was trying to get a further reading on Gabe from the room. It was unconventional and expansive, with each area serving a definite purpose. One area held a TV and a recliner. Another corner resembled a small meeting room. There was an elaborate stereo system opposite the desk and the computer.

"This room looked as if no one had been inside it for ten years. Evicting the spiders was a major project." Gabe laughed and led Lynn over to the wall closest to the desk. "I had to redo the wiring throughout the house. When I moved in there was one electrical outlet in the whole room. I keep saying I'm going to finish the interior work. It needs new carpeting, and I already have bought the paneling for that bedroom wall. But," Gabe said with a shrug, "there never seems to be time. It's livable as it is."

"It serves you well, doesn't it," Lynn observed.

"I wish you could get my old man to see it that way. He hates this place."

Lynn stiffened at the mention of Judge Updike but forced the emotion away. "As long as you like it, that's the only thing that matters."

Gabe had noticed the sudden tensing of Lynn's muscles. For several hours he'd been able to ignore the feeling that there was more to Lynn's story than she'd revealed in the park. Now the sense was back again. There was still a wall between them.

He hated that wall. Gabe had had women in his bedroom before. He'd told those women about the house's history, watched their wary unease around Ranger and sensed that they didn't understand why a man would live on property more suited for storage than a home. But he hadn't cared what they thought, for those women were in his room because, although he didn't like admitting it, he'd had only one thing in common with them.

It was different with Lynn. Gabe didn't yet understand the difference, only that she was much more than a body and warmth and someone to spend the night with. He wanted to take more steps with her but didn't know how.

"I wish it were that simple, but my father won't let things rest," he said. "My father's a formidable man. For years he intimidated me, but then, maybe because I discovered certain skills I could take pride in, I started to stand up to him. I've tried to make him understand that there's more than one yardstick for measuring success in life."

Lynn came close, so close to telling Gabe that she did know the judge and could sympathize with Gabe, but at the last instant she held back. Tonight was as close as to perfect as she'd ever experienced with a man. She was terrified of testing that perfection. "You care what he thinks, don't you?'' she pressed. "If you didn't, you wouldn't have brought it up."

"What are you?" Gabe turned Lynn toward him so she had no option but to meet his eyes. "A psychiatrist? Are you trying to analyze my relationship with my father?"

"Hardly. I'm the last one to be an expert on family relationships." Lynn ducked her head momentarily, but finding strength in Gabe's touch, fastened her eyes on his again. Their dusty quality had taken on new depth. "But you aren't happy the way things are. You'd like to be accepted for what you are."

"It'll never happen." Gabe's resigned smile was ragged around the edges. "I know that."

"I'm sorry," Lynn started before a thought reached her. "I think it's more complicated than that," she hurried on. "You'd like your father to acknowledge your life-style, and yet I think you're putting deliberate barriers between you. This house, for instance." Her eyes strayed to the window and its view of a flatbed truck. "It's a monument to the fact that you've rejected your father's values. Tell me if I'm wrong, but I'm guessing that the home you grew up in is as different from this as it's possible to be."

"Are you saying I'm using this place to defy the judge?"

Lynn sensed Gabe's denial, but because she'd expected it, she continued. She didn't believe that what she was saying would jeopardize what they'd started. "Gabe, I've seen your business. I don't know how much money you make, but I have to believe it's enough to allow you to live just about anywhere. You don't have to stay here unless you want to, unless you have something to prove by it."

"It's a little more complicated than that. There are facets of my business neither you nor the judge are aware of." Gabe released Lynn and turned away. He was facing the window when he spoke again. "I need storage space for the machinery I don't want to leave on the construction site. When I meet with my foremen and architects, I don't want to do it in a sterile office, and there isn't room in the trailer. This place symbolizes what I am for the people I do business with."

"It also symbolizes your rejection of your father's values." Lynn ached with the need to feel Gabe's arms around her, but she didn't think it was the right time to reach out for him. She'd taken their relationship along a rocky path by telling him about her growing-up years. They were on another rocky path now; she wasn't going to try to smooth the journey with her body.

Gabe was a long time in responding. Lynn watched his unmoving body. She could have ruined everything with her words, but she didn't think so. He simply needed time to think.

"What do you know of my father's values?"

He had her now. Or perhaps he didn't know how close he'd brought them to her remaining secret. Either way, Lynn wasn't going to avoid the question. "He's a judge," she said. "True, he isn't involved with juvenile cases now, but the system isn't big enough that juvenile workers don't know most of the judges in Denver. Besides..." She paused, wishing she could see his eyes and not his back. "His reputation gets around."

Gabe turned around. "Is it that bad?"

Lynn didn't read anger in the dark eyes searching her in the darkened room. And yet something hung between them. "Let's just say that Judge Updike's opinions were formed many years ago. He hasn't changed them."

"Let's just say that he's an opinionated bastard. But he's a good provider for his family. And he kept Brook and me from getting into trouble because he had goals he expected us to meet. I respect him for that. But I will admit he is hard-nosed.''

Lynn nodded. ''Don't you see?'' She spread her arms in a questioning gesture. The movement lifted the hem of Gabe's T-shirt, but she didn't think it mattered. ''He's probably the same at work as he is at home. I know what you've had to contend with.''

''And you think I'm rebelling against his beliefs by living here?''

There was a questioning, almost tentative quality to Gabe's words that told Lynn he was no longer angry with her—if he ever had been in the first place. She wondered if he could sense her tension or if he was locked too tightly within himself. ''I think so. I think that's why you've never finished the work on it.'' She dropped her hands to her sides. He looked magnificent silhouetted against the window, a physical bear of a man with a sensitivity that was just starting to be revealed to her.

''You may have a point. I'll try to think about that. But later.'' Gabe ate up the space between them in three steps. His hands were light on her shoulder. ''In the meantime, what are you doing with the rest of the evening?''

''Oh, I don't know. Why? Would you like me to help with the paneling?'' Lynn leaned forward. She felt as if she were being sucked into eyes and muscle and warm flesh that were capable of absorbing her. And she didn't mind the feeling at all.

At least she told herself she didn't mind.

''We'll panel later. Then there's the matter of the carpet. There's no telling how long you might have to stay here.''

''I'd like to find out if we can remodel a house without getting into a fight. We should at least have decorating skills in common.''

That wasn't the only thing they discovered they had in common before the night was over. Lynn learned that Gabe liked to surround himself with music when the mood called for it, and although his stereo system was much more sophisticated than her small radio at home, the effect was the same. Music framed the mood before, during and after their lovemaking.

The first time they'd made love, Lynn had felt hesitant and virginal. This time she was more confident that he found her desirable. She was no longer afraid to satisfy her curiosity about his body. She didn't think it bothered Gabe to learn that the uncertain woman he'd taken to his bed earlier had now turned into a woman who had become fully a partner in lovemaking.

"Stay the night, please," Gabe asked after they'd turned the bedsheets into a hopeless tangle. "I want to wake up with you next to me."

"I want to wake up next to you, too," Lynn whispered back. She buried her fingers in his beard and rested her cheek on his shoulder. The last sound she heard was that of his heart beating.

Taking over her own heart sounds.

Chapter Six

Brandy had changed. The last time Lynn saw her older sister, Brandy had been in what she now called her "gray" stage. As a brand-new stockbroker, she'd felt it necessary to dress like a clone of the men who made up the bulk of her profession. That called for wearing blazers and slacks and nondescript skirts. Her blouses had nothing as daring as a ruffle. But the past two years had given Brandy confidence. Now, as the two women met for dinner at a small, elegant restaurant, Brandy was ready to have heads turn in her direction. Her soft yellow sweater was just low enough to reveal enticing mounds and expensive enough to set off the silk pants she wore.

"No, I'm not kidding," Lynn was saying. "I've never been here. Sis, juvenile officers go to McDonald's, not places where you need reservations and no one can pronounce the names of the wines."

"I'll have to take you to New York with me one of these days." Brandy wrapped a professionally manicured hand around her wineglass. "Not that I think you're a hick, Lynn. I'd just like you to see another slice of the world. I know I'm different now that I've experienced things I never dreamed of as a child." She lowered her voice. "I was so damn scared when I started out as a broker, I wanted to blend into the woodwork. But, well, I have more guts now.''

Lynn had already taken in enough of her sister's outfit to realize that "self-confident" was exactly the word that described Brandy. Although it was a little hard to reconcile the slim, poised woman with Lynn's memory of braces, knobby knees and a thin nose constantly stuck in a book, Lynn sensed that Brandy was much happier with herself than she'd been when they were growing up. Brandy had always known she was smart; now the rest of the world knew, too.

"I wonder," Lynn started to say slowly. "I wonder if the confidence you have now wasn't there all the time; you just had to grow up in order to bring it out."

"Maybe. With all the moving around we did, it was hard to make friends or feel confident." Brandy leaned closer so that the flickering light from the candle on their table accented the lightened strands around her face. "And maybe we change more than we realize as we grow older and start having control over our lives. You aren't the same person you were as a child, either."

"I was a mess." Lynn tried to laugh. "Even I couldn't read my handwriting."

"You scared me sometimes. I never told you that, but there were times when I really was afraid of you."

Lynn winced. She hated hearing that from her sister. "I'm sorry. I didn't mean—"

"No," Brandy interrupted, "don't apologize. You couldn't help it. It's just that you were so damn angry. You never took that anger out on anyone except yourself, but Lynn, that's what scared me."

"I don't understand," Lynn said, although maybe she did.

"I was afraid you might give up."

Lynn wrapped her hands tightly around her wineglass. It would have helped relieve the tightness in her if she could shatter the glass and to hell with the consequences, but Brandy was right. Lynn never had taken her anger out on anyone but herself. "You thought I might commit suicide? I never knew—"

Brandy nodded. "That's why I'm so thankful you have your act together now. The folks should know that."

"They could ask."

Brandy took a sip of her wine, her eyes on Lynn's white knuckles. "It hasn't gotten any better, has it? You still don't see them?"

"It depends on what you mean by 'see.' We were together at Christmas. We talked about Dad's upcoming retirement and the price of gasoline and whether Mom should try contact lenses. There's this invisible line none of us cross." Lynn knew she sounded stubborn; she didn't like that characteristic in herself. But Brandy had been busy with her own growing up. She hadn't been the one weathering the arguments, the insinuations that all Lynn had to do was try harder in order to bring her grades up. Her parents had allowed her to be placed in foster homes. They hadn't done a thing to stop the legal machinery that sent her to a residential center for delinquents.

"I'm sorry." A shadow settled into Brandy's eyes. "Sometimes I wish I could lock you and the folks in the same room and not let any of you out until everything has been hashed over."

"You might have to wait a long time." Lynn was resigned to the way things were. She didn't often think about what couldn't be changed. "Brandy, this isn't your problem. I've learned to deal with it, and I'm sure our folks are relieved not to have me around, ramming my fist through their walls, anymore."

"The point is, you aren't ramming your fist through any walls. I wish they could see that. I wish you could tell them what life's like for you now."

"So do I," Lynn whispered. It hurt, more than she could say. "Look, my life's on course. I'm not interested in dredging up the past. We get through the holidays by tiptoeing around each other."

Suddenly, Brandy smiled. "Speaking of having one's life on course..." She held up her left hand to show an impressive diamond glittering on her ring finger.

Lynn clamped a hand over her mouth in surprise. "How could I not have noticed? You—you're engaged?"

"Yep." Brandy pasted on a smug grin. "The dedicated career gal is engaged, to a man who believes in engagement rings; can you believe that? Don't worry, I'm not going to chuck my suits and put on an apron, but I've come to that point in my life when I want to belong to someone." Brandy shook her head as if not quite believing what she'd said. "I didn't think that was ever going to happen to me. I love my work. I thought that was going to be enough."

"I'm surprised," Lynn admitted. She was grateful for being allowed to share Brandy's happiness. "You always said you were the original career woman. Together. That's what you said. You had your life together."

"I thought I did, too." Brandy was still smiling, but her voice was sober. "But that together life was lonely. Is that a contradiction in terms? I think it's because we were so rootless as kids. It's time for me to experience commitment."

While their salads were being placed in front of them, Lynn mulled over what Brandy had just said. "I'm happy for you. You know, you've always done what I felt I should be accomplishing myself. It looks as if everything you could ever want is falling into place."

"And you don't resent that?"

Lynn didn't try to sidestep her sister's serious question. "No, and I don't think I ever did. I didn't hate you even when you were getting all those academic scholarships and I was flunking every class I was in except phys. ed. It—" Lynn stopped long enough to allow the wave of emotion to wash over her. "I desperately wanted to believe I had a brain, but I didn't begrudge you your brain."

"That's a relief." Brandy had been toying with her salad, but now she put down her fork and covered Lynn's hand with her own. Tears glistened in Brandy's eyes. "You have a brain. It took too long for that brain to be tapped, but all that's behind you now. What I'd like now is for you to find someone."

Lynn blinked back tears of her own. It hurt to think that she and Brandy had wasted years that could have been spent close to each other, but that was the past. Lynn believed in living in the present. "Your fella wouldn't happen to be interested in polygamy, would he? He sounds like a prize."

"Them's fighting words, sis. My clothes I'll share. My man's another story."

"That's all right," Lynn said lightly. "I don't need to share."

Brandy blinked. "There's someone? My independent, strong-willed sister?"

"Yes, there's someone." Lynn opened her mouth to tell Brandy about Gabe, but she couldn't find the right way to begin. She didn't know what words, if any, would convey the special, precious emotions that were coming to life in her. Or her fear.

As if she understood Lynn's confusion, Brandy pressed forward. "Let's start with the basics. He doesn't have a criminal record, does he?"

Lynn laughed. "Not as far as I know. He owns his own construction business."

"Does he have a name?"

Lynn spoke without thinking. "Gabe Updike."

Brandy was silent too long. "As in Judge Updike?"

Lynn hadn't thought Brandy would remember. "Yes, Gabe is the judge's son."

"Does he know?" Brandy shook her head at her question. "Of course he knows who his father is. What I mean is, does he know of your past involvement with his father?"

Lynn wanted to say no, but that didn't take things far enough. "Not yet," she amended. "I—I have to tell him. I just don't know how."

Lynn was no closer to an answer to this problem by the time she and Brandy had finished their dinner. Brandy once again tried to talk Lynn into joining her while she ran over to Salt Lake City to visit their parents, but Lynn backed off. Her explanation that Brandy had a great deal to tell their parents and didn't need Lynn around as a distraction fell a little flat, but to Lynn's relief, Brandy didn't press the issue. Instead, her older sister simply asked Lynn to give serious thought to having a heart-to-heart talk with their parents.

Fortunately, Lynn had more than a flawed familial relationship to think about when she woke up the next morning. Although she had eight hours of work ahead of her, there was still the evening with Gabe to look forward to. He had called the day before to ask if she minded sharing a sandwich with him at the construction site. He explained that he was going to be working late for the next several days, but if she didn't mind a casual setting for dinner...

Lynn pointed out that any meal she was involved in would be casual. Then, because he'd called during working hours, she asked him a few questions about the boys on his pay-roll. "I keep telling you to become a civil servant," she wound up. "You sound too much like a workaholic."

The eight hours crawled by despite three emergencies that wreaked havoc on her originally planned schedule. Lynn vacillated between clock watching and mentally picturing what Gabe was doing at 10:43, 1:05 and 3:31. She could imagine him shucking his shirt as the temperature climbed into the eighties, the sweat from his day's labors holding his T-shirt tight against his finely honed body.

At four-thirty she gave up all pretenses of work and signed out for the day. Gabe had promised to pick up deli sand-wiches, but Lynn wanted to make the meal as special as possible. She might be a disaster in a kitchen, but she'd been known to go grocery shopping a few times. She drove to a local farmers' market and bought fresh peaches. On im-pulse, she added chilled apple juice to her purchase and headed toward the construction site, hoping she'd find re-frigeration there.

Lynn arrived just in time to watch a solid line of cars and trucks leaving the construction site—a fleshed-out skeleton of a shopping center. When at last she was able to drive past the outer fencing, there were only a handful of vehicles left. She parked near the trailer bearing the words Updike Con-struction and pulled the key out of the ignition. It now seemed incredible that she'd been here a few short weeks ago and had somehow not sensed that her life would be changed before that day was over.

After changing into practical tennis shoes, Lynn ran her fingers through her hair, lifting the thick locks away from her temples. Today she'd worn a light summer-weight sweater and dark blue slacks that could survive hours around dust and dirt. The moment she stepped out onto the hard-packed surface of the construction site, Lynn left behind all vestiges of her professional life. This evening she was eager to soak up as much as possible of her new environment. This was Gabe's world. She wanted to become part of it.

The sound of masculine voices drifted toward her, borne aloft by a mountain-scented breeze that kept her sweater from being too warm. Despite not being able to see who was speaking at the far side of the massive earth-moving equipment, she was able to isolate Gabe's voice. It wasn't the deepest, nor was it the loudest. It was simply the one she had to hear.

The first time Lynn had come here, she'd felt a little shy about invading this masculine enclave, but Gabe had given her access. She had a right as well as a need to be here. Pleased at the prospect of having the site to themselves, Lynn boldly walked around a piece of machinery with tires taller than she was. Gabe was talking to the solidly built man with the oversized belly whom Lynn had met the first day, while two other men in more formal attire stood opposite them with clipboards and briefcases held in their hands. Lynn didn't need anyone to tell her that Gabe was controlling the ebb and flow of the conversation.

When the men acknowledged her presence, she nodded but didn't try to join them. Instead, she stood leaning against the monster-sized machinery, listening with half an ear while the men finished their conversation about load-bearing walls within what was going to be the largest structure. Although the two men in slacks and dress shirts referred to their forms several times, regulations and figures rolled easily off Gabe's lips.

"Red tape." As the two men reached their car, Gabe shook his head both for Lynn and his foreman's benefit. "We're going to be crushed under regulations one of these days."

Gabe's foreman shifted his hard hat from one hand to another before reaching for his car keys. "Like I keep telling you, don't worry about it. There'll be a new regulation to replace this one tomorrow."

Lynn shared a laugh with the men but waited to speak to Gabe until they were alone. "Problems?" she asked. It shouldn't be hard to carry on a normal conversation with Gabe. He looked different today and she, too, felt different from the last time they'd been alone together, when they'd been lovers.

"Nothing new. You look so damn good! Do you have any idea how tired I get of seeing nothing but men in blue jeans?" Gabe was holding his arms at an awkward angle as if unsure of what to do with them, resisting the impulse to embrace her publicly.

Being together again is as special to him as it is to me, Lynn acknowledged to herself. She took a tentative step forward, but the need to have everything perfect stopped her. She wanted to put her arms around him and feel his lips against hers, but she lacked the courage to make it happen. It had been two days since she'd seen him. Two long days!

"I missed you last night." Gabe still hadn't made a move to touch her.

"I had dinner with my sister last night. I hope you can meet her someday. I think you'd like her." Damn! This wasn't what she wanted to talk about. But she was afraid; what if their minds and bodies no longer fit? What if she found a name for the quiet fear she'd been living with?

"What did you talk about?"

"You."

Gabe took the final steps to close the space between them. His voice was husky as he enfolded her in his arms and held her against his tired body. "I was that important?"

Yes, Lynn wanted to say. Yes! But they'd had so little time together; they were still so new with each other.

"Your name did come up." Lynn lifted her face for the kiss she'd been dreaming of for two days. Not for the first time was she grateful for Gabe's power. Without him holding her tight, she wasn't sure there was enough strength left in her legs to keep her from collapsing. A kiss shouldn't be capable of doing this to her; it had never happened before.

"Lord," Gabe groaned a long minute later. "Maybe you shouldn't have come."

Gabe's words brought Lynn back to earth. She wanted to be sure around him, but she wasn't. "Don't you want me here?"

"You're the only thing I want. But I meant it about having to work." Gabe shrugged ruefully. "If I do what I want to right now, my men aren't going to be able to accomplish anything tomorrow."

It took a far greater strength than she knew she possessed, but Lynn managed to pull back enough to look up at Gabe. The darkness spreading over their surroundings was captured in his eyes. "Then I guess we'd better get dinner out of the way, so you can get back to work."

Hand in hand they walked over to the trailer. Lynn reluctantly let him go while she hurried over to her car for her purchases. He was holding the trailer door for her when she stepped into it. There was something overwhelmingly intimate about being the only two humans in the middle of thirty acres of gravel and machinery. "Tell me something?" Lynn asked. "The first time you saw me, what impression did you get?"

"What kind of a question is that?" Gabe cocked his head. "You want the truth? I thought, What the hell are they doing sending her?"

"Because I wasn't wearing a gun?"

"Because I thought it was going to take muscle to get that kid out of my trailer. And like it or not, Ms Tresca, muscles are not your most obvious attribute."

"Oh, yeah." Lynn dropped her load on Gabe's desk and turned to challenge him, hands on hips. "Are you saying a person has to have muscles to come here?"

"I'll make an exception in your case." Gabe made a show of testing the strength of her upper arms.

"You're a little late," Lynn teased. "I already feel comfortable here. If this is supposed to be an all-male enclave, I'm sorry, but I'm thinking about changing that."

"What's with you tonight, lady?" Gabe ran his fingers along her arm to her throat. "Are you trying to pick a fight?"

"I was just thinking how comfortable I feel here. I'm not sure why, but I think it's because I know the boss." Lynn stood on tiptoe long enough to give Gabe a whisper-light kiss. "Your dinner is going to get warm."

"Warm?" Gabe was staring at her with a puzzled look.

"I brought fruit and a chilled drink. You need your vitamins if you're going to be burning the midnight oil." Lynn stopped speaking. She wasn't sure she was capable of another rational sentence. If she weren't absorbing Gabe's warmth from his encircling arms, it might be easier.

With a shake to bring himself back to reality, Gabe turned toward a small battered refrigerator half buried behind a large coil of copper wire. He didn't speak as he pushed aside the coil and opened the refrigerator. Silently, he handed her two paper-wrapped deli sandwiches.

A half hour later, with their supper finished, Lynn went for a walk alone in the dark while Gabe sat hunched over reports and blueprints. Despite Gabe's contention that he wanted her around while he worked, Lynn was unable to simply sit still and watch him. As Lynn idly followed the trail of marker flags to the far end of the site, she realized she was totally at peace with her environment. Despite being surrounded by dark craters awaiting concrete and stark gray walls devoid of doors and windows, Lynn wasn't going to run from what held only a promise of reality. She wasn't used to being comfortable with the dark and with silence. Darkness had always brought back memories of the small closed-up room she'd been locked in at the juvenile center. Silence had given her thoughts too much time to flail helplessly at the quicksand of her early life.

The quicksand was gone now. Where it was and what had replaced it were questions Lynn wasn't ready to answer. It had, she believed, something to do with the man back in the trailer.

But admitting that simple fact would mean having to admit how essential he'd become to her life in so short a period of time. It was, she believed, dangerous to depend that completely on another human being.

Her heart was racing full speed ahead into something from which it might never recover. The suspicious woman who had been taught the hard lesson of relying on no one wasn't yet ready to fight those years of conditioning. She couldn't deny that there was a warm thread reaching out from Gabe to her in the dark. That thread carried the light and warmth she needed to explore the deepest shadows. She simply wasn't going to give that fragile thread a name. Not yet.

A few minutes later, Lynn was sitting atop a piece of earth-moving equipment she'd had to claw her way onto. She sat with her hands around the controls, body hunched forward as if poised for the first downward thrust that would displace tons of clay and rock. There was power in her hands, a sense of control she'd never experienced before. Maybe... Lynn ran her palms lightly over the controls, soaking up feelings left behind by the men who'd mastered the clawing monster under her. She could understand why men were drawn to the strength of steel and machinery.

She could understand why construction was more than a word on the side of a battered, dirty trailer.

This was Gabe's world, his domain. Lynn understood that a man like Gabe could have a steel mistress. He needed to feel that there was more to him than two hundred pounds of muscle and bone. He needed backhoes, skip loaders and jackhammers around him.

Lynn shivered and leaned forward, the oversized steering wheel taking most of her weight. She wondered if Gabe ever tried to find words to explain why what he did was essential to his happiness or whether he felt more comfortable keeping those emotions to himself.

She wondered if she wanted to get close enough to him to ask.

Although he didn't call out to her, Lynn sensed when Gabe left the trailer and came looking for her. Perhaps his shoes made a faint sound on the hard-packed granite; perhaps Lynn was simply tuned into Gabe enough that their bodies were already communicating without words.

She waited until she felt that he was standing next to the machine on which she was sitting. "If I asked you to teach me how to run this, would you?" she asked. "I might need a job someday."

"I thought you were afraid of the dark," he replied instead. "What are you doing out here?"

"Waiting for you. You didn't answer me." His deep tones were swirling round her, emotionally pulling her down to him.

"If you want to learn, I want to teach you."

It was the right answer. Although there was no one to see her expression, Lynn smiled before lifting her body out of the hard seat. She felt Gabe's hands first on her legs to steady her and then around her waist as he helped her down. She waited until her feet were on the ground and then turned toward him.

With his arms around her, Gabe pressed her back against the cold column of steel, but his lips on her mouth were so gentle she was aware only of the kiss. Lynn wrapped her arms around Gabe's neck, undone by her need to feel him strong and alive against her.

"I thought you had to work," she whispered. It was incredible to her that a man—any person—could be capable of touching emotions buried so deep inside.

"I'm done now but I kept thinking about you out here alone." He took her mouth again. "I had to find you," he said after he released her.

"I'm glad. Gabe? Were you serious about our working together on your place? I'm not very handy."

Gabe shook his head. "Tonight we're going to your apartment."

"You're sure of yourself."

"With you I'm not sure of anything," Gabe admitted. "You don't mind, do you? Going to your place, I mean."

"No. I don't mind." She was grateful for his hesitancy. If he'd been self-confident, she might have drawn back with an instinct aimed at self-preservation.

Gabe walked Lynn back to their parked vehicles. He was aware of her dependency on him in order to place one foot in front of the other and wondered at his own body's ability to do certain things without assistance from his brain. He'd told Lynn only half of the story when he'd said he'd finished working. Although he'd sat staring at the material covering his desk, his mind was filled not with thoughts of load-bearing walls but of the soft, whispering laugh of a woman who hadn't laughed enough in her life, who hadn't shown him all he wanted to know of her potential for laughter.

She was beside him now; he never wanted to let her go.

"Tell me about your sister," Gabe said when they were on the road leading to her apartment. "Are the two of you close?" It wasn't a casual question.

"We are now."

Lynn's hip brushing against his made it impossible for him to concentrate, but he had to try. "Now?"

Lynn's sigh was a little shaky, but when Gabe wrapped his arm around her shoulder, she continued with newfound strength. "Brandy and I used to live in two different worlds, or at least I thought we did. She was a bookworm. I believed books had been put on earth to torture me. That didn't give us much in common. But..." Although he couldn't see her smile, Gabe could sense it. "I guess she's decided I'm not as crazy as I used to be. We're getting to know each other now. Brandy's getting married and I'm happy for her. I just wish..." Lynn's voice trailed off.

Gabe waited a minute, but when Lynn didn't finish her sentence, he prompted, "You just wish what?"

"She wants me to try to clear the air with our parents."

Gabe could have told Lynn that he shared Brandy's concern. He could have said that maybe this estrangement between daughter and parents didn't have to continue. But he didn't. "You'll do that when you're ready to," he said instead.

Lynn was silent for a minute and then said, "Thank you."

"For what?" He turned his head just enough to touch the top of her head with his lips.

"For not putting pressure on me. I got enough from Brandy. Damn." The oath was so soft that for a moment

Gabe wasn't aware that she'd sworn. "I wish it wasn't so complicated."

"Life's complicated," he replied with a wisdom he wasn't sure he could be credited with. "And I am putting pressure on you, Lynn. Your sister's right; we have to talk about that. But not tonight," he amended.

They made love in Lynn's bed after leaving a trail of clothes leading from the front door to the bedroom and the latch still hanging limply instead of locking them in and the world out. When Lynn slipped his T-shirt over his head and found the fastening on his jeans, Gabe thought back to their first time together, when he'd made all the moves. Now her hands moved freely over his flesh as if trying to commit him to memory. Even as his own hands traced their way over her breasts and belly, Gabe wondered how many other men had felt those small warm fingers on them.

Not many, he believed. The knowledge gave him comfort. When he made love to a woman, it was because he found something in her mind that appealed to him as much as her body did. He liked believing that the same held true for the woman moving restlessly underneath him. He wanted to give and to receive something that would last longer than one night.

And then Lynn's hands and his own stripped away conscious thought, and Gabe was flown to that place where only sensations could reach him. He was ready for fingers on his stomach, buttocks and chest; he was ready to surrender to her touch.

With her fast breath on his cheek and neck, Gabe slid over Lynn and entered her, surrendering his separate self. He was taking and giving, his need making him vulnerable, desire making him bold. As the torrent filled him, Gabe could only grasp briefly at a thought. With Lynn he could receive more than physical satisfaction.

Lynn tasted salt. She didn't try to lift her head from Gabe's chest when her tears began to fall. A few minutes ago they'd been lovers; now she was lying with an ear pressed against the flesh and bone separating her from Gabe's heart. It was the sound of that strong beat that had started her tears.

"You're crying."

Turning his words over in her mind, Lynn decided that he wasn't demanding an explanation, but gave him one anyway. "I'm not... Gabe, I'm not used to feeling close to someone. I wasn't ready for this."

"Ready for what?" Gabe sounded uncertain.

"I'm letting my guard down so much. That's the way I feel," Lynn said through her tears. Although her voice quavered, she didn't feel embarrassed about crying. Just the reason. "I never used to cry," she explained. "I didn't dare. And... it never did any good."

"I wish you wouldn't. You're scaring me."

She shook her head. "I don't mean to do that. Just call it a case of arrested development. I feel secure enough to cry these days. I know—" she laughed at herself, laughter mingling with the other emotion "—it sounds like a contradiction, but it takes courage to let someone see me cry."

Gabe ran his fingers over Lynn's back, the journey taking a long time. "How many people have seen you cry?"

Only one. You, Lynn thought. "My nose gets red, and my eyes puff up." Her answer was an evasion, but his question was pointed. She needed a moment to get used to it.

"I don't mind. I just want to know why you're crying when it happens."

"I'll try to remember that. It isn't always easy for a woman to explain her emotions."

"It isn't any easier for a man."

Gabe's words stopped Lynn's tears. She didn't know how many men felt sure enough about themselves to admit their frailties; she appreciated having Gabe tell her that. It made him even more precious than he already was. It also scared her to know how far they'd come with a few short words.

"No," she said slowly. His beating heart was hard to think around, but she had to try. "I don't imagine it is. We build so many defenses around our emotions. That's sad. I don't think it's healthy."

"It has to do with vulnerability." Gabe's fingers were resting on the swell of her hips; the contact went beyond physical intimacy. "Adults are afraid of admitting their vulnerability," Gabe concluded.

"I'd like to get past that. I just don't know if I'm capable," Lynn said, her words blowing breaths of warm air across Gabe's chest. "A child lets its parents see every emotion. A child is a window with no curtains. I don't know why we lose that ability when we grow up. I wonder if we do it consciously."

Gabe was breathing deeper than a minute before. "Is this a professional observation you've made, Ms Tresca? Something they taught you in college?"

"It's something I've learned as a result of dealing with delinquents." Their conversation was turning down new alleys with almost every sentence, but Lynn didn't feel the need to try to direct it. Somehow, she hoped it would come out right in the end. "Kids—the kids I work with, at least—have learned to lock their feelings up inside them. The hardest thing I do is try to unlock those doors. But it's necessary. That's the only way they're going to learn what they want out of life."

"You're committed to what you do, aren't you. It isn't just a job."

"You have to ask?" Lynn laughed to lighten the impact of her question. "I wouldn't be bringing my work home with me if I cleaned carpets for a living. Dealing with kids in trouble means carrying bits and pieces of them around with me."

"I think it also means sometimes finding yourself in them."

Lynn turned what Gabe had said around in her mind. He understood her so well that it was more than a little frightening. Maybe he understood her better than she did herself. The safe response would be to draw away, to deny what he'd said. But that would mean drawing away from the man as well, and Lynn didn't want to do that. "I think this conversation is getting too deep. You know, you'd think that a man who has his own construction company would know a few things about the art of conversation." She touched the tip of her tongue to his warm skin.

"Don't," Gabe warned. "Not if you want to get any sleep tonight."

"I'm not interested in sleep," she answered.

Chapter Seven

It was Sunday afternoon. Gabe and Lynn were watching a football game on TV at Gabe's place, with Ranger sleeping just outside and the remnants of their lunch still on the coffee table. Gabe sat sprawled on his aged couch; his lap served as Lynn's pillow. The game was into the second half, and although Lynn had never watched an entire football game in her life, she was content to watch this one until the final gun. Quarterbacking one of the teams was Gabe's younger brother.

She'd enjoyed the short interview between Brook and a sports reporter before the start of the game almost as much as she appreciated the close-up shots of him cocking his powerful arm, almost a twin of the one resting on her shoulder. Although his helmet obscured much of his face, Lynn read intensity in Brook's every fiber. It was obvious that his love affair with football was as total as what Gabe felt for turning raw materials into a man-made structure.

Lynn shifted her weight, but Gabe didn't move his arm. She was aware of his warmth, his breathing, everything about him. Laying her head on Gabe's lap had taken more courage than she wanted to think about. It was a submissive gesture. *It'll get easier,* she told herself. She wasn't sure she believed that.

"Stay in the pocket, damn you!" Gabe muttered for at least the fifth time that afternoon. "I swear, I don't know what that fool's thinking. The protection's there. He has to use it."

Lynn wanted to tell Gabe to relax, but she knew that he was only half aware that she was in the room. "You could be there, too, you know," Lynn observed, her words muffled by the bony pillow that was Gabe's knee. "I bet you could have made the pros."

"And never know when I was going to be put on waivers? No, thank you. I'd much rather be am employer. They can't fire the boss."

"I think I've heard that before. What's the real appeal? All that job security?"

"You better believe it. No headaches. Nothing to do but sit there and count my money." Gabe still hadn't taken his eyes off the screen.

"If that's the case—" Lynn held out her hand "—how about a loan of a few thousand? I figure I can start paying you back in about twenty years."

"Don't count on it, lady," Gabe said in his best gangster imitation. "I'll send my goons after you if you're five minutes late. They don't ask twice."

Lynn was going to say that she wasn't exactly trembling in her boots, but the words never got out for she became involved in the action on the TV screen. As she watched, Brook moved back to relative security behind his front line, the way he'd done dozens of times already today. Even when the huge defensive lineman charged in, dumping Brook, neither Lynn nor Gabe took it seriously. Brook had been sacked before. Only this time he didn't get up when the lineman was no longer sprawled over him. Brook moved not a muscle.

Gabe leaned forward; he seemed to be holding his breath. "Get up, you fool. Come on, kid."

Lynn watched, not fully understanding why the cameras stayed on the inert quarterback. She'd seen other players injured throughout the course of the game. Usually the stop in the action was an excuse for a commercial break. But not this time. The announcer wondered whether the second-string quarterback was sufficiently warmed up to take over. When Gabe stirred and then rolled onto his side to grab his right knee, the announcer didn't say anything more. Brook's pain-twisted face said it all.

"Not the knee." There was agony in Gabe's voice. "Anything but that damn knee."

"What's wrong?" Lynn asked, but Gabe was staring, unblinking, at the TV screen. She sat up and leaned forward, not believing that she was actually seeing first several coaches and then a stretcher come onto the field. The noise level from the crowd had been cut in half. Then the announcer started up again. He said something about Brook Updike having a history of knee injuries and being in obvious pain. Another announcer broke in with hollow words about hoping to see Brook back in the game before it was over, but Lynn knew better. Someone had removed Brook's helmet; the look in his eyes tore Lynn apart.

"He's done it this time," Gabe said with rough finality. "There goes the season," he added when Brook threw his head backward in pain as he was being lifted onto the stretcher.

"Gabe?" Lynn ventured when the picture switched to a commercial. "Are you sure? I mean, maybe it isn't so bad."

"It's bad enough. There's only one weak place on my fool brother's body, and that's his knees. I wonder if Dad's watching."

The phone rang as if in answer. Gabe picked up the receiver, his clipped responses telling Lynn that Gabe held no hope of seeing his brother throwing a football again today. She didn't say anything after he'd hung up. She wanted to save him from having to answer questions.

"We'll just have to wait and see," Gabe supplied. "Mom's pretty upset."

And what about your father? Lynn thought.

"It isn't the first time," Gabe muttered as if trying to reassure himself. "Brook's hurt those knees before. Maybe it isn't as bad as it looks. His career—"

"How can we find out? I mean, is there someone from the team you could call?" Lynn ached to soothe away the frown lying heavily between Gabe's eyes but knew it would be a futile gesture. Worry couldn't be brushed away with a touch. She could only give him her companionship and hope he understood that she wanted to carry some of the load.

"He'll call." Gabe sat back down, his eyes fastened on the TV screen as Brook's replacement took over the quarterbacking chores. Lynn settled down beside him, knowing that the easy companionship they'd been sharing wouldn't return. She didn't try to distract Gabe with her presence; neither did she feel slighted because he seemed to have forgotten that she was there. If she'd seen someone whom she loved injured . . .

Lynn closed her eyes, surprised by what she'd just learned about herself. She felt love for Brook Updike, although she'd never met the man and might find little to talk to him about when she did. But he was Gabe's brother, and because of who he was, she loved him. She could feel his pain; she could fear for Gabe's brother.

The knot of disquiet that had settled in her stomach had to be a twin of the one Gabe must be feeling. "I wish there was something I could do," she offered.

"There's nothing anyone can do. But thanks for saying it." His lips brushed her forehead. "I'm glad you're here. There isn't a damn thing you can do, either, but I'm glad you're here."

"Do you want to go see your folks?" Lynn asked after the game was over. "Maybe they know something by now."

Gabe shook his head. "Brook will call me. I'm sorry, Lynn. This isn't the way I wanted today to turn out. That damn fool!"

"Because he's a football player?" Lynn had been putting away the remnants of their lunch, but now she came to where Gabe was staring out a window and draped her hands over his shoulder. She couldn't give him false assurance; all she could give him was her support in what she hoped was a comforting gesture. He had, after all, said he was glad she was there.

"Yeah. No. I wouldn't want to take that away from him even if I could." Gabe stared down at her, but his eyes were somewhere else. "It's his decision. It's what he wants to do with his life. But if it's bad—"

If it's bad, you'll be there for him. Lynn held the thought close, not wanting Gabe to know that she was experiencing the emptiness of all the years when she'd felt she had no one who would do that for her. "Where will they take him?" she asked. "I mean, does the team have its own doctor?"

Gabe answered her question but didn't turn back toward her until she was no longer touching him. Only when she'd broken the silent contact did he spin around and press her close. "I'm sorry. I'm not much of a host, am I? Look, do you want to go out for dinner or something?"

"No, I don't want to go out for dinner or something. I don't have to be entertained. We'll wait for the phone call." *We.* Lynn wanted to be part of the waiting, the call, the words that would be said when they knew whether Brook would ever throw a football again.

When the phone rang, Lynn was telling Gabe about a runaway who'd shown up on the front steps of the police department because that was the only place with lights on at three in the morning. Gabe gave her a quick, questioning look before answering it. "Yeah, I saw," he said carefully into the instrument. "What'd they say? Damn! When's the surgery? Don't give me that. Of course I'll be there."

He hung up the receiver and turned to her slowly. His eyes were hollowed out; Lynn knew that nothing she could say or do would take that away. She waited. "Brook's scheduled for surgery tomorrow morning," Gabe explained in a life-less voice. "They won't know anything until after that, and maybe not then."

"How is he?" she asked, taking Gabe's strangely cold fingers and pressing them against the side of her neck.

"He isn't in pain anymore." Even though Gabe was star-ing at her, Lynn sensed that he was in a southern California hospital and not here with her.

"That isn't what I meant," Lynn amended. "How is he up here?" She tapped her forehead.

"Scared. One hundred and eighty pounds of scared kid. He's been under the knife too many times. There isn't much left to work with. Football has been his dream, his life, since he was eight years old. I don't know if he can live without it. At least not while he knows he's still young enough to have some playing years yet."

Lynn took a deep, calming breath. "Does he want you there?"

Gabe nodded. "He didn't say so, but I know. That's why he called. There isn't anyone else, not really." Gabe dropped his eyes, his voice little more than a whisper. "It isn't easy being the quarterback, especially one who gets all the press.

He doesn't really have a best friend on the team, because quarterbacks are set aside due to the nature of their position. The pressure. And . . . there's no one woman for him. At least I don't think there is." Gabe laughed bitterly. "Sure, there'll be all kinds of coaches and owners and reporters circling him like buzzards, but there won't be anyone who wants to hear what he's feeling in his gut. He can't tell anyone he's scared."

"That's why he called you, Gabe. He needs his big brother," Lynn pressed. She felt the hot weight of tears behind her eyelids, but because she wanted to be strong for Gabe, she fought them off. "You're the one he can show his white knuckles to."

Gabe brought his eyes back up and stared at Lynn for so long that she lost contact with any sense of time. Finally, he spoke. "I wonder if I can get on a flight tonight?"

Lynn took Gabe's hand and guided him to the telephone. "Call. And make that reservation for two."

Gabe blinked. "You want to come, too?"

Lynn was saying so much, maybe too much, about her need to be part of Gabe's world, but she didn't draw back now. Tomorrow she might need her own physical and emotional space back, but not now. "He's your brother."

"Oh, God. How did I find someone like you?" Gabe's words were almost lost in the slow, deep kiss that followed, but Lynn understood. She gave him what she could of herself, knowing that their kiss was for understanding and not passion; knowing their relationship was taking a giant leap that might have to be retracted—later. She stood with her arm wrapped around his waist as he made reservations for a 10:00 P.M. flight and then helped him think through how construction was going to continue on schedule for the next few days without him. It wasn't until Gabe had called his foreman that she asked about his parents.

"Brook said he'd talked to Mom before he called me," Gabe explained. "Of course, they're going to be there. Mom wants to see that her baby's all right. And Dad?" Gabe's tone was bitter. "Dad has to make sure that nothing goes wrong with his investment."

"That isn't fair, Gabe," Lynn pressed despite the cautioning inner voice that said she was treading on dangerous turf. "Of course your father cares about his son."

"He'll be there because he can't stand any flies in the ointment. He's set up a means of assuring my brother's financial success. No setbacks allowed."

Lynn wondered how many other people had heard Gabe talk like that about his father. Not many, she guessed. That she was being shown a glimpse of a complex relationship meant more to her than she had the words to express. "I think we'd better pack," she said.

Within five minutes Gabe had thrown a change of clothes into a suitcase and declared that he was ready to take Lynn to her house to pick up her things but she was able to convince him to pack at least one more outfit in case Brook needed him for several days.

Lynn tried to take as little time as possible to pack, but she, too, had phone calls to make. She informed her supervisor that she would be taking several days of personal time and then called her co-worker Chuck Rubin to ask him either to reschedule appointments for her or, if he could find time, to contact several teenagers whose problems wouldn't wait.

"You're having to do more juggling than I am," Gabe observed after she'd called her supervisor back to ask him to make sure a court report she'd completed was sent over to juvenile court.

"Don't worry about that," Lynn assured him. "Maybe they'll see how indispensable I am. About two hours ago you offered to take me out to dinner. Does the offer still hold?''

Lynn brushed off Gabe's apology. She didn't expect him to be concerned with the state of her stomach when his mind was occupied with his brother. As Lynn suggested that they grab a quick hamburger and then go back to Gabe's place to make arrangements for Ranger's care, she realized that it was she who was taking charge tonight. Gabe had made the decision to go to Brook, but it was she who was focusing on the details. She wondered if Gabe was aware of that but didn't make a point of it.

The last hour before they left for the airport lay heavily. Lynn managed to get Gabe to tell her more about what he and Brook had been like as teenagers, but there was no way she could keep his eyes from straying to the clock every five minutes. "I'm lousy company; I'm sorry," Gabe muttered after she'd had to repeat a question twice. "I don't know why you're here. You'd have more fun with a statue."

Lynn had been perched on the arm of the couch where Gabe sat, but she now slid down next to him, pressing her hip against his. "I'm learning something new about you tonight," she said as she fought off unexpected depression. She simply wanted to be with him; she hoped he knew that. "What you feel for Brook is beautiful. Thank you for letting me see that."

Gabe turned toward her, the emptiness that had lain in his eyes turning into something she knew was for her alone. "Thank you for not asking me to explain," he whispered. "I love my kid brother. When I'm not thinking about wringing his not-so-scrawny neck, that is. I just don't know how to put that emotion into words."

Lynn brushed a finger gently over Gabe's eyelids. "It's in your eyes. You don't have to say anything."

"It's the way men are raised, I guess." Gabe's expression became thoughtful. "We aren't supposed to cry. To care too much."

"I don't believe that's possible." Lynn felt so close to Gabe, so set apart from the rest of the world at this moment, that it was frightening. Still she couldn't deny him what he needed to hear. "Maybe men are taught not to show their emotions, but that doesn't stop the emotion."

"I don't think I've ever thought of it that way." Gabe blinked and brought his eyes back into focus. His mouth, which had been pulled into a taut line for several hours, softened. "You're making me think about a lot of things in ways I never have before. Between you and my fool brother I'm being given a run for my money. This isn't the way I wanted today to turn out. I was looking forward to a Sunday for us. For... I'm not sure what for." He stared at his hand for a moment before touching her cheek. "Just for being us, I guess."

Lynn didn't ask for more of an explanation. At times what she felt for Gabe Updike threatened to engulf her. The only way she could retain self-control was by denying the depth of those emotions. "I've never flown before," she admitted. "I hope I don't get airsick."

Gabe's look said he understood she was trying to change the subject, but he didn't push the issue. Instead, the kiss they shared in the minutes before they had to leave for the airport was filled with an intensity that had to be sidelined earlier. Lynn felt her body's response to his mouth, his arms, his body. She acknowledged that her response was far more powerful than any instinct to preserve what she'd been before meeting him could be.

When, reluctantly, Lynn watched Gabe pick up their suitcases and head for the door, she knew that although there was now physical space between them, she had left an essential part of her essence with him. If something came between them now, she might never have that part of her self back again.

LYNN WASN'T AIRSICK, but neither did she particularly enjoy the flight. Because it was night, she could see nothing of the earth below them. There was something lonely about the businessmen going through their briefcases or trying to sleep. She was eager to reach their destination, and Gabe's restlessness only added to her sense of unease. They held hands during most of the flight, an act that Lynn noticed didn't set well with the attractive young stewardess who asked Gabe if he wanted a drink at least three times.

She supposed she should have expected the Los Angeles airport to be operating on a twenty-four-hour schedule. Still, it surprised her that it was possible to rent a car in the middle of the night and reserve a motel room near the hospital without having to leave the airport. Once they'd been given directions to the motel and collected their luggage, they entered a highway system that boggled Lynn's mind with its complexity. "I'm glad you're driving," she admitted. "I'm so turned around I have no idea where we're going."

Gabe explained that he'd been to Los Angeles before both on business and to watch Brook play. "I think we should try to get a few hours of sleep and try to be there before he goes in for surgery."

Lynn kissed Gabe's cheek. She could have remained silent, but she didn't. "Thank you."

"For what?" Gabe ventured a look in her direction before concentrating on driving again.

"For including me in everything." It could be a dangerous thing to say.

"Of course you're included. I don't want it any other way."

WIN A GREAT PRIZE

▲ If you are NOT signing
up for Preview Service, DO NOT
use seal. You can win anyway.

FILL IN BIRTHDAY
INFORMATION BELOW

MONTH   DATE

This month's featured prizes—a
dream come true MINK or FOX
jacket, winner's choice + as an
added bonus, a world renowned
delight, Godiva Chocolates for 101
other winners.

Harlequin American Romance™   Free Gifts–Free Prizes

YES I'll try the Harlequin Preview Service under the terms specified herein. Send me 4 free books and all the other FREE GIFTS. I understand that I also automatically qualify for ALL "Super Celebration" prizes and prize features advertised in 1986. I have written my birthday below. Tell me on my birthday what I win.

154 CIA 1513

PLEASE PRINT

NAME

ADDRESS   APT #

CITY

STATE   ZIP

PLEASE PICK FUR JACKET YOU WANT ☐ FOX ☐ MINK. Gift offer limited to new subscribers, one per household, and terms and prices subject to change.

If card is missing write:
Harlequin
"Super Celebration"
Sweepstakes
901 Fuhrmann Blvd.
P.O. Box 1867
Buffalo, NY 14240-186

Harlequin
"Super Celebration" Sweepstakes
901 Fuhrmann Blvd.
P.O. Box 1325
Buffalo, NY 14269

PLACE
1ST CLASS
STAMP
HERE

Lynn closed her eyes. She'd felt some of her life force merging with Gabe's back at his house. Now he was taking even more of her, and that scared her. Just the same, she wouldn't try to pull away.

Gabe had requested a single room at the motel. She needed to be with him; the form their togetherness took wasn't the essential thing. Lynn unpacked her nightgown but didn't know whether to put it on or not. It was utilitarian, not alluring. Gabe might interpret the sedate collar and long sleeves to mean she was putting barriers between them. It wasn't that at all. It was just that Lynn had never wanted to dress for a man at night before.

Gabe stopped her before she had a chance to claim the bathroom to change in. "We're going to be here a day or two," he said as he sat on the side of the bed, removing his shoes. "I hope we'll have time for us, but now..." His voice trailed off for a moment. "I just wish I could tell Brook that we're here."

Lynn draped her nightgown over her shoulder and kissed the tip of Gabe's nose. "You're doing enough worrying about that brother of yours for three people. That leaves him with nothing to do except getting a night's sleep. I hope you're not that way when you have kids. You're going to drive them crazy." She started to turn away, but Gabe took her wrist, stopping her.

"I can't help it, Lynn. I'm sorry. I'm as much fun to be around as a dead mackerel."

"I've never been around a dead mackerel." Lynn nipped teasingly at Gabe's nose. "I'm willing to bet you smell better than one. Gabe, I'm here because I care about you and your brother. Because I wasn't going to let you come to Los Angeles without getting in on the action. I'm not asking to be entertained."

"I just can't believe it." Gabe had to let go of her, but his almost desperate sigh held her. "Here I am in a motel room with a beautiful woman and all I can think of is getting to the hospital in a few hours."

"I understand," Lynn whispered before leaving him. "Believe me, I understand." When she returned a few minutes later, he was still sitting on the side of the bed with a rather sheepish grin on his face.

"I've never had this happen before," he said, continuing the conversation he'd started earlier. "I mean, here I am in a motel with a woman. The old hormones should be taking over, but they're not. You understand that, don't you?"

"Are you asking if I've figured out that you're more man than male? Yes." Lynn helped Gabe to his feet and loosed his belt for him. He looked so tired that she wanted to mother him. "It makes me feel good to know you can be honest around me. Don't ever try to be anything but what you are."

Slowly, Gabe took over the chore of shucking off his jeans. "I feel comfortable with you. Maybe 'comfortable' isn't the right word." Gabe's eyes slid to her breasts which disrupted the smooth line of Lynn's gown. "I can't imagine ever taking you for granted. But I don't have to pretend around you. I guess that's what I mean by comfortable."

Lynn pulled down the coverlet on Gabe's side of the bed. She patted the bed and waited until he'd sat down on it. "How about if we continue this psychoanalysis business in the morning? Don't forget, it's been a long day for both of us. You're going to be a walking zombie if you don't get some rest now," she ordered. She walked around to her side of the bed. "We'll talk when we're both a little more coherent."

When Gabe reached for her, Lynn willingly nestled against him, but she made no attempt to distract him from the sleep she hoped would claim him. In a few minutes his breathing deepened, and his muscles relaxed. Only then did Lynn ease his arm off her. She felt both trapped and content, emotions she couldn't reconcile any more than she could understand them.

Lynn was able to sleep a little herself, but when Gabe got out of bed at dawn, she joined him. Gabe shaved while she showered. She took the small motel towel he handed her and started toward the bedroom to dry herself and dress. They were acting, she thought, like a long-married couple.

"Do you have any idea how good you look this morning?" Gabe asked as he placed himself between her and the door. "I hope you were able to get some sleep."

"Enough. What about you?" Gabe was wearing only shorts, the soft blanket of hair that covered his chest inviting her touch. The towel she held in front of her was all but useless when it came to modesty.

Gabe touched her hands clutching the towel but made no attempt to remove it from her. "The world takes on a different perspective in the morning. Maybe it's just convincing myself that Brook's in good hands; maybe it's knowing I'll see him soon, but I think I have a handle on things now. I can be strong for him now."

"I'm glad." There wasn't anything else Lynn could think of to say. The silence between them was both awkward and electric, the potential for a spark less than a breath away.

Gabe took that breath. When he touched her towel, she didn't try to stop him. Her hands dropped heavily to her sides as the towel was removed. She'd never given much thought to her body in a sexual way, but she could see it in Gabe's eyes. What he was seeing pleased him.

"We have a few minutes."

"I know." Lynn barely got the words out.

Despite the cramped quarters, Gabe lifted her in his arms
and carried her to the rumpled bed. As air touched her still-
damp flesh, Lynn trembled, but a moment later Gabe's
body took away the cold and turned her into a quickly
building flame. Last night she'd been content to only listen
to his breathing; this morning she needed more. He was the
man who made her feel as if she were giving up her personal space; he was also the only one she'd allow to get that
close.

He gave himself freely, holding back until she was ready
and then finding the release that hadn't come last night.
Lynn held onto him with arms and legs that didn't need to
hold tightly in order to possess. Her fingers could move
softly over his shoulders and not grip desperately. Her kisses
were by turns light and lingering, never reckless. Even when
self-control had become nothing more than instinct, she still
touched him with feathering strokes. Raw animal emotion
wasn't what she wanted between them. There had to be tenderness, a communication that went beyond the physical.
She was looking for an end to the unease that ebbed and
flowed whenever she was around him, and for a few minutes she found contentment.

"We're going to be late," Lynn muttered. She felt as if she
were still floating above herself, looking down at the two
limp bodies that had felt so much a moment ago.

"I want you here. Always. Lynn, it's good between us."
Gabe ran his mouth down the side of Lynn's neck, the act
recharging her numb nerves.

Always. A forever word. One she wasn't sure she believed in or even wanted to before Gabe. An emotion that
lived uneasily within her. Someday, soon, she would have to
talk to him about that.

The sound of the shower propelled her out of bed. By the
time Gabe was out of the bathroom, Lynn had dressed and

was using a blow dryer on her hair, which she'd forgotten to have cut since meeting him. She felt self-conscious as he watched her until she caught the faint smile he didn't try to suppress. "I've never watched a woman dry her hair before. I didn't realize it could be such a fascinating experience for the watcher. Do you have to do that every day?"

"The price of beauty," Lynn explained. "It can't be any worse than having to shave."

"What we don't put up with under the guise of civilization," Gabe observed. "If we were cave dwellers, I'd be snuggled under my saber-toothed-tiger skin, waiting for you to bring home—what was it I told you to get for breakfast?"

"Get your own breakfast, caveman," Lynn shot over her shoulder. "This woman doesn't slay any prehistoric creatures for any man. In fact, you can consider yourself in big trouble any time I venture into a kitchen."

Although Gabe seemed relaxed while they were driving to the hospital, he stiffened perceptibly once the sliding-glass doors at the entrance to the institution closed them inside. Lynn took his hand, finding it, as she expected, cold. She winked up at him, when he glanced at her, but she wasn't surprised when he didn't speak or smile. She filed under miscellaneous information the knowledge that he didn't like hospitals. Convincing the volunteer manning the patients' information desk that Gabe had a right to see the hospital's most famous patient took even more out of Gabe. He was tight-lipped and uncommunicative while they were in the elevator and in no mood for another quizzing from the third-floor nursing staff.

"Do you think I flew here from Colorado because I'm his fan?" Gabe snapped as he shoved his driver's license in the head nurse's face. "He's scheduled for surgery in a few minutes. I have to see him right now."

By the time the head nurse relented, Lynn was shaking with both anger of her own and concern that Gabe would indeed lose his temper. She let Gabe lead the way down the hall, trying to put herself in Brook's place. Surely the last thing a healthy young man wanted was to be surrounded by hospital walls.

Brook was everything she'd imagined and more. Even stretched out under the sheet with his heavily wrapped leg sticking out, Brook Updike impressed Lynn as a man who had no business being in a hospital. Except for his leg he was a well-tuned machine. If anything his hands were larger than Gabe's. His face, less weathered than his brother's, was the epitome of a health-conscious generation. She understood perfectly why Brook was always referred to as a handsome bachelor.

Brook had eyes only for Gabe. "Where the hell have you been?" he asked, his voice slowed by the presurgery medication. "Did they give you a hard time? I told them my brother was going to be here. I told them you were the only one I wanted to see this morning."

"Have the folks been here?" Gabe asked. He'd punched Brook lightly on the shoulder, but now he stood with his hands hanging at his sides.

Brook blinked as if he were having trouble focusing. "Not yet. I hope to God I don't have to see them until later. If Mom starts crying—"

"Our mother cries every time you get thrown on your can. What makes you think it's going to be any different this time? Brook, I want you to meet my...I want you to meet Lynn Tresca."

Brook turned his head. Although his study of her took longer than Lynn would have liked, she appreciated his honest appraisal. "Hello, Lynn Tresca. He hauled you along with him, did he?"

Lynn took a step closer to the bed. She would have given anything to take both men away from this place. "No, I asked to come."

"Yeah?" Brook looked confused. "He's a strange one. I don't know why you'd want to bother with him." Brook nodded in his brother's direction. "Stubborn as hell."

"And you're not?" Gabe broke in. "I was yelling at you all afternoon, 'Stay in the pocket.' You never did listen to me."

"I was in the pocket when there was a pocket. It wasn't my fault I got sacked."

"Excuses, excuses. If you were faster on your feet—"

"Which is it going to be?" Brook interrupted. "First you're on my case because you want me to stay put and then you chew me out for being slow. Do you think I planned this?" He jabbed a finger at his knee.

Lynn drew back a step as the brothers continued the argument, which she realized Gabe had started in an attempt to keep Brook's mind off what was ahead of him. Looking at Gabe now, she would have never guessed he'd been tied in knots a few hours ago. He was reaching beyond himself, trying to place himself in Brook's position, giving his brother something to focus on. He was exactly what she would have wanted if it had been she waiting to go into surgery.

"The doctor who's doing the surgery?" Gabe asked. "Does he have any idea what he's doing?"

Brook took so long to answer that Gabe had time to throw Lynn a look. "He should," Brook said slowly. "He handled my last two operations."

"Tell him he gets a percentage of what you earn playing the rest of this season," Gabe suggested. "That should keep him on his toes."

"I don't think there's going to be any more playing for me this year."

Brook's words hung heavy in the sterile air. Lynn breathed deeply to control her own emotions so she would have strength to pass on to Gabe. She didn't speak or move, but from the way Gabe locked eyes with her, she was sure he had correctly read her emotions. He didn't jump in to dispute Brook's words, and when he did speak, Lynn felt her heart swell in response. Gabe wasn't going to attempt to deny Brook his fear. "We don't know that yet. And if it is, we'll deal with it," he said softly to the droopy-eyed man. "Let's take this one step at a time, kid."

Lynn wasn't ready to have the two attendants enter Brook's room. She wanted more time before Brook was taken from them. "We'll be here when you wake up," she promised before allowing the men access to Gabe's brother.

"Thanks," Brook said sleepily. He fought off the helping hands of the attendants and, despite the effort showing in his face, managed to hoist his solid frame onto the stretcher that would take him to surgery.

Lynn wrapped her arms around herself tightly as Brook was pushed out of the room. It was crazy to feel this way. Brook was going to have injured muscle and bone repaired; his leg wasn't going to be amputated. But tension was something she could smell and touch in the room. She had no defense against it.

When she looked at Gabe, she found the source of that tension.

On numb legs Lynn went to Gabe and pulled him close. She felt nothing except compassion and understanding. And maybe something even deeper. "I was proud of you," she whispered into his chest. "Brook was able to tell you what he's feeling. It helped."

"I can't remember him ever being this uptight before," Gabe whispered back. "God, I'm glad you're here. I'd hate to have to be doing this alone. I don't know if he thinks it's worse this time or if he's just tired of being injured." He waited until Lynn looked up at him and then continued. "It's going to get rough around here when the judge shows up. I hope you know that. I can quote you chapter and verse what he's going to tell Brook."

Lynn had no thoughts other than continuing the communication flowing between them. They were merging; right now that was the only thing she wanted. "I want to be part of that. I hope you understand...." She didn't finish. If words were needed to explain why she wanted to be part of the bad as well as the good, that would have to wait. All she had was the emotion.

"I think I do." What hesitancy lingered in Gabe's voice was erased from Lynn's mind when he kissed her. It wasn't until she heard the voice from her past that she remembered where she was.

Chapter Eight

Judge Updike had made an uneasy truce with age. His hair was a little thinner and a lot grayer. There were more lines in his face, but because they only accented what Lynn knew about the man, she barely noticed them. He seemed to have shrunk somewhat, a fact that meant little, since the man still led his way through life with his chin. His eyes were smaller than his sons', and buried so deeply in his skull that they appeared to be connected directly to his brain.

By contrast, his wife was a small moth of a woman who walked a half step behind her husband as they entered the room. Lynn wondered if that said anything telling about their relationship. By the time the judge said his first words, Lynn had her answer.

"I wanted to see him before surgery. Where is he?"

"You're too late. They took him away a minute ago," Gabe supplied. It wasn't a meaningless gesture when he placed himself between her and his father. Lynn was grateful.

"When I talked to Brook last night, he said surgery was scheduled for nine o'clock. It's only a few minutes after eight." The judge spoke indignantly, as if this were somehow Gabe's fault.

Gabe shrugged. "There must have been some kind of mix-up. He was pretty sedated, Judge. He probably wouldn't remember anything you said, anyhow."

Lynn knew Gabe was lying to protect his brother. She wondered how many lies the sons had told over the years. She swallowed, knowing that the time would come when Gabe would have to introduce her.

She wasn't ready. She needed more time before Gabe put his arm around her and pushed her gently toward his parents. Just the same, she held out her hand, her mouth locked in a frozen smile. The judge's hand was dry, the skin scratchy; its size told her where the sons had inherited theirs. Gabe's mother's hand was as soft as her husband's was leathery, her handshake tentative enough to tell Lynn that she wasn't comfortable with the gesture. For two seconds longer than necessary, Lynn gripped the older woman's fingers, seeking her eyes.

"You flew here with Gabe?" the judge asked. "That's a new one. I'm surprised to see him here, let alone with a woman in tow."

Lynn sensed Gabe's tension. The words were what Lynn expected. "Why would you think Gabe wouldn't come here?" she baited. She was in no mood to tiptoe around the emotional land mines Gabe and his father were setting up.

"If you've known Gabe for any length of time, young lady, you know by now that that business of his is his mistress. How did you manage to tear yourself away, Gabe?"

Lynn wasn't surprised to have the judge dismiss her. She suspected that concern for Brook had honed a fine edge to the judge's always sharp tongue. That she understood. Despite everything else, he was a father.

"He asked us. He needed us, and we came," Gabe was saying. His voice grated on Lynn's ears, telling her of the effort it took for him to remain civil to his father. The real-

ization that she had found a direct line to Gabe's emotions
grew even clearer. His thoughts were hers.

"Us?" Mrs. Updike asked. "Gabe, why didn't you tell us
about—Lynn, is it?"

Lynn stiffened at the sharp glance the judge threw his
wife's way. "I was watching the game with Gabe when
Brook was hurt," she supplied. "You might say I tagged
along." It wasn't the whole truth; she needed to acknowledge Gabe's mother's curiosity and yet not expose her
emotions where Gabe was concerned. "Brook looked pretty
good just before they took him away," she continued. "He
didn't seem to be in any pain."

"Brook's used to pain," the judge cut in. "The damn
fool's going to have to find out the hard way that there's a
limit to what he can take."

"Let's talk about this later, Judge," Gabe said through
taut lips. "Why don't we hear what the doctors have to say
first?"

"You know damn well what the doctors are going to say.
His knees have had it. I just hope they get that through
Brook's head this time."

Gabe was speaking. "Don't hit him with that right after
he gets out of surgery. His defenses are down now. Give him
a little time."

"Don't tell me what to say." The flint in the judge's voice
sucked Lynn back in time. "I know what's best for Brook."

"Just like you know what's best for me," Gabe was saying, but Lynn couldn't listen. She hadn't wanted this to
happen. She'd hoped that with Gabe beside her she'd be
able to shake herself free of her childhood and face the
judge as an adult. But the old bonds still existed. She didn't
think that would ever change.

It wasn't until she felt Gabe's hand hard on her shoulder
that she surfaced. The strength in Gabe's fingers said he

needed to get out of the room as much as she did. "We're going to look for some breakfast," Gabe was saying. "There won't be any word on Brook for at least an hour."

Gabe propelled Lynn toward the door without asking his parents to join him. Despite the release of tension Lynn felt once she was no longer in the same room with the judge, it bothered her that a family couldn't pull together at a time like this. "Maybe they haven't had breakfast, either," she said low so her voice wouldn't carry.

"Do you want to eat or to watch my father and me take potshots at each other?" Gabe asked sharply. They were at the elevator before he spoke again. "Damn. I'm sorry, Lynn. I didn't want to get you into this. That's the last thing I want."

I'm already in deeper than you know. "Gabe?" She stopped him from touching the Down button. "If we're going to be together..." She faltered. "If we're going to be together, there'll be rocky times as well as good."

Gabe punched the button, his body ramrod straight until the empty elevator swallowed them. Even then he didn't speak but looked down at Lynn, making her wonder if any part of her wasn't under scrutiny. She didn't shy away. They were standing on the brink of a turning point in their relationship. No matter what direction that might take, she was going to face it.

"Hold on, Lynn." Gabe folded her against him and enveloped her in his strength. "You're going to see rocky times today, all right. I just hope...I just hope you're around when it's over."

"You aren't going to get rid of me that easily," Lynn said. "Think about what I do for a living. I'm used to crises."

"Yeah. I guess you are."

"Gabe?" Lynn took a breath. "I don't want to make light of what is happening in your family. I didn't mean for it to sound that way."

"I understand that." Gabe leaned back so he could look at her. "What I said about wanting you around when this is over? You haven't said anything about that."

"I know I haven't." Lynn touched her lips to Gabe's. "We have—"

"I know. We have to talk."

There wasn't time for Lynn to reply because the elevator stopped at the next floor and two nurses got on. Lynn stood beside Gabe at the rear of the elevator, gripping his hand so tightly that by the time the elevator stopped again, her fingers ached and there were oval indentations on the back of Gabe's hand. He'd been the one to resist coming into the hospital, but now she was having to fight the claustrophobic effect of the elevator's confines. Gabe said he was looking at their future. Lynn had no experience with wanting that. With admitting she wanted a man in her future.

Gabe took the first step when the elevator stopped on the ground floor. At the same time, he held Lynn's hand against his hip so that she felt the swell and roll of muscle. It wasn't fair of him to do that to her, not now. She had to fight to remember why they were here and who was here with them.

If Gabe was aware of what she was going through, he gave no indication. He'd entered the elevator believing that his father's presence would follow him. But Lynn's words, her body beside him, had surrounded him until there was nothing left to think about except that Lynn, a woman he had just met but knew with every fiber in him, was standing beside him. She hadn't asked questions last night when he couldn't make love to her; she'd accepted what he had to give when desire rose in him this morning. She'd weathered the first meeting with the judge and had made no judgments about what father and son were saying to each other. He'd seen the concern in her eyes as she watched his mother. More than that, maybe she understood what Brook was facing and how that touched his brother.

He loved her ability to become part of his world. He was stunned by his need to have her enter that world. That's why what she'd said—or rather, didn't say—in the elevator scared him.

"If we're going to be together..." she'd said. Changing uncertainty into certainty was a journey they'd already started. What the result would be he didn't know; all he knew was that the woman standing beside him was, at this moment, as precious as breathing itself.

Gabe ate more to pass the time than because he was hungry. He didn't try to hide the fact that he was watching Lynn's every move. There was a grace in her gestures that hadn't been there when they'd gone to high school together. At least he hadn't sensed it then. The grace, he decided, came from a self-confidence that had been missing before. The meshing of the muscles and bones in her hands fascinated him. The easy rhythm of her lungs became his rhythm. For the first time, he thought of how she'd helped him pack and her parting words to Ranger. If there was one thing she knew, it was how to stand on her own feet. She was her own person. He didn't know how much of that person he'd been allowed to see.

"I wish I could take you sight-seeing," Gabe said. "Here we are surrounded by shopping centers and you probably won't have a chance to test the limits of your credit card."

Lynn stared into her coffee. "I've never been much of a shopper."

"I'm shocked. I thought that was what all women loved doing."

"I don't know much about other women." She met his eyes. "I guess shopping is something I never got into the habit of. Or cooking."

"What are you into?"

"Kids." Lynn drew out the word. "Spring and summer. Football. Ghost towns."

After eating in the hospital cafeteria, they went first to a sheltered sun room where several patients were enjoying a California morning and then wandered into the pediatric ward. Gabe felt out of place around the scaled-down furnishings, but it was obvious that Lynn was able to see past the wary looks of the children and find ways of bonding with them.

He stood back, watching while she talked to a five-year-old who happily admitted that trying to play Superman from the roof of a building wasn't what mortal legs were made for. She didn't try to speak to the preadolescent girl under an oxygen mask but stood at the door to her room, smiling gently until the girl acknowledged her presence. The slightly built woman who knelt in front of a boy in a wheelchair wasn't the same one who could hold her own in an argument with a juvenile delinquent, and yet she was. In each case, Lynn was communicating with a child. No wonder she said she was into kids. And football and ghost towns. She wouldn't have said that a few weeks ago.

"I'm sorry," Lynn said when he finally suggested they leave the ward. "I didn't mean to take so much time."

"Time's something we're going to have a lot of today. I'd much rather spend it watching you butter up little kids than staring at Brook's empty bed. Lord, I hate that room! See what happens when you're a hotshot. They won't even let you have a roommate." He was aware of a look from a male doctor as he put his arm around Lynn's shoulder. He knew the doctor had been watching Lynn with interest, but the woman was already spoken for.

"You said we wouldn't know anything about Brook for an hour. Is that all the time you think the operation will take?"

They were standing in a deserted hallway leading from the pediatric ward, a fact that Gabe took advantage of by bringing Lynn closer to him. "I've been through this with my fool brother before," he explained, his mouth near enough to Lynn's that the lure of her was almost more than he could resist. "That's all the time it takes."

"But then he'll be in recovery for a while, won't he?" Lynn's voice trailed off. Gabe wondered if she was as aware of their closeness as he was.

"For a while. Brook throws off the drugs quickly. He'll be . . . he'll be asking questions pretty soon." Gabe couldn't remember what had been on his mind when he started that last sentence, nor was he clear on how he'd finished it. The emptiness of the hall was too rare, too precious to let go by. He could kiss her and no one would notice. And if they were discovered, it didn't matter. After what they'd been to each other already, a kiss was such a little thing. Besides, he needed her. The day's real trial was ahead of him—ahead of both of them.

Lynn rose on tiptoe, reaching for the mouth she'd been conscious of for so long. She'd managed to focus on other things while they were eating. She prolonged the trip through the pediatric ward because she hoped it would give Gabe something to think about other than what his brother was undergoing. But all that time she'd wished she were a magician capable of transporting them back to the motel so they could be alone. He'd given her so much this morning. It should have sustained her for the day, but it hadn't. She'd never felt this close to someone before. Never been so afraid of that emotion in herself.

"I—we're taking chances," she managed to say. She wasn't going to think about fear. It could overwhelm her and make her forget what was so good about him. "I don't think this is the best place for this. It's probably against the rules."

"I don't care. Lynn?" Gabe touched her cheek with exquisite tenderness. "Did I tell you I'm grateful for your being here. I'm glad you came."

"Yes, you did tell me. This morning. You don't *have* to be anything, Gabe," she said. Speaking was almost impossible, but she tried, anyway. There was so much she wanted to tell him. It was just that words didn't go far enough. Or maybe it was because she didn't understand herself enough for words to work. "I wanted to be here. I had to."

"Then—" Gabe drew out the word "—I think we'd better go back to Brook's room."

Nodding, Lynn forced herself out of the cocoon of his arms and led the way back to Brook's room. Gabe's parents were there. Lynn had had enough time away from the judge to wrest herself free from the past. She now saw a woman with a pinched face and eyes that strayed toward her husband for reassurance. She saw a man who kept his emotions locked away from everyone, even the mother of his children. Maybe even from himself.

"They should be bringing him back in a few minutes," Gabe's mother said. She nodded her head as if trying to convince herself of that fact. "The surgery didn't take long. That's a good sign, isn't it?"

"You know what I told you," the judge supplied. "It could also mean they found damage that couldn't be repaired. You have to look at the facts, Grace. That boy's playing days are behind him."

You don't know that, Lynn thought, but the need to restrain Gabe left her with little time to ask why the judge was being so fatalistic. "Why don't we let the doctors make that decision?" Gabe was saying in a voice that couldn't be contained in a small room. "And Brook. In the end it's his decision."

"Not if he doesn't have his head on straight," the judge pressed. "Someone has to pump a little logic into that kid."

"Your brand of logic, you mean."

Lynn shot Gabe a sharp look, but it wasn't necessary. She could tell that he already regretted his remark. Without taking time to weigh her words, she told Gabe's mother that she'd dealt professionally with the judge in the past. It was a way of changing the subject. "He was still hearing juvenile cases when I first came to work for the department," she explained.

"Oh." Grace gave Lynn a blank look. "I'm sorry I didn't guess, but we don't talk about work much."

That stopped Lynn. She blundered on into a conversation about their tour of the pediatric ward. Grace Updike mentioned that she did volunteer work at the hospital back home, but because the men remained silent, the discussion soon bogged down.

Fortunately, Brook was wheeled into the room before the silence could become any more uncomfortable than it already was. Although Gabe and his parents tried to talk to Brook, it was clear that the quarterback was more in need of sleep than conversation. They were informed that the doctor was already tied up with another surgery and wouldn't be able to answer questions for several more hours. Gabe left with a nurse to pass that information on to the sportswriters, who had been hounding the hospital staff, which meant Lynn had to struggle through several minutes of strained conversation about the size of Brook's bandages, and the inadequacy of the room for a man with a multimillion-dollar professional sports contract.

"Brook's agent is on the phone," Gabe explained as he came back in. "You wanted to talk to him?" he asked his father.

"I've been trying to get in touch with the man all morning." The judge grabbed Grace's arm and hurried her out of the room.

"I didn't mean to leave you like that," Gabe apologized. Gabe had started out the day with a crisp, clean shirt, but it was limp and wrinkled now. "You could have come with me. I hope he didn't put you in the position of having to defend me."

Because she knew the time was coming when Gabe would have to side with her or his father, Lynn dug deeply for the reserve of strength she needed. "I'm not looking to hang on to your shirttail. It probably was good for me to spend a few minutes with them. And no, you were not the subject under discussion."

"That's a switch. Let me guess. He was planning a press conference. To do Brook's talking for him. You haven't seen the man in action yet. Wait until he starts rolling."

Lynn knew exactly what the judge was like, but she didn't tell Gabe that. Instead, she told Gabe that since it would be a while before they could talk to Brook, they might do a little sight-seeing to kill time. "Do you think we should ask your folks to join us?" she asked, although that was the last thing she wanted.

"No, I don't. Dad's going to be holed up with Brook's agent for God knows how long, and Mom won't take a step without him. Besides, I like the idea of being alone with you. Who knows when we'll get here again?"

Gabe and Lynn left before Gabe's parents returned. Lynn floated out with Gabe's words whispering around her. She was determined to make the most of what she could out of the day, not because a tour of Los Angeles excited her but because they might not be this close again. Although they drove past places Lynn had only daydreamed about before, she took little note of yards landscaped with plants that would never survive a Colorado winter, men and women wearing mere scraps of clothing and endless miles of highway system. Even the southern California heat failed to reach her. They could have been on another planet for all she cared. She was aware only of Gabe and a communication that didn't need words.

"Do you think you'd be happy in a place like this?" Gabe pointed to what they could see of a black-on-white monstrosity behind a locked gate. "I don't imagine these people mow their own lawns."

"The people there are probably working too hard to have enough time to mow their lawns," Lynn pointed out. "Maybe that's why I stayed in Denver. The snow cuts down on the yard work."

"Hmm." Gabe pretended to be studying her critically. "A lazy woman. I don't know how I'm going to handle that."

"I wasn't aware I was up for inspection."

Gabe shook his head at the sight of a tiny sports car overflowing with teenagers. "Well, you are. And so far your grades are excellent."

"Gabe . . ." She didn't know how to go on.

"I know." He sighed. "I'm pushing, aren't I?"

"A little."

"I'll try to remember." He touched the top of her head. "But it's hard to concentrate around someone who smells like jasmine in June."

"Soap," Lynn amended. "I smell like motel soap."

"Whatever." Gabe shrugged off her remark. "You don't have to be a stickler for detail when I'm waxing eloquent."

"I'll try to remember that." Lynn rolled up her window in a futile attempt to place a barrier between them and the sounds of hard-rock music coming from the car in the right-hand lane. They were closed in, cut off from the others in the endless stream that gave the road life. Lynn wanted to say something to soften the impact of her words a minute ago, but nothing seemed right. He was moving too fast. Either that or she was moving too slowly.

Although they'd left the hospital little more than an hour ago, Lynn didn't argue when Gabe suggested they return to see if Brook was awake. Gabe's parents were already in Brook's room. Grace was seated in a molded plastic chair in a corner of the room, while the judge had planted himself beside Brook's bed. He barely acknowledged his elder son's presence; obviously he was losing no time in amassing his arguments with Brook. Although Brook's eyes were open, Lynn wasn't sure how aware he was of his surroundings.

"You haven't talked to the doctor yet; I have," the judge was saying to the man with an IV hooked to his arm. Lynn glanced at Grace but could read nothing in the older woman's blank stare.

"What did the doctor say?" Gabe asked. "What were his exact words, and not how you interpreted them?" He took up a position near his brother and father.

"I'm not sure this concerns you," the judge countered. "It's not your decision."

"He's my brother, Judge," Gabe's body language told Lynn all she needed to know. Gabe didn't want another fight with his father, but he accepted it as inevitable. "When will the doctor be seeing Brook?"

The judge dismissed Gabe's question. He turned his attention back to the unmoving athlete on the hospital bed. "There's scar tissue. And there's going to be more after this surgery heals."

"I figured that." Brook's voice was soft but alert. "What I want to know is how much strength and mobility I'm going to have left."

"What the hell does that matter?" the judge asked.

Although she knew she was an outsider, although her opinion would probably only add to an already splintered family's problems, Lynn had to speak up. She was goaded on by years of having struggled herself, when giving up would have meant a life unfulfilled. "Isn't what Brook wants the essential thing?" she asked. It was more of a statement than a question. She took a step forward, separating herself from Gabe and moving into the sphere of the judge's power. She could be damned by what she was saying, but she'd risk that. "He's the one who has to live with any decisions that are made."

"This is none of your affair, young lady." The small, deep eyes drilled into Lynn. "I don't know why Gabe brought you here, but I'd thank you to stay out of things that don't concern you."

A few weeks ago Lynn would have fled from the judge's words, but they were discussing Gabe's brother. The man with the still-heavy eyelids came out of the same mold as the man who'd made love to her that morning. That, Lynn believed, gave her the right to speak. "I disagree," she said, mindful of the tension radiating from Gabe. "What you need is an objective voice. Someone who can bring logic to an emotional issue. I believe it's Brook's decision. No one else's."

The judge's snort told Lynn that her argument had been dismissed. "What this man needs to consider is that his professional football career is over. However—" the word was drawn out for emphasis "—there are ways to capitalize on his record on the football field. But it has to be done now, before the fickle public forgets who Brook Updike is."

Lynn could have interrupted again, but she didn't. She was curious to hear what the judge had to say. Also, Gabe was silent.

The judge continued speaking as if he and Brook were the only two people in the room. He pressed home the point that Brook's agent had connections in both the business and entertainment worlds. Although the judge believed that Brook's name would open many doors in the business world, he also believed that more money was to be made in the entertainment industry. Brook wouldn't be the first former athlete to capitalize on his highly visible status. Brook, the judge pointed out, was handsome, articulate and intelligent. If they moved quickly, they could take their pick of those eager to take advantage of his many attributes.

Lynn couldn't believe what she was hearing. It wasn't that she was shocked because the judge wanted to map out his son's future; she expected that. What turned her stomach into a hard knot was the callous way the judge was willing to go about it.

"I want to talk to my doctor." It was the first time Brook had spoken since the judge began. "When is he going to be in?"

"Haven't you heard anything I've said?" the judge snapped. "Your career's over, Brook. You'd be a damn fool to hang on."

"I want to hear it from the doctor." Brook's voice was weak but determined.

"He isn't going to tell you anything I haven't already. Listen to me. You—"

Gabe, who had remained motionless, although Lynn sensed a slowly building flame inside him, now stepped forward. "We're talking about a man's life here, Judge," he said in a voice so deadly calm that it chilled her. "He isn't looking to trade a car. Why don't you want Brook to talk to the doctor? Are you afraid he's going to tell him there's still a chance he could play?''

Lynn marveled at Gabe's ability to keep his voice controlled. She could almost reach out and touch the effort it took for Gabe to force his hands to remain at his sides. Earlier today she'd been able to sense his emotions. It was happening again. "I agree," she said softly, not really aware that she was going to speak until she heard the words. "Things have happened so fast. Brook needs time to—''

"What Brook doesn't need is you butting in!" The judge paused long enough to shoot Lynn a withering glance. "You know you'd do all of us a favor by keeping your opinions to yourself.''

That was it as far as Lynn was concerned. She had tried to remain civil to the judge because he was, after all, Gabe's father. She didn't want Gabe placed in the position of having to choose between them. But the judge had dismissed her once; he wasn't going to do it again. She ignored Gabe's "That's uncalled for," and pushed her way to the head of Brook's bed. Although she was aware of the judge's attempt to force her out of the way and Gabe's quick move to protect her, she took Brook's hand.

"You're the only one who hasn't said much," she whispered. Her total attention was riveted on Brook's drug-dulled eyes. "What do *you* want?"

It was there. The answer they all had to understand was in Brook's eyes. She'd seen the same look in her own eyes when she first started to believe that she could be like other people. She understood Brook's dreams and prayers and desperate longing.

"I want to play football."

"No one wants to see some cripple trying to hang on." The judge's words sliced through Lynn, making her wonder how much deeper the wound was for Brook.

"That's enough! You can't live his life." Gabe's voice reached Lynn, but she couldn't tear her eyes away from Brook. She felt as if she could tell Brook about her dyslexia, and he would understand, because he'd fought as hard as she had. "Let him make his own decision," Gabe finished.

"Please, I can't stand any more of this fighting! I want all of you to stop," Grace Updike whimpered. "I don't feel well. I need something for my head."

It was only after Grace had managed to get her husband to go with her while she went to search for some aspirin that Lynn realized that the woman wasn't as helpless as Lynn thought she was. Although Lynn couldn't approve of Grace's methods, she had found a way of getting her husband to pay attention to her needs. Grace might be withdrawing from a confrontation, but she was also skillfully defusing an explosive situation.

Gabe placed his arm around Lynn's shoulder and brushed his lips briefly against her temple before speaking. "You stood up to the old man." His voice was husky. "I wish it didn't have to be like that, but I'm proud of you."

"Are you?" Lynn asked shakily. She was reacting to the aftermath of the judge's harsh words, but Gabe's warmth was a salve for her nerves. She could have done as Grace did; she could have stayed in the background. But she hadn't, and it hadn't harmed what existed between her and Gabe. Today was going so fast; nerves were so raw. And yet—

"You better believe it." Gabe kissed her temple again before turning his attention to his brother. He still held her close. "That man! Talk about putting in the screws when a man's down and out. I think we should have had this woman around before. She knows the right questions to ask.

You're right, Brook. You shouldn't make any decisions until you know what your doctor found out.''

"I'm scared. Isn't that a joke?'' Brook's laugh fell flat. He ran his free arm through his tangled hair. "I'm not supposed to feel like that am I? Iron man, they call me. But Gabe, what if I can't play? It's the only thing I want to do. In a few more years, yeah. I'll be ready to move on. But not now. Not so soon.''

Lynn couldn't stop herself from touching Brook any more than she could deny her need for Gabe's presence. She hadn't felt this alive emotionally in years. "If you can't play, you go on with your life. We'll be here.''

We. Gabe ran the word around in his mind for a moment before gripping Lynn even tighter. She fit so naturally against him. She had a place in his family, understood its imperfections. When the judge had attacked her, it was all he could do to keep from flattening the man. He hadn't expected his protective instinct toward the woman in his arms to be this powerful. She was a competent adult who had just proved that she could stand on her own two feet. She, not he or his parents, had reached the core of the conversation. She'd been the one to make Brook admit that playing football was still the dream.

And yet he still wanted to protect her, show her that he was there. What he felt for her was that strong.

But because dealing with his feelings was something that would take more privacy than they had now, he turned to the safer topic. "There's one thing the judge hasn't considered,'' he told his brother. "What if no one wants to look at your ugly mug? I sure wouldn't pay to watch you—what is it you can do except throw a football and land on your can?''

"Beats me." Brook laughed for the first time since he'd been injured. "They turn old racehorses out to stud. Maybe that's something I can do."

"Who says you're ready to be turned out to stud?" Lynn was still holding Brook's hand. She gave it a comforting squeeze. "You're entitled to another shot."

"Unless the doctor says I'm washed up."

"Then we'll be here."

The judge was back in the room. Gabe knew that without having to turn away from the flickering hope in his brother's eyes. "That's about enough of that kind of talk," the judge said before the door closed behind him. "You may mean something to Gabe, Miss Tresca, but you aren't family. You don't know what we're dealing with."

"The hell she doesn't. She just proved she does. Lynn is entitled to an opinion just like the rest of us. Maybe more. We didn't think to ask Brook if he still wanted to play. She did."

"What she hasn't considered is what it's going to do to his financial future if he forces himself out there again." The judge steered his wife in the direction of the plastic chair, but his eyes flashed between Gabe and Lynn.

Lynn didn't bother to try to argue the point with the judge. Neither did she try to explain why she didn't feel like an outsider. She and the judge were light-years away from common ground. All she knew was that she couldn't throw off the emotion behind Brook's words when he said the word "football." The sport was as essential to him as the ability to read was to her.

"Maybe I'm not interested in my financial future," Brook said.

"Not interested! Don't be a fool, Brook," the judge snorted. His face had paled, and that scared Lynn. She hadn't heard that the judge's health was anything but perfect, but the situation now was explosive. She had to try to defuse it.

"You said that Brook has already made a great deal of money," she started tentatively. "That means he has a certain freedom most of us don't enjoy. I don't see that there's all that much wrong in letting him make the most of that freedom. He's young. He has time."

The judge took a step forward. His face was less than a foot from Lynn's. "You don't know what you're talking about."

Lynn tried to restrain Gabe, but her grip on his arm slid off as he whirled toward his father. "I mean it," Gabe growled. "I'm not going to put up with you talking to her like that."

Lynn was both frightened and moved. Moved because of the stand Gabe was taking in her behalf and frightened because the Updike family was splintering before her eyes. Desperately she tried to pull the fragments together.

"It's Brook's decision," she repeated. "I'm sorry if I've offended anyone by what I've said. Maybe I am the last person to have a say here, but there are more important things than money."

"Such as?" the judge challenged her.

"Such as self-respect and pride. Such as doing what a person loves with his or her life. That's why I work with juveniles. That's why Gabe does what he does. That has to be why you're a judge." She wasn't sure that was true. Power might be a greater motivation for the man.

Gabe's breath was feathering the hair on Lynn's neck; she knew that the intensity of his breathing came from anger, but her skin recorded it as something far different. She didn't dare look at him. If she did, his parents would know that they were lovers—and more.

"We're not dealing with abstracts, young lady." The judge brushed aside her words. "This is not the time for idealism."

"You're wrong, Dad. It's my life we're discussing. I'm the one with the decisions to make."

Lynn glanced at Brook, caught the depth of his conviction and turned toward Gabe, because she wanted to share the moment with him. When their eyes met the emotion she saw in them sliced a molten path to her heart. She knew she had never felt this close to another human being before.

Chapter Nine

Gabe hung up the phone for what must have been the fifth time in the past half hour. If he'd had his way, he would be ripping the instrument from the wall, but he understood Brook's need for communication with the outside world. Since Brook's release from the hospital the day before, he'd been contacted by more media people than Gabe knew existed. Their questions were always the same—what were Brook Updike's future plans?

At least Gabe had an answer. Don't count Brook out of football.

Now as he stood at the entrance to Brook's bedroom in the oversized and overpriced apartment his brother leased in the hills overlooking Los Angeles, he actually envied Lynn. All she had to do was wait on the invalid. She didn't have to put up with the skeptics.

Brook was already arguing that he didn't need Gabe and Lynn waiting on him, but Gabe wasn't rushing their departure. Brook had been operated on three days before. His knee was in a cast, which made moving around a major undertaking. But that wasn't the only reason Gabe was hanging on. He wanted to be sure that Brook wouldn't suddenly turn around to find depression and fear staring him in the face. He wanted to be sure that, deep down, Brook was as confident about his recovery as he sounded to the press.

Damn the judge. The surgeon hadn't said anything about Brook's career being washed up. He'd laid it on the line: Brook was the only one who would know whether the knee had enough mobility left for the NFL. And that couldn't be determined until Brook started physical therapy. His brother thrived on challenge. As long as there was a chance, he'd rise to the top of the challenge. As long as they could keep the judge from planting the seeds of doubt too deeply, Brook might lead his team again next season.

They. There was that word again.

From the moment the decision was made to come to Los Angeles, Lynn's thoughts had dovetailed with his. It was as if they shared the same brain. Although he had brought up the advisability of moving in with Brook instead of staying at the motel, it had been Lynn who packed their few clothes and loaded them in the rental car. She was the one who suggested they arrange a meeting between Brook and his agent without the judge in attendance. Then, once the agent was in the room, she sat quietly, listening but letting Brook talk. While he was trying to keep Brook confined to his hospital bed, Lynn had waylaid the surgeon and sprung Brook a day early.

Now she was reading a newspaper article to Brook, exaggerating the misquotes from the team's coaches, with the result that Brook was laughing instead of fuming.

She fit here. There was no other way of looking at it. A few weeks ago Gabe hadn't known Lynn existed, and now she was so much a part of his world that the thought of going on without her frightened him. They hadn't made love last night because they didn't want to disturb Brook who was sleeping in the next room. Yet the closeness they'd shared while wrapped in each other's arms continued to cling to the edges of Gabe's consciousness. He wondered if they were ready for what he was going to ask of her. It was such a little thing. Hell, no! It was the hardest thing he might ever ask. And yet he had to. Someday.

"You wouldn't be conning us, would you?" Gabe asked his brother, because the intensity of what he felt for Lynn at this moment could overwhelm him if he allowed it to build. "You don't sound like a sick man to me. It's about time you answered your own damn phone calls."

"I've answered my share," Brook shot back. "I don't know why you're complaining. You're getting to talk to some of the biggest names in the sports world."

Gabe snorted and walked into the bedroom. He placed his hands lightly on Lynn's shoulder and acknowledged the tide of emotion that swept over him. He could speak to her without words, make love without the physical act. "You get the big names. I get the flakes from the *Podunk Daily*. What did the judge say when he called?"

Brook and Lynn exchanged a glance before breaking into guilty grins. "I picked up the phone," Lynn admitted, nodding toward the bedside phone. "I told him that Brook was sleeping."

Gabe ran his fingers up the sides of Lynn's neck. He was rewarded when she turned toward him with shining eyes. "Did he buy that?"

"I don't think so." Lynn's voice sounded a little vague, as if she were distracted from what she was trying to say. "I'm not his favorite person."

"Get a number and stand in line." Brook shook his head. His eyes were on what Gabe's fingers were doing, their expression saying that he understood what was happening. "My agent says the judge is threatening to have him fired, now that he won't go along with the judge's determination to get me to retire."

Gabe stepped forward, nearer to Lynn, until the back of her head was resting against his chest. He held her close and strong against him, loving her smell, her softly curling hair. She'd mentioned needing to get it cut, but he liked its slightly ragged look.

"He isn't going to give up," Gabe told Brook.

"Neither am I," Brook said firmly. "I owe it to you, Lynn. Just after the operation, when I was still drifting in and out of consciousness, the judge's argument made a lot of sense. Who needs to go through this all the time?" He stabbed an angry finger at his knee. "I tried to picture my mug advertising life insurance or whatever it is they'd want me to promote. Then you started talking about people having dreams and the decision having to be mine, and I knew you were right. I"m not ready to give up."

"Because you love all that money," Gabe challenged.

As Gabe expected, Brook shook his head. "No, because I love football."

"I knew it." Lynn's voice was a gentle contrast to the deeper masculine voices. She didn't look up at Gabe standing behind her, but Gabe felt as if she were speaking to him, reaching him through the silent communication they were capable of. "When a person loves what he is doing with his life, a setback isn't going to kill that love. Or end the struggle. You worked so hard to get where you are. Commitment isn't a light you can simply turn off."

"You should have been a nurse," Gabe told Lynn while Brook was on the phone with a staff reporter for *Sports Illustrated*. "Brook used to give Mom such a hard time about staying in bed that she always let him up."

Lynn had been working on a shopping list, but now she turned from the open refrigerator. "I take it you were the model patient. Always doing what you were told."

"I don't remember being sick. At least—" Gabe smiled at a memory "—I don't remember admitting it."

"I like it here," she said, indicating the apartment. "And I like your brother."

"More than me?" Gabe took the step that erased the distance between them.

"No." Lynn drew out the word. "Not better than I like you."

Gabe took the notepad from her fingers and leaned forward for a brief kiss. "That's what I wanted to hear. I will not be upstaged by my brother."

Lynn placed her arms around Gabe's neck and stood on tiptoe. "Was there any doubt of that?" Her lips were only an inch away.

"No. No." The second "no" came after a kiss that lasted the better part of a minute. "Did I tell you thank you—for everything?"

"Yes, you did. About a dozen times." Lynn's eyes said it all.

"I wasn't sure. You've done so much. Put up with so much."

"Don't." Lynn stopped him by placing her fingers over his lips. "Gabe? When you—when I care for someone, doing for them comes easily."

Gabe folded Lynn close against him and breathed in her scent. He had no idea how long they stood wrapped in each other's arms, only that the gesture reinforced what he'd been feeling since they sat in his living room, watching Brook on television. Since before that, even. "I want time for us," he said when Brook called out to let them know he was off the phone. "We need it."

"I know."

Later that day, when the judge and Grace dropped by Brook's apartment, Gabe tried to make his father see that

Brook wasn't interested in logical arguments, but Gabe was wasting his breath. The dinner Lynn and Grace prepared in the bachelor kitchen was a strained affair. Gabe wished he was the one confined to a bed and couch instead of having to sit across the table from his father. Although his mother praised Lynn's stab at cooking, the judge barely acknowledged her presence. Obviously he had no inkling that Lynn was more than someone who'd insisted on trailing along after Gabe.

Gabe wanted to tell his father how wrong he was. He wanted to hold Lynn in his arms and present her to his parents as his woman. But he didn't. Lynn wasn't "his" any more than he was "hers." What they were becoming to each other, what they were still to become, wasn't something that could be painted with words. When he found a private moment to lock eyes with her, it was as if she'd pulled away a curtain that had been there before. She was giving him access to a deeper layer of herself that maybe no one else had ever seen. Although she was no more comfortable with the situation than he was, she accepted this uneasy grouping as something that had to happen. She was accepting everything he was part of, not just the good.

They stayed that night and most of the next day until a woman named Rachael, who'd called a half-dozen times, came by and convinced Gabe that there were things she could do for Brook that his brother couldn't. "He isn't your little brother," Lynn teased when Gabe stalled their leaving. "He doesn't need big brother looking after him all the time. Not when Rachael's willing."

Gabe had to admit that Lynn was right. Brook was in no hurry to have this particular guest leave. Besides, with a couple of other team members living in the neighborhood, Rachael had muscle to call on if necessary. After making their plane reservations, Gabe and Lynn again threw their rumpled belongings into their suitcases, said their good-byes and caught an evening flight back to Denver. Once again, it was the middle of the night when their plane touched down.

Lynn had been dozing, her head pillowed on Gabe's shoulder. He hated having to disturb her and having her take her warm presence even an inch from him. But in a few minutes they would be the only people left on the plane.

"You aren't going to try to go to work in the morning, are you?" he asked once she stirred. "Call and take the day off."

Lynn gave him a sleepy look. "What about you?"

He hadn't given that much thought. His mind, when it wasn't on Lynn, had been back with his brother. "I don't know. I guess I'll call and see how things are going."

"We could spend the day together."

Gabe stood up and moved aside so that Lynn could get into the aisle, but now he stopped her. "Are you saying what I think you are?" he whispered.

Lynn nodded. "I want to be with you." Her voice was muffled. Her eyes caught his and held on. "Please."

Gabe pushed her gently ahead of him, somehow holding on to her at the same time. The tone behind her plea rocked him. It would take more than a narrow aisle for him to lose contact with her. He didn't know where his head had been. He should have been thinking about the reality of their having to separate physically because of the responsibilities in their lives, but he hadn't. He wasn't ready to face their separation. They'd functioned as one for days; ending that was cruel.

And now she was postponing the pain. She hated it as much as he did.

They spent the next thirty hours together, sleeping, making love, talking, making contact with their respective worlds, eating and making love again.

"I wish I understood your mother better," Lynn whispered in the middle of the night. Her head rested against Gabe's chest. Her hair made a home for his fingers.

"I don't think she understands herself very well. She's talked about leaving the judge, but I don't think she ever will. She needs a man to run her life. And she likes the lifestyle being married to a judge affords her."

Lynn ran her hand over Gabe's ribs. "But if there isn't love... I'm sorry. It's none of my business."

"Don't say that, Lynn," Gabe said, even though she was making it hard for him to concentrate. "When we were all together? I felt as if you'd always been part of my family. That's what Brook said, too."

"He did?" Lynn said, but she didn't sound surprised.

"You wouldn't have put a spell over him, would you?" Gabe teased. "He certainly was taken with you."

"Someday he's going to make a woman very happy," Lynn said as her fingers marched from Gabe's ribs to his throat. "Your brother loves life as much as you do."

Gabe concentrated on breathing evenly so that she wouldn't know how much her answer meant. "Do you really believe I love life?"

"Yes, I do. Gabe? That's why I'm here." She trembled for just a moment. "Because there's so much about you that's good."

Even after she'd left to return to work and he had nothing but the scent of her shampoo left in the bathroom, Gabe felt as if he could reach out and touch something of the aura she'd left behind. He didn't like being alone, and yet he wasn't. Not really.

The only thing that bothered him was a kind of gut desperation he sensed in their parting kiss. She didn't want to leave. He understood that.

What he didn't understand was why his promise to see her again as soon as possible didn't wipe away the desperation.

IT WASN'T EASY for Lynn, either. Physical exhaustion and her very real need for Gabe had allowed her to separate what they'd been yesterday and early that morning from the other thing he was. But because the other thing was that he was Judge Updike's son, Lynn couldn't escape the reality for long.

She'd dodged a bullet while they were all together, but the danger remained. She could, she knew, keep silent about what the judge represented to her, but if she did that, she'd be lying to Gabe as much as to herself. And she couldn't lie to Gabe. Not ever. He was essential to her, too essential for anything except the truth.

During a break in her schedule at work, Lynn called Gabe and invited him over for dinner. "We have to talk," she said before her courage could fail her. She didn't like leaving things like that, for Lynn understood Gabe well enough to realize the impact her words would have on him.

No matter how many times she told herself not to be afraid, Lynn's mouth felt like cotton, and her hands were both hot and cold when Gabe showed up at her apartment that night. He'd shaved since she'd left him at dawn and had changed into a clean outfit before coming to see her, but she forced herself not to be sucked into thinking about that. She was almost undone when he handed her a small rose. "From my yard. The bush survives despite me. I figured you'd had a hectic day and might appreciate this."

"I do." Lynn held a small amber flower close to her nose. It smelled of everything good in life. She started to babble, telling Gabe of having to run from one commitment to another in an attempt to make up for the time she'd taken off, but Gabe wasn't fooled.

"You said we had to talk."

She saw the harsh worry lines that hadn't been on his face before and chided herself for saying words that turned him into knots. Even so, it eased things a little to realize she could do that to him. He wouldn't be on edge if he didn't care. She could only pray that his caring was enough to see them through this.

She was still holding on to the rose. "Yes." She collapsed into a chair but didn't wait for Gabe to sit down before beginning. "I'm sorry. I didn't handle that well, did I?" She swallowed and forced herself to speak more firmly. "There was no way you could know, but what I said to your father in the hospital wasn't just for Brook."

Gabe waited.

"I was speaking for myself."

"And this is what you want me to hear? Lynn, I'm not following you. I have no idea what you're talking about." Although Gabe was too far away to be able to touch her, when he looked at her, she felt touched.

"You will," she said with the courage he'd given her. "Gabe, I spent today making a decision. It hasn't been an easy one. But I want honesty between us."

Gabe couldn't breathe; it didn't matter. Even though he was terrified of what Lynn might say, he would not try to stop her. He could take it—as long as he didn't have to walk out of her apartment alone afterward.

Lynn took a breath deep enough to strip the room of much of its air and then said, "I thought about telling you when we were with Brook, but somehow the time was never right. There were other, more important things on our minds. No, that isn't the truth, either." She shook her head angrily. "I should have told you the moment I learned your last name."

"Told me what?"

Lynn searched Gabe's eyes for strength, found it and went on. "When your father walked into the hospital room, it was as if I were sixteen all over again. Gabe, your father is the man who sent me to the detention center. He—" She faltered. "It's strange—isn't it?—how one person can make such an impact on another's life."

Gabe didn't speak, but Lynn didn't really expect him to. There wasn't anything he could say. She lowered her eyes and stared at her hands, lightly folded around the small blossom Gabe had given her. After the years of living with dyslexia and forging a niche for herself in life, the moment when she'd heard Judge Updike sentence her to two years in what was essentially a prison now seemed like a pinprick in time. She could have buried the memory, but finding Gabe brought it back.

She wasn't aware of Gabe getting up and kneeling in front of her, but when he reached for her, she went to him. She'd imagined all kinds of horrible things; the most horrible was that he'd leave her. He wasn't going to do that at all. She buried her face in the shelter he was offering, but she had no tears. The past was dead. Buried. She wasn't going to cry for what couldn't be changed.

"Do you hate him for that?" Gabe asked.

It should have been a question she could anticipate, but she wasn't ready. Hate wasn't an emotion she spent time with anymore. "It was so long ago, Gabe," she whispered. "I just wanted you to know."

"You had to tell me because you can't look at the man and not remember what he did to you. Tell me something, Lynn. Do you think of that when you look at me?"

No! It wasn't that at all. It would never be like that. "I didn't think you'd have to ask that." Lynn forced herself away from him, but only because she wanted to answer with gestures and not words. She lay the rose on the table nearby and ran her finger lightly across Gabe's cheekbone and down over his beard until her finger met his jaw. Her finger felt as if it had been made for fitting over those contours. Even his beard couldn't diminish that feeling.

"I wish you'd told me earlier," he said before turning his head so that her finger was now brushing his lips. "You didn't answer me. Do you hate him?"

Gabe could have drawn away from the confrontation, but he was as eager as she to have it resolved. She could be honest and he wouldn't walk out on her. "I don't know if hate is the right emotion," she tried to explain. "I spent two years of my life living with his words. Every time a door locked behind me, when I wanted to be outside and couldn't be, it was because he'd sent me to that place. Gabe, his control over me was total. I hated it being that way." Lynn stopped speaking, hoping Gabe understood, for she'd said as much as she could.

Gabe ran his hands over her knees, slowly moving upward. Lynn knew the gesture was meant as a comforting one, but she had to stop him before she lost control of her thoughts. "Do you understand?" she whimpered.

"I'm trying to." His voice was husky, or maybe it only seemed that way because she had so much emotion invested in the conversation. "You blame my father for treating you like a criminal."

"He didn't listen," she gasped. "I was hurting, and he didn't care."

"I know, Lynn. I know." Gabe gripped her upper arms and pulled her off her chair and onto the floor beside him.

"Remember, I grew up with the man. But Lynn, there's something else you have to think about."

"What?" She wasn't sure she wanted to hear what that was.

"Where would you be if he hadn't sent you there?"

"I wouldn't have been locked up. I wouldn't have those fears."

"And maybe you would have never learned what was wrong with you."

That wasn't fair! She didn't want to give the judge credit for what had turned out to be her salvation. No way could he have known what was ahead for her when he had stared down at an angry rebel and told her she had no place in society. "He didn't know I was dyslexic." She tried to draw away, her voice bitter. She'd had one image of the judge for years; she didn't want it changed. "He's probably never heard of dyslexia."

"You may be right." Gabe hadn't released her, but his hands on her arms weren't punishing. "Don't get me wrong, Lynn. I'm not asking you to see my father as some white knight. He'll never be that. I'm sure his only thoughts were to remove you from the community. But, honey, can't you put what he did to you behind you and think about the good that came out of the experience?"

Honey. The word was so potent that Lynn was afraid to examine it. "I've tried." She gave up the struggle and sagged against him. He was strong and sure, everything she wasn't at that moment. "I thought I'd succeeded, until I met you."

"But I brought it all back, didn't I? No wonder you acted like a scared rabbit when I said I remembered you."

"Something like that." Lynn tried to laugh. It was getting easier. She'd told him everything, and he was still here. Holding her.

"Tell me something." He waited until she looked up at him before continuing. "What did you think was going to happen when you asked me over here today?"

"I don't know." In spite of her fear while she was waiting for him to arrive, she hadn't really been able to picture him walking out on her. "I just knew I had to tell you."

"Good." Gabe let his breath out on the tail end of a heavy sigh. "Now we have that behind us."

"Is that all you have to say?"

"There's nothing more to say. I can't change what the judge did to you. But you can't deny that his action turned your life around. I know what my old man is. But it still turned out all right for you. I want us to live for today. For us. I hope you can do that."

Lynn was still clinging to the old order and Gabe wanted her to dismiss it. "Do you really think it's that easy?" She was bitter—but what he said made sense.

"Of course it isn't easy." Gabe was touching her with his words. "But it's today and us that matter. That's what I'm asking you to focus on."

She could do that. She had Gabe beside her to guide her. "You sound pretty sure of yourself," she ventured.

"I'm not. I don't think anyone ever is, at least not if they're honest with themselves. Ah, Lynn, we've already been through so much together. I hope someday we'll have nothing more important to talk about than whose turn it is to do the dishes. Everyday things."

Gabe's hands were taking her away from rationality. He was taking her yet another step in the joining they'd begun. He was right. They were living in the present. The past couldn't touch him if they didn't allow it to. "I don't do dishes," Lynn informed him. "At least not willingly."

"Neither do I. I think we have a problem."

"What do you think we should do?" Lynn asked.

"I think we have better things to do than dishes," Gabe informed her, and proceeded to show her what he had in mind.

Her old blouse parted under his expert touch. Her slacks slipped off her hips and fell unheeded to the floor. Dressed only in her underwear, Lynn pressed her body against his, inhaling his life force. "You seem pretty sure of yourself," she said. She didn't try to stop him.

"I'm never sure around you, Lynn Tresca. I just hope that this, now, is right for us."

It seemed to Lynn that they made love for hours. Time wasn't a concern. She was hungry, then satisfied and satiated, and then hungry again. Each time Gabe was ready for her, his emotions echoing hers. At times during the night they slept, but then their need for each other would surface, and they would reach for each other again. She was acting out of thankfulness, because her fears had been unfounded. He understood how she felt about his father and wanted her despite that. She should be shocked by her behavior; surely she'd never demanded to be appeased before.

But there was no shame in her bedroom that night.

Finally, just before dawn, Gabe rolled away from her, his deep breathing lulling her to sleep. Her last thought was of a key. Gabe's father had used one to lock her up; the son had one, too. Gabe had reached her heart.

Only she wasn't ready for that.

Neither of them woke until sunlight streaming through the window forced its way past their closed eyelids. Lynn was the first out of bed. "Don't touch me," she whispered when Gabe reached for her. She had to remain free. Her last thought had come back. "I have to go to work."

"I'm not going to stop you." Although his eyes were half closed, she could read their message; he reveled in his power over her, challenging her to argue the point.

"You will if you touch me," she admitted.

"Is there anything wrong with that? Lynn, I want us to be that close."

"Don't push me, Gabe." She hated what she'd just said, and yet she had to. "I've been on my own for so long. Changing what I am isn't easy."

Gabe sat up and slid his legs over the side of the bed. "I've been alone a long time, too, Lynn, but I'm willing to let that change."

Lynn turned back toward him. She refused to let last night dominate her. "We're different people. We come from different backgrounds."

"That's a problem only if you let it be."

They were both dressed and ready to leave when Lynn gave voice to the thought that had surfaced while she was in the shower. There was something she had to do for herself. And for Gabe. Especially after the words they'd spoken in her bedroom. He wanted them to be more than they now were. She didn't know if that was possible, but there was one step she could take. "I want to see your father."

Gabe's hand froze on the front door. "Why?"

"I think you know." Lynn lowered her eyes momentarily, but she owed Gabe more than that. "I've been thinking about what you said last night."

"I didn't know you were thinking about anything," he said teasingly.

Lynn shot him a look of mock anger. "I'm not going to debate that point, but I have been thinking this morning. Gabe, I want to tell your father who I was and what I've become."

Silently, Gabe pulled her close. "He doesn't care, Lynn. Believe me, he's dealt with so many delinquents over the years that he couldn't care less what happened to one of them."

"But I'm not just one of them." Surely Gabe believed that her ties to the Updike family already ran deep and might run deeper still. Despite her fear of getting too close to anyone, and especially to Gabe, it was happening. "I don't think he has many kind thoughts about me right now. But . . . I hated not having the courage to tell you about myself." She leaned her head heavily against Gabe's chest. "That feeling won't go away until I've talked to your father, too."

"I thought you were the independent one. The one who doesn't want people getting too close."

"Don't," Lynn warned. "All I know is that I want to talk to your folks."

He can hurt you. Squash your pride. Those thoughts kept Gabe silent for a moment, but he couldn't deny Lynn her conviction. He was so damn proud of her courage; that courage was part and parcel of what made her precious to him. If she had been like the other women who'd flitted around his life, he would have tried to talk her out of it. But Lynn wasn't like other women. He had no words and only whirling thoughts for what she was. He knew she was part of his present, and maybe his future, and because of that, the past had to be laid to rest.

After that, he'd make his own request. Push her further than she was pushing herself.

That evening he picked her up at work and drove her to the exclusive neighborhood nestled in the foothills around Denver. Lynn was silent, but Gabe didn't try to cover up with words of his own. He was seeing the neighborhood through Lynn's eyes, feeling as out of his element as she must feel. Where his parents lived wasn't for people who lived from paycheck to paycheck.

"I feel as if my heart's climbing up my throat and I can't swallow it," Lynn admitted while Gabe waited for her to get out of his pickup. "I haven't been this nervous since I was brought before him for sentencing."

Gabe willingly gave her what he could of his strength. He didn't let go of her hand as they started up the walk to the trilevel house. "Would you like me to punch him out for you?"

Lynn's weak smile told Gabe that his attempt at humor had helped a little. "It's a tempting thought. Are you sure they're expecting us?"

"Now you're dreaming up things to worry about. I called Mom earlier. She was shocked to hear that I was coming of my own free will. She didn't say much when I said you'd be with me. You don't suppose—" Gabe laughed "—you don't suppose she thinks we're going to tell them that we're getting married?"

Lynn didn't respond, and Gabe dropped the subject. "I told her not to fix dinner," he went on. "I hope she was listening. My mother's idea of dinner takes about three hours to wade through."

"I don't think I could eat." Lynn was watching Gabe's finger on the doorbell. He had to know that a part of her wanted to turn and run.

Gabe's mother opened the door. She was wearing a designer original, not, Gabe knew, in honor of his visit but because that was the way she believed the wife of a judge should always dress. For a moment he could do nothing more than absorb the wave of compassion he felt for his mother. He'd never want his wife to live through him.

"Gabe, you don't have to ring the doorbell. You're always welcome here," Grace said before stepping aside to let her visitors in. When Gabe pressed his hand against the small of Lynn's back, she jumped. She was putting herself through the wringer by coming here; he wondered if the judge would be aware of that or would care.

The judge was waiting in his study. At least that was the name Lynn gave to the paneled, book-lined room on the main floor that Grace led them to. The older man had removed his tie and was wearing slippers, but his shirt looked far newer, far crisper, than Lynn felt. She started to turn toward Gabe for reassurance but stopped herself. She didn't know how to lean on anyone for anything.

Fortunately, Grace filled in the first few moments by telling them of a conversation she'd had with Brook earlier in the day. Lynn was aware of the tight line around the judge's mouth when Grace mentioned Brook had already begun physical therapy. "I don't suppose you bothered to point out that he's wasting his time," the judge interrupted. "As long as you give that boy silent approval, he's going to continue in this fool endeavor of his."

Grace gave her husband a blank stare, but before it was over, Lynn saw something she hadn't expected. Grace's conversation with her youngest wasn't as innocent as it seemed on the surface. Lynn wondered how long ago Grace had learned ways of working around her husband's edicts. Without putting it into words, Grace was telling Brook that she approved of what he was doing.

Lynn actually felt sorry for the man being swallowed up in his oversized recliner. Because he didn't know the meaning of give-and-take, the people around him excluded him. Gabe had had his arm around Lynn, but now she stepped away and settled herself into a wooden rocker, the only other chair in the room. She took a deep breath and began.

"I don't expect you to remember me, but we go back a long way."

"You're right. I don't remember you."

Lynn ignored the sharp comment. If he was going to shoot from the hip, she would do the same. "I was under your jurisdiction once. You sent me to the juvenile treatment center for two years."

Grace sucked in a deep breath, but Lynn didn't take her eyes off the judge. She felt strangely numb now, aware of very little except Gabe's presence as he took his place beside her. *It's almost over now,* she told him silently. "Gabe wasn't sure I should tell you that, but I felt it was necessary," she said.

"Why?"

Good question. A question designed to throw her off balance. "Because . . ." Lynn took a moment to weigh the wisdom of her answer. "Because of your son. Judge, when I first learned who Gabe's father was, I wanted to run. But it didn't turn out that way. I guess what I'm saying is, I'm hoping there can be honesty between you and me."

"So you came here to tell me what a bastard I was." The judge spoke without moving.

"No," Lynn said slowly, carefully, keeping her eyes steady on the man sitting across from her. She wasn't going to be cowed now. "That was what I thought for a long time, but Gabe made me face something else."

The judge glanced at Gabe before fixing his eyes on Lynn's again. "I have a pretty good idea what my son said."

"I don't think you do," Lynn said softly. "Because of Gabe, I'm here to thank you."

The judge snorted. "Why don't I believe you?"

Gabe leaned forward, but Lynn reached for his hand, stopping him. "Let me finish," she said quickly. With a brevity of words she explained the circumstances that brought her before Judge Updike. "I still believe there were things you could have done besides make sure I was locked up for two years. I was a runaway, not a delinquent." She pushed herself beyond what couldn't be changed. "But that place turned out to be my salvation."

When the judge only continued to look at her without expression, she finished with her explanation. She didn't waste time explaining the effect of dyslexia on her early years, concentrating instead on the anger, fear and frustration that controlled her as a teenager. "For too many years I resented you because you didn't take the time to try to understand me."

"If you're expecting me to apologize—"

Lynn held up a hand. She was coming to the hard part; she didn't want to be sidetracked. "I hated you for being judgmental. You didn't ask why I wouldn't stay in school, why my parents and I couldn't speak to each other without tying ourselves in knots. All you were concerned with was getting yet another troublemaker out of your court."

This time the judge succeeded in making his point. "We don't live in a perfect world, Ms Tresca. The resources available to me were limited. I'm sorry if you thought I should have found family counseling for you and your parents. If I sent you to the center, it had to be because attempts to find a place for you in society had failed."

Lynn couldn't dispute that. She'd been through three foster homes before being sent away. "But you didn't ask me why that was. You didn't ask why I wouldn't stay in school. I needed compassion; I didn't get any."

As if bored with the conversation, the judge stood up. "This all took place years ago, Ms Tresca. What does it have to do with today."

"Let her finish, Judge," Gabe warned.

"Maybe it has nothing to do with today. Maybe everything," Lynn admitted. She realized that perhaps nothing she'd said would register with the man, and yet she had to try, for Gabe's sake. "I want you to know that I don't blame you anymore. Sending me to that center was the best thing that could have happened. My life's on course. I have to thank you for that."

The judge took a half step as if to follow through on his decision to leave the room but then stopped. He stared at Lynn for so long that the silence became uncomfortable. Lynn reached back and covered the hand that was on her shoulder. Gabe had warned her that his meeting might solve nothing.

"Are you staying for dinner?" the judge asked.

"You haven't heard a word she said, have you?" Gabe challenged. "You really don't give a damn what happens to the people you sentence."

"There have been so many. You can't expect me to keep tabs on all of them."

"That isn't the point," Gabe was saying. Lynn knew she should be speaking for herself, but Gabe was doing so well. His strength was taking over, now that hers was exhausted. "Do you have any idea what it took for Lynn to come here tonight? Of course you don't. You've never tried to put yourself in other people's positions.

"Oh, why bother!" Gabe challenged as he helped Lynn to her feet and guided her to the front door. She glanced at Grace and received a look of infinite sorrow in return. Lynn wasn't going to look at the judge. Gabe was standing beside her. That was all that mattered.

"Wait a minute. I'm not finished." The judge's order was as binding as any rope. Although Gabe was still trying to steer her toward the door, Lynn stopped.

"When Grace told me you were coming here tonight, I didn't believe we had anything to say to each other," the judge went on. "But you've proved me wrong. You may turn out to be the one woman I'd choose for my son."

Lynn didn't speak. She knew her eyes were asking the question.

"You know about life's hard knocks. You have strength. That's something I can admire. I didn't think Gabe could find a woman like that. Maybe I've underestimated him."

Lynn reeled under the impact of what she'd just heard. Even Gabe seemed to have been caught off guard. "If I have strength," she began, "you had a great deal to do with that."

It wasn't until five minutes later that Lynn took her next conscious breath. Gabe was taking her back home, leaving behind a man she might never understand.

"He underestimated me. I never thought I'd hear that," Gabe whispered. "Do you feel up to dinner?"

"I'm not sure I can keep anything down." Lynn scooted closer to Gabe in the cab of his pickup and let him support most of her weight. She hadn't wanted to do that earlier, but now it felt right. "That might be the most incredible experience of my life. I feel as if I've been through the wringer."

"You have. We both have. But you came through the experience in one piece. Now there's only one more hurdle ahead of you."

But Gabe didn't say what that hurdle was.

Chapter Ten

It could all go up in smoke.

That was why Gabe kept his thoughts to himself for the week after the meeting between Lynn and his father. She'd already faced the man who once controlled her life. He was proud of her for that, but more than that, he was grateful for the new dimension in his relationship with his father. He didn't expect the judge ever to be capable of seeing things through his eyes, but at least they were speaking without throwing up the old roadblocks. He had Lynn to thank for that.

And that was why he had to try. Maybe do for her what she'd done for him. Maybe push her further than he had a right to.

"Who says it's going to work?" he said out loud on his way to Lynn's apartment that evening. "Even if she agrees to this, it could blow up in her face. She could wind up blaming you."

Dropping his bomb took longer than he thought it would. First he kissed her hello; that simple little act took them into the bedroom and an hour of sharing that stripped him of every emotion except loving what she was capable of bringing out in him. Then he had to tell her about the call from Brook.

"It's official, I guess," he explained while they were still in bed. He ran his fingers lightly over her side, relishing her quick response. "He's inked in for the quarterbacking slot next season. Of course, it all hinges on how well the physical therapy goes."

Lynn grabbed his hand and brought it back to safer territory. "It'll go fine," she reassured him. "Being able to swim helps. Rachael says she'll have him out jogging by next week. Did he tell you he's back in the gym working on his upper body already?"

"Wait a minute." Gabe stopped her. "How did you know all this?"

Lynn grinned. "Brook called me last night. I talked to Rachael, too. I'd have a talk with that kid if I were you. He's going to break a lot of hearts if he spends much more time with that one."

"So my brother's been calling you. I'll have to talk to him about that."

"Don't you dare. We're getting along just fine without you."

Gabe nipped at Lynn's nose. "Mom likes Rachael."

"What did your father say?" Lynn asked, as he knew she would.

"That's why I was late. I dropped by the house to tell them about Brook's position with the team. I guess Brook didn't want to break the news over the phone. He let me have the honor." Gabe chuckled. "Mom was glad. I could see it in her eyes while she was waiting for Dad's reaction."

"And what was his reaction?"

"Nothing. He hardly said a word." Gabe cocked his head, remembering. "There was none of the ranting and raving I expected. He didn't run for the phone, either, which surprised me."

"Gabe?" Lynn shifted positions but didn't pull herself away from Gabe's answers. "Do you think he was hurt?"

She understood. Sometimes Gabe wondered if there was anything she didn't understand. "Yeah." He drew out the word. "I think he was hurt that Brook told me and not him. But—"

"Gabe, it isn't easy for a man to admit that his sons can't tell their father what's going on in their lives."

"It's a little late for him to be figuring that out." Gabe didn't mean to be bitter, but old wounds took a long time to heal.

"Better late than going through life never knowing what your children are like."

It was the opening he'd been looking for. All he had to do was open his mouth and begin, but the soft, trusting look in Lynn's eyes momentarily froze his words. "It works both ways, Lynn." He was taking the coward's way out, but easing his way into what had to be said was the only way he could do it. "It's taken me a lifetime to get to know my father. Really know him."

"The job isn't over yet," Lynn pointed out.

"At least I've started." Lynn couldn't possibly understand his need to hold her close, to feel her heart beating in tempo with his, to blend their body heat, but the need was too strong for Gabe to deny. For a long minute he lay with one leg over her body, their lips locked in a kiss that extended throughout the length of his body. His reaction rocked him but gave him strength. "You don't know your family at all," he said. The words were muffled, because their mouths were so close. "You see them a few times a year and play word games, but you don't really know them."

She stiffened just as he knew she would. "Gabe," she warned.

"No." He placed a hand over her mouth to stop her. "Hear me out. You owe me at least that much."

"I don't owe you anything."

"That isn't true," he pressed. "And even if you don't owe me, what about what we are to each other?"

Lynn took a long time to answer. "I told you. I'm used to being on my own."

"So get up and walk out of the room."

"Gabe?"

"I'm sorry." Gabe covered her shoulder with his hand. "You have to know I don't mean that. I don't think I could handle it if you did that."

"I—I needed to hear that. Gabe, I take life one day at a time. I've never asked for more than that."

Because he was aware of what he was putting her through, Gabe refused to take her literally. "I'm not asking that much. Why can't you get to know your parents, for me?" he pressed.

Without leaving the bed, Lynn managed to withdraw from Gabe. She held herself tightly in a small corner of the bed, a blanket pulled protectively around her. "My parents and I are doing okay. I'm not interested in dredging up the past."

"You did exactly that when you faced my father," he challenged, hating himself for what he had to say.

"That was different."

Gabe fought the need to touch her and allowed her her own space. But no matter how much he wanted to, for her sake, he wasn't going to skirt away from what he'd brought up. "Because the judge can't touch you personally? Because no matter what he did to you, he didn't create you? You're afraid. You know that, Lynn? You're willing to spend the rest of your life tiptoeing around your parents because you're afraid."

"What are you trying to do to me?" Lynn was out of bed before Gabe could react. "Leave me alone, Gabe! I mean it. I've run my life for years. I can continue to do that without your help." She stalked naked from the bedroom, slamming the door behind her as she left him.

Gabe didn't give himself time to think; instead, he reacted with the instinct of a man determined to hold on to what was precious to him. He was in the living room when he caught up with her. She was standing beside the drooping rose he'd brought over earlier. When she turned to face him, he wasn't thinking that neither of them wore a scrap of clothing. All he saw was agony and anger glinting bright in her eyes. The pain he'd promised he wouldn't inflict.

"Please." He held out his hand, needing her more than he'd ever needed anyone before but knowing his need couldn't possibly match hers. "I don't want to hurt you. Believe me, that's the last thing I want."

"Then why'd you say it? I can tell you what will happen if I talk with my parents. They'll tell me I failed them as a daughter. That they tried so hard, gave so much. And got so little in return. That's a hell of a thing to hear."

He shouldn't back down. He knew they'd accomplish nothing that way. But he could sense the aftermath of her words lashing around her. Wounding her. She was too precious for him to do this to her. "I shouldn't have," he heard himself say. His hand was still reaching for her, but he knew he would have to say more before she would respond. "I...Lynn, you've helped me mend fences with my parents. I was hoping I could do the same for you."

Her words were heavy; they saturated the air and then lingered. "Gabe, I haven't really talked to my parents since I was sixteen. We pretend a lot of things never happened."

Let it go. You were wrong. Let it go. "I'm sorry," he said, even though the thought that started things refused to die. "You're going to get cold standing there."

Lynn lowered her eyes and stared down at her legs as if they were alien things. She wrapped her arms around her waist, leaving her breasts exposed. It was her utter vulnerability that made Gabe forget that he was as naked as she was. Because he sensed she still wasn't ready to be touched, he went back into the bedroom for his jeans and for a bathrobe to place over her shoulders. She let him come that close, but when he tried to put his hands on her, she drew away.

It wasn't until she'd wrapped the lightweight gown around her and was curled up on the corner of the couch that she spoke. "You don't understand what it was like. If I brought the past up, it could destroy what relationship we do have. They tried. They really tried." Her tone told him how desperately she needed him to believe that. "But...I guess they got tired."

"You're not the same person you were at sixteen," was what he wanted to say. But once again, the words refused to come out. She looked alone, utterly alone. Maybe he could take that away, but not if they lived anywhere but in the present. He wanted to give her more than that but didn't know how. "I'm sorry," he said again. "Sometimes when I'm with you, I say things before I know I'm going to."

"I don't think so." She looked at him with a wisdom that made her a hundred years old. "Gabe, I care for you. So much it scares me sometimes. I'm not used to feeling that way about someone. I—I'm used to making my own decisions. That happens when you haven't dared let anyone get close for as long as I have."

"Are you saying I don't have any right to tell you how I feel?"

Of course he did. It was that realization that pulled Lynn out of herself and forced her to try to see things Gabe's way. He hadn't tried to stop her when she insisted on going to see his father. He'd let her bare her soul, stood beside her when he could have left her standing alone. His strength, his commitment to her, gave him the right to enter her life.

But she wasn't ready for the ramifications of that right. She might not be able to throw off his challenge, but she could postpone it. Disarm it. She wasn't ready to face her parents.

"Is that why you came over here tonight?" she had to ask. "To try to talk me into having a knock-down-drag-out with my parents?"

"I came here because I wanted to see you."

That, she believed, was the truth. Surely her body, attuned as it was to his beating heart, would know if he was lying. Because his words filled her, she was at last able to take his offered hand and let him pull her close. As his mouth covered hers, she thrust everything else away. She had him; she didn't need anything else.

A WEEK LATER, Lynn still believed that when he asked her to arrange for a three-day weekend. If she agreed, they were going camping in Rocky Mountain National Park. She wondered if the trip had been planned in an attempt to put certain things behind them. If that was the case, Lynn was grateful to Gabe. He could have chosen to stay in the city and filled their time with activity. Instead, he was setting the stage for them to be together without any distractions.

"You can't help having been deprived of certain experiences. And I'm willing to forgive you if you don't have such essentials as a sleeping bag and a backpack," he pointed out while she was still trying to picture herself forsaking Denver for barren mountain peaks.

"What's wrong with going for more of your back-country drives?" she stalled. "I loved doing that. How cold does it get in the park?"

"Very cold. I'm talking about sleeping above the timberline." Obviously Gabe was enjoying himself. "I don't know how you call yourself a native of Colorado until you've been camping in the park."

Despite her apprehension, Lynn accepted the challenge. She needed the time away from work; so did Gabe. But more than that, they needed each other. Lynn was ready to admit that. She still didn't know what she was letting herself in for, but Gabe was confident enough for both of them. She'd be safe. She wouldn't freeze.

By the time they'd left Gabe's truck behind at the entrance to Beaver Meadows, strapped on backpacks and started on the trail that led to Loch Vale in the southern part of the 410-square-mile park, Lynn's concerns didn't go as far as nightfall. She'd never given much thought to the national park northeast of Denver. Now she wished she'd taken the time to get her lungs in shape. It wasn't that the trail was hard, but the high altitude demanded a great deal of her. Maybe it wouldn't have been so bad if there'd been more to think about than Gabe's broad back forging ahead of her and a skyline saw-toothed with jutting granite.

At first she'd at least been able to hear the cars on Trail Ridge Road. Now, except for the cadence of her heart and lungs, there was nothing except the eerie stillness of the mountains. Although she had to push herself to stay close to Gabe, she refused to allow the distance between them to grow. He was all that stood between her and total aloneness.

They'd covered what seemed to Lynn to be hundreds of miles, but was probably closer to four, when he paused to point out Longs Peak rising over fourteen thousand feet into the heavens. Because they were already near the timberline above which evergreens wouldn't grow and because Longs Peak was surrounded by other peaks almost as tall, it was a minute before the impact sunk in. "There isn't any radio reception here, is there?" she said in an understatement. She was thinking about being alone with a mountain man. Alone with the one man who was making her question so many things about herself.

"No civilization. Does that bother you?"

Lynn didn't have a ready answer. Gabe had taken her away from civilization before, but his truck had been nearby. This time, if she wanted to surround herself with the sounds that had been so vital to her security, she would have to backtrack those four miles. Because it was still daylight, she didn't turn around. Neither did she want to look ahead to night.

When, two hours later, they reached their destination, they had Bear Lake near Loch Vale to themselves. Lynn caught the distant scent of a campfire, but she had no desire to infringe on the other campers' privacy. She was of little help to Gabe as he set up camp, but because she had brought along a camera, she was able to occupy herself by running off a roll of film. It wasn't until Gabe called her that a simple, undeniable fact sunk in.

They had no tent. There would be no curtain tonight between her and their primitive surroundings.

"The weather forecast isn't for rain," Gabe pointed out when she asked. "I wanted to enjoy our hike, not have to haul around a heavy tent."

"Oh." The word seemed so ineffective, but Lynn had no one but herself to blame for not having asked more questions before leaving Denver. She'd placed everything in Gabe's hands; trusted him with all the decisions. Now she would have to live with those decisions.

That was easy to do in the hours of daylight left to them. Although the silence of their surroundings ate away at Lynn's subconsciousness, she was able to dismiss it because Gabe's voice was there. She followed him around the lake, peering down for a glimpse of fish. She smiled when he pointed out the imprint of an elk hoof in ground formed by glaciers aeons ago. She even identified the work of a beaver in an aspen sapling.

Hand in hand, they tramped over rock and around brush while he told her about a mountaineering school he hoped to have time to attend someday. Lynn wasn't sure she'd ever want to do that, but looking up at the challenging peaks all around, she could understand where Gabe's desire came from.

After the sun set, they returned to camp and shared in the task of preparing a simple meal. Once again, Lynn was struck by the trusting way she'd let Gabe make all the plans. If it hadn't been for him, they'd be eating pine needles and drinking lake water for dinner. It was dark by the time Gabe introduced her to the sweet stickiness of roasted marshmallows surrounded by chocolate and graham crackers.

"I have no idea how you got to voting age without roasting marshmallows over a campfire," Gabe observed. "It's one of the rites of passage kids are expected to go through." He was sitting down with his back against a rock. Lynn was between his legs, his chest her backrest.

"I've never camped out," she pointed out, although surely Gabe knew that. She could see nothing except the flames from their fire, feel nothing save Gabe's warmth surrounding her. There were night sounds, maybe sounds that had been there all day without her knowing it. She wasn't a juvenile officer; he didn't own a construction company. They were simply two people together.

"I hope you like it, because I'd like us to do it again."
Gabe's voice reached Lynn like a thin whisper, as if
the mountain air needed to claim some of his voice for its
own.

"Wait until morning. Then I'll tell you. I haven't slept on
the ground yet." Lynn tilted her head back until it was resting on Gabe's chest. She could hear his heart. It was, she
discovered, in harmony with the wilderness sounds.

"Our sleeping bags zip together."

"Oh." Of course, they would sleep together tonight.
There was no one here who cared what they did. Lynn's eyes
had been drooping, but now she opened them. Night hadn't
been this black since they'd locked her in a cell. But then
Gabe wasn't with her. Without his warmth and strength she
would have run screaming into the mountains.

But he was here. That made all the difference.

"Have you ever made love on the ground before?" she
asked. She wasn't probing for knowledge about past lovers. She simply needed to know more about the man who
could take away the sharp loneliness of night for her.

"If I did, I'm not sure I'd tell you about it, but the answer is no." Gabe ran his lips over the top of Lynn's head,
a gentle gesture that made its way down to her feet. "Tonight will be a first."

There had been many firsts with Gabe Updike. Lynn
wondered how many more were ahead of her. She'd been
right to follow her instinct when she said an unthinking yes
to his suggestion they come here. Testing herself, she tried
to summon up images of night creatures, something walking out of the blackness toward her. It wouldn't happen;
Gabe was here.

"I feel so safe," Lynn admitted. "Are you sure Davy
Crockett wasn't one of your ancestors?"

"No mountain man, but I'm not so sure about Tarzan types." He wrapped his arms even closer around her. "I wasn't sure you'd want to come here."

"Why?"

"You're the one who said it. You're used to standing on your own. You have to depend on me here."

"I do, don't I?" It wasn't the first time she'd thought about that. "I had a choice when I was released from the center," she told him. "I could either rejoin my parents or enter college through a scholarship program available for people with learning disabilities. I knew I couldn't go back home. I found an apartment, saw a counselor. At his suggestion, I spent a year working before entering college. I took night classes that year and thought a lot about what I wanted out of a college education. I had to work part-time to supplement the scholarship. Gabe, there wasn't anyone to help me with those decisions. The counselor told me what my options were, but he didn't try to help me make up my mind. I've been on my own for a long time. I—"

"You're used to calling your own shots. I understand."

"Do you? Do you understand how hard it is to let someone in?" Lynn stopped her thoughts in the only way that made sense. She twisted toward Gabe and offered him her mouth. He took it, erasing what little rational thought still remained.

"You'll let someone in when the time is right," he said.

I hope so. God, I hope I can do that!

Gabe had planned ahead, a fact that didn't occur to Lynn until later. But when kisses weren't enough, he helped her to her feet and took her to the joined sleeping bags that were ready to receive them. Lynn shivered when Gabe exposed her shoulders to the night air but waited until he slipped her out of the rest of her clothing before dropping to her knees and pulling the warm fabric up over her. She couldn't see

Gabe undressing, but her ears told her everything she needed to know. She was reaching for him when he knelt to join her.

"I don't think there are any rocks under us," he whispered, even though there was no one to hear them.

"I won't feel them," she whispered back. She realized that he was cold, too, and accepted him along the length of her body. A moment later they stopped shivering.

"You taste like chocolate," Gabe said after kissing her.

"You taste like graham crackers. The campfire we smelled earlier—do you think those campers know we're here?"

"Would you like me to invite them over?" Gabe's fingers touched the swell of Lynn's breast. "We could spend the evening playing cards, singing campfire songs."

"You could teach me how to whittle." Lynn circled Gabe's beard with her mouth and spoke through clenched teeth. "You do know how to whittle, don't you?" She ran her leg over his.

"What I do know is much more interesting than whittling." Gabe placed his hands over Lynn's ribs and pushed her upward until her shoulders were out from under the sleeping bag. Then he ducked his head and found with his mouth the exquisitely soft mound that had been filling his hand. Despite the hot pounding in his temple that demanded more, he moved slowly, his hands still on either side of her rib cage. His tongue explored her soft fullness, the hardened tip that told him all he needed to know about her response. When her breath came in ragged gasps that had nothing to do with the mountain air on her shoulders, he relished his mastery of her. At sixteen she'd fought like a wildcat for her freedom; he hoped that the woman she'd become was secure enough to allow for sharing. For him.

She moved her hips toward his, missing contact because he was controlling. He would give her satisfaction, give her what she needed and had a right to, but not yet. First he had to learn how much she needed him. Force her to admit that in herself.

"Gabe?" Her voice was strangled. Her fingers were intertwined with his beard, as if ready to pull his mouth off her breast should she sink too deep.

He didn't answer her. He knew what she was asking, but it felt as if he'd been waiting a lifetime to feel his teeth gentle against her breast. He explored the hard tip with an impatient tongue until she groaned, rewarding him. Only then did he give her back that little bit of privacy.

It didn't last long. This time he sought the narrow valley between her breasts. His tongue was inches away from her heart, her swollen breasts surrounding his face. He was no longer in control. He wondered if either of them was. As her searching hips and thighs found his and her fingers tightened around his hair, he felt it all slipping away.

It didn't matter. He was safe with her. He could give her his heart; there was no danger. "Thank you," he whispered.

"For what?"

"For coming here. For trusting me."

"I do, don't I?" she said with a wonder that told him more than words could. "Don't let me go, Gabe. Please don't let me go."

"I won't, my love."

A moment later Lynn was burrowing deep in the sleeping bag. Her movement forced his tongue from between her breasts, but the lips she offered him were the perfect substitute. Despite the hard ground under them, Gabe could have been on a down mattress. His thoughts, what there were of them, were on the female body asking and giving, searching and finding. He'd never felt this close to anyone before, had never wanted to be this close.

She turned on her back and gripped his shoulders. Under him her legs were spreading. Gabe groaned, lifted his face for a draft of air and entered her.

THE SOUND OF AN OWL was the first thing that registered on Lynn's saturated senses. Gabe had fallen asleep with her arm as his pillow. His sleeping gave her no cushion between herself and the strange timeless world surrounding them. She was alone with their surroundings.

Although Lynn had never heard an owl at night before, she recognized the sound immediately. She tried to picture the solitary creature perched on a branch high above her, voicing whatever sentiments owls voiced. Owls never saw the night as an alien thing; they relished the dark, since that was when nature had ordained that they should come to life.

The thought was simple but one that Lynn had never had before. There were, after all, creatures who embraced night and darkness, who had no need to hide from it, as she'd done for too many years. An owl might cower from light if it was forced into what was for it an unnatural setting, but the night creature was totally at home in an environment that, until tonight, had been Lynn's enemy.

It wasn't anymore. Although she had only Gabe's gentle snoring to keep her company, the old fears no longer lay heavily around her. Instead of wanting to hide from the mantle of night, for the first time in years Lynn welcomed it. Examined it.

There was a peace, a sameness, to an unlit world she'd never appreciated before. The distractions she'd sought in her well-lit, sound-filled apartment had been stripped away, leaving her with nothing except her thoughts. Gabe was beside her; she could at least examine what she'd refused to acknowledge since she was sixteen.

The memories were coming back now in the aftermath of the owl's lonely call. Lynn remembered the cold sweat that had invaded her body when the state-owned car pulled up in front of the training center that was to be her home for the next few years. She hadn't spoken then; instead, her eyes turned black and unreadable. It was important for her to keep her emotions safe from prying eyes. Her back was locked into a straight, hard line, eyes unwavering as she took the steps leading to a barred door. Tough one, they'd called her. Nerveless. They'd been right—and terribly, terribly wrong.

Inside, Lynn was dying. She continued to die until she was touched by a teacher who carried the key to her salvation. The teacher, Phillip Jacobs, didn't care about the failures of the past. "You can read," he told her. "You aren't stupid." Slowly she came to believe him. Phillip Jacobs couldn't unlock the door to her cell, but he could unlock her mind.

For that she would always love him. Call him miracle worker.

Lynn shifted positions so that she was looking up at the sky. It was alive with stars, the moon a cool beacon. She'd denied herself those memories of her years at the center for too long. It wouldn't happen again. Because the man sleeping beside her had given her courage.

He'd done it in a way she didn't recognize until the act was finished. Somehow, without her knowing it, Gabe Updike had stripped away the painful links to her past and replaced them with a new present.

"I love you, Gabe," she told the moon as cool tears ran down her cheeks. "You've given me so much. You've given me yourself."

The intensity of her emotions frightened Lynn. She was used to dealing with the hard knocks that beset the juveniles she worked with, but their problems had always been a little distant. It was their lives, not hers. Tonight she wasn't listening to someone else pouring out his heart. She was listening to the sounds of her own heart, remembering both black nights and days with Phillip Jacobs.

It was almost too much. In the past, Lynn would have turned up the stereo and found escape from her emotions. She wouldn't have thought about that very special teacher and where she'd been when her life finally righted itself. But there was no artificial sound here. She had nothing but an owl and Gabe's breathing.

Slowly, steadily, Lynn regained control. Tears still washed away at the hollows in her life, but she didn't fear letting that happen. Like a man covered with the grime of his life, Lynn bathed herself in her tears. She was naked, newborn. But because Gabe was here, there was no sense of vulnerability.

A man, one man, had changed everything.

Lynn didn't know how much she slept that night, but she awoke with a sense of renewal that transcended the aches and pains that were part of sleeping on the ground. She was first aware of Gabe's stirring, and then he reached for her.

"There's a crease on your cheek." Gabe touched the mark as if it were something to be cherished. "I'm afraid I can't offer you a hot shower."

"No breakfast in bed?" she asked in mock horror. Breakfast was not what she wanted.

Gabe's fingers left her cheek and found the hollow at the base of her throat. From there he inched his way lower, letting her know that food wasn't what he was thinking of, either. "I had a dream," he said. "You don't happen to know how to fly, do you?"

"Is that what I was doing?" Lynn was trying to command her body to remain still, but it was rebelling.

"Actually, you were floating." Gabe's grin told Lynn that he knew of the struggle she was going through. "Over a lake."

"Wh—what were you doing?"

"Fishing."

Lynn never knew whether Gabe was telling her the truth or not. Things other than speaking were more important. By the time they became one, Lynn wondered if she'd ever want to wear bedclothes again. The simple reality of having Gabe's body next to hers filled her with wonder. He could, she believed, be anywhere with any woman. He'd chosen to be here. With her.

Much later, while they were hiking back to civilization, Gabe told her a little about the glaciers that formed the park and pointed out a spot where he'd once seen a number of bighorn sheep, but Lynn's thoughts were the owl she'd spent the night with. She hoped that his night had been as precious, as deeply satisfying, as hers had been.

A thought had been born last night. It refused to die. What she and Gabe had experienced during the night, and almost from the moment they'd met, was a flawless crystal. He might not love her tomorrow; he might not love her now, although her eyes and body were making her question that possibility. But no matter how long this feeling lingered, she wanted to make it as perfect as possible. And there was one thing she could give him that would tell him that.

She stopped in the middle of the path, took Gabe's hand and leaned against him. For a moment she was silent. "Next time I want to pick the place we go."

"Next time?"

If that's what you want, she thought of saying, but she'd gone beyond that point. "Gabe? Have you ever wanted to tell someone something but been afraid—because you didn't know what the reaction was going to be?"

Gabe pulled her against him and let her sense his beating heart. "Don't play word games with me, Lynn. If you're afraid to say it, then I'm afraid of hearing it."

"Oh, no. No, Gabe," she whispered. She closed her eyes and let Gabe's strength engulf her. "It . . . I don't ever want that to happen."

"Then what is it you want to tell me?"

Lynn took a deep breath. There was still an emotion called freedom to be worked through, but she was willing to take this step. She had to. "I love you."

"Lynn—"

"Is that all you're going to say?" It was so hard to breathe.

"No." Gabe sighed deeply. "No. Oh, God, Lynn, I love you, too."

He loved her! Thank you, she wanted to cry. Where do we go from here? she wanted to ask. But they'd come so far and had so far yet to go. The words they'd spoken were enough for now. She could only look up at him with shining, tear-filled eyes and then wrap her arms around him.

GABE HAD LEFT his house closed up while they were gone. While Gabe fed Ranger, who had been looked after by a neighbor, Lynn went around opening windows to let out the stale air that went with old houses. She was unlacing her boots when he joined her in the living room. "You need plants in here," she observed. "It is rather austere."

"Austere?" Her observation took Gabe by surprise. True, he was aware that the place where he hung his hat lacked the finishing touches most people associated with a home, but he'd never given much thought to the worn vinyl in the kitchen or the frayed carpeting where the front door dragged across it when opened. In fact, the place felt more inviting today than it had since he first moved in. The woman he loved, the woman who said she loved him, was here.

"You know." She shrugged. "Pictures on the walls—that sort of thing."

"Maybe. I haven't given it much thought."

"Do. I loved having that rose you brought me. There's nothing wrong with a man needing the same things." She nodded. "Let me do that for you. I'd like it to feel more inviting."

"The ladies' bridge club isn't going to meet here. I don't have to impress anyone. Besides, the refrigerator's stocked," he said. "What more does a place need?" Just the same, maybe he would look into new carpeting. Lynn would like that. She deserved to be surrounded by the trappings of a home. "I think I'd like having flowers around. But real ones. Not those plastic things."

He helped her pull off her boots, and then she did the same for him. "Tired?" he asked when she remained seated on the floor.

"No." The word came out on the trail of a long breath. "I was thinking."

"About what?" The way she was looking at him scared him.

"About something you said the other day. You really want me to talk to my parents, don't you?"

Chapter Eleven

Lynn had been wrong. There was nothing austere about the room they were sitting in. Her eyes were bright enough to warm everything they touched on.

Instead of immediately asking questions, Gabe took a minute to let what she'd just said sink in. A few days ago she'd been adamant that nothing could be accomplished by talking to her parents. But something had changed her mind. Except for that one exquisite moment when they told each other everything, she'd been quiet during their hike out of the park. Then he'd attributed her silence to emotion, but now he realized that this, too, must have been on her mind.

He'd been so sure a few days ago that she would be truly able to go forward with her life only if she put the past to rest, but he was no longer convinced that it was for the best. In perfect worlds parents and children bridge their estrangements. In the imperfect world in which he and Lynn lived, happy endings weren't assured.

But they had each other. The black sheep of two families had found something neither of them expected. Maybe that was enough.

"Are you sure?" he asked, aware of how inadequate his words were on the tail of what she'd just said.

"No, of course I'm not sure. I'm scared to death." Her suddenly too-large eyes mirrored her words.

"Then don't do it."

"What?" Lynn's eyes had been glazed, but they sharpened as she focused on him. You're the one who—"

"I know what I said." His anger was at himself, not her. "But Lynn, honey, I don't want you hurt."

"Hurt is a fact of life."

She was right. "Don't do it just for me."

Lynn was shaking her head. For a moment he was afraid of meeting her eyes; when he did, there was no saving himself. She sucked him down and into her soul. Captured all there was of him. "Gabe, I owe you so much. Last night, that's when I realized what you mean to me. That's why I said what I did."

"Last night?" he repeated stupidly. God, she was beautiful! Beautiful inside, where it counted the most.

"I've been afraid of the dark, of silence, for so long that I'd forgotten there was any other way to be. But—" she faltered, as if knowing she was stripping herself naked for him "—last night we were alone in the middle of the wilderness, and I wasn't afraid anymore. You did that for me."

She was crying, there were tears in her eyes. Gabe started to brush them away but stopped himself. Her tears deserved a life and time of their own. "I didn't do anything special."

Yes, you did. You gave me yourself. Lynn fought her way around the thought, which was almost more than she could handle. "Maybe you don't think you did. But Gabe, you're part of my life. You came in without my knowing it was happening. I've—no one's ever done that before. No one even tried. I always thought I had to stand on my own. To be brave for myself. Maybe I don't have to do that anymore."

"No, you don't, if you don't want to." Gabe wanted to say more, to tell her that he wanted to be there always for her, but he'd never said that to a woman before. He, too, was taking new steps. "You're an easy woman to be around," he said instead, because the conversation had come too close to the edge. "Have you thought about it?" he pushed. "About what you're going to say to your parents, I mean?"

Lynn shuddered. She was trying to be strong for Gabe, but it wasn't easy. In her mind she saw two people with eyes hooded over to stop her from seeing all their emotions. The last time she'd seen them, they hadn't touched each other when they said goodbye at the end of the visit. "I have no idea what I'm going to say to them. I haven't dared think of it, so how can I say it?"

Then don't do it. I couldn't stand to see you hurt. The thought flitted through Gabe's mind, but he stopped himself from saying it out loud. Her decision had come at no small cost. He could do nothing less than stretch out his hand and give her all the support he had to give. "When would be a good time?" he asked.

Lynn frowned. "The weekend. Dad works as a mechanic now and works regular hours, just like everyone else. You know, all those years when Mom wanted him to light in one spot? It took the recession to make that finally happen."

"It won't be easy."

"Of course it won't." She'd been sitting cross-legged on the floor in front of him, looking small and vulnerable and brave. He wanted to pull her up onto the couch next to him, but she needed to concentrate on the mountain she'd placed in front of herself. "Do you want to call them now? I can either stay or leave the room. Whatever you want."

"Now?" The word was unsteady. "Maybe...later. I want to get cleaned up first. *Coward!* Lynn admonished herself.

Gabe had really asked only one thing of her since they'd met. In turn, he'd given her so much. Surely she could do it—for him.

"Of course," he was saying, as if all the logic in the world were behind her stalling. "Would you like to flip for the first shower, or do you want me to be a gentleman?"

She could still laugh. The sound rolled easily off her lips. "Be a gentleman. I fight dirty when it comes to a hot shower." She was on her feet and headed toward the bathroom before he could ask her to reconsider his offer. Although he was waiting to get in, Lynn lingered under the hot spray. She was sweaty and dirty from their trek in the wilderness, but that wasn't why she was standing with her arms wrapped around her waist. It felt right to be here. She'd called Gabe's house austere while she was opening windows, because there wasn't enough of him in it, but now she could sense him everywhere. All it had taken to change things was for him to walk into the house and take it over.

"What about me?" Gabe opened the door to the shower a crack. "Aren't you going to take pity on a smelly old man?"

"Get out of here!" Lynn wadded up her washcloth and threw it at Gabe. "Haven't you heard of privacy?"

Gabe hung a towel over the top of the shower door for her. "You're in real trouble if there's no hot water left."

"There's plenty of water," Lynn observed as she stepped out of the shower, a towel tied securely around her. "If there's one up-to-date thing about this house, it's the hot-water heater. An army could move in and stay clean."

"There's only one person I'm interested in having move in here, Lynn."

Lynn's fingers tightened around her towel. Although the room was hot and steamy, she began to shiver. "Are you asking . . . ?" Her voice faltered.

"Am I asking you to move in here?" Gabe had been studying his beard in the mirror, but now he gave up that pretense. "Yes, I am."

"Oh." Lynn wanted to say more. There were a thousand things crowding her mind, but nothing was ready to come out.

"Oh, what?" Gabe picked up a hand towel and started to gently wipe the drops from her forehead. "Say something, Lynn."

"I don't know what to say." The bathroom was too small. She had to get out. She reached for the doorknob, but Gabe stopped her.

"You either say yes or no." His voice sounded as if he'd been inhaling too much steam.

"It isn't that easy, Gabe." Lynn still wanted out of the bathroom but not as much as she wanted to explain things. If that were possible. "I thought you wanted a shower."

"All right." Gabe pulled his T-shirt over his head and let it drop onto the floor. "I'll get my shower. Then we'll talk."

Lynn was ready by the time Gabe emerged from the bathroom. She'd had to put on one of Gabe's shirts, but she was more concerned with thoughts and emotions than appearance. She smiled tentatively at him but continued to fluff her hair. "Do you know how long I've been alone?" she asked as he sat on the bed and reached for his socks. "Since I was eighteen. And I felt alone long before that. At those foster homes, in the training center, I never felt as if I could share my emotional space with anyone. As if I wanted to."

"I want to. That's what I'm asking." Gabe sat motionless, his socks dangling from his fingers.

"I know that. It's—Gabe, I haven't shared a bathroom since I got out of the center. I'm used to being alone."

"Did you mean it when you said you loved me?"

Lynn gave up the pretense of caring what her hair looked like. She moved toward the bed but stopped just out of his reach. "I meant that more than I've ever meant anything in my life."

"Then why don't you want to live with me?"

It was a simple question. The answer should have been just as simple, but it wasn't. "Because... Oh, Gabe, I don't know how to make you part of my life. What if I fail?"

"I won't let you fail." Gabe leaned forward.

"You can't promise that." Lynn laughed gently, loving him. "No one can guide another through life. That's something we have to do on our own." Lynn raked her hand through her hair, destroying the order she'd created a few minutes ago. "Gabe, from the time I was a little girl, I've kept certain things, my emotions, to myself. That's how I kept going. When I decided to become a juvenile officer, it was a decision I made on my own. I didn't discuss it with anyone."

"Because there wasn't anyone to discuss it with. It's different now."

"Is it?" Lynn moaned. "Do I know how to change?"

Gabe picked up his socks again and rammed his right foot into one. "You will if the motivation is strong enough." He looked up from his task, his eyes easy on her. "Besides, I'm not sure all that much is being asked of you. I want us to be together because I happen to believe we have something special going. I'm not asking you to make yourself into something you aren't."

"But what if you don't like who I am?" Lynn sighed heavily, tired of the argument. "Please be patient with me. My batting average with relationships isn't the best. This time I don't want to strike out. Particularly not this time."

"You aren't going to strike out." Gabe patted the bed next to him and waited until she sat down and their shoulders were touching. He took her hands in his and held them gently. "Ranger likes you, and he's the best judge of people I've ever known."

Lynn lifted her chin and turned toward him, because she knew Gabe's lips were waiting. "I just don't want either of us to regret anything. I don't think I could handle that. Gabe, I don't think I can make any more decisions until I've talked to my parents.

"All right." Gabe's lips were an inch away. "But I want you to think about something. There aren't any guarantees in life. All we can do is live that life to the fullest extent possible. Take chances. Extend ourselves. Sometimes it comes out right."

You're so wise, Lynn thought as she returned Gabe's kiss. *I just pray I haven't been alone too long to let that wisdom reach me.*

"Are you hungry?"

Lynn's consciousness swam toward Gabe's voice. Something was expected of her, but until he repeated his question, she was unable to concentrate on more than the masculine tone. "I don't know."

Gabe laughed, the sound pulling her closer to reality. "That's not much of an answer. We haven't eaten since morning."

"What time is it?"

"Time to feed you. A woman can't live on love alone."

Love. Lynn opened her eyes, but Gabe was already getting up. His back was to her. She wanted to touch him, make him turn around, say the word again. "I want a pizza."

They ate at a neighborhood pizza parlor. Gabe talked her into sharing a pitcher of beer with him. Despite having never had more than a sip before in her life, Lynn relished the experience. It wasn't that she particularly liked the taste; rather, she liked the fact that this was what couples did for a spur-of-the-moment meal. Tonight, they were no different from anyone else.

"I want you to spend the night," Gabe whispered as they were leaving. "There's going to be a football game on TV tomorrow, and I don't like watching football alone."

"Brook isn't playing," Lynn pointed out.

"But he'll be watching. He'll call afterward."

Gabe didn't have to say any more. He wanted her to be part of his night and his lazy Sunday. To share a phone call from his brother. Those simple, intimate gestures were what other women took for granted. She had to discover whether those things were right for her or whether it was too late and she was too locked into her aloneness. At least after a night in Gabe's arms, maybe Lynn would have the courage for a phone call of her own.

She waited until after the game was over and after a fifteen-minute phone call between the brothers before she looked up her parents' phone number. She wanted to tell Gabe that she didn't mean to forget the number, only that it was part of being dyslexic, but her mouth had suddenly become too dry for wasted speech.

Her fingers shook as she punched the numbers, but she didn't dare look at Gabe for support.

Lynn's mother answered the phone. For too long Lynn could think of nothing to say. Finally, she shot Gabe a beseeching glance and swallowed. "Mom, it's Lynn."

The silence on the other end of the line told her that she wasn't the only one thrown off balance. "Lynn, is anything wrong? Where are you?"

"In Denver." Oh, God, what was she going to say next? "I . . . how are you?"

"Fine. Your father isn't here."

The inane conversation continued for another minute as Lynn tumbled around memories long buried that refused to come to the surface. At last, Lynn put an end to the strain. "I'd like to see you and Dad. There are some things we need to talk about. Important things. Do you think that would be all right?"

"Of course," her mother breathed, and then, as if afraid to postpone things any more than necessary, suggested that Lynn come over to dinner next weekend.

"I'd like to bring someone with me," Lynn added before hanging up. She turned toward Gabe. "I think Mom was in shock" was all she could get out before seeking the comfort Gabe was offering her. "I think she knows we aren't going to discuss what clothing styles are in."

Gabe would have given anything to tell Lynn to call back and tell her mother that she wouldn't be there, after all. He wanted to wrap her in a blanket and carry her back into the mountains. The only world there was the one they had created, nestled amid the towering mountains; there they would be safe.

But that would solve nothing. Eventually they'd have to return. Lynn would still have her past to face. They couldn't get on with their future until she did.

"Are you sure you want me there?" he asked. "Maybe you won't want an outsider around."

"You aren't an outsider. You'll never be that."

Gabe sighed. He wondered if she knew how deeply her words touched him. "I don't think I can help. I hope you know that."

Her eyes were brimming with hope and fear. "You've already helped more than you'll ever know. I'm not asking you to come because I'm going to lean on you. Gabe? You've let me be part of your life. You..." She almost laughed. "You let me speak my mind to your father. I'm not going to shut you away from my family."

She didn't add that she'd been shut away from any true relationship for years, but that was what Gabe was thinking about when he held her later that night. Not long ago he hadn't been able to think about lovemaking because he was worried about his brother; now it was Lynn's turn to simply be held. Gabe hadn't been sure what his response would be when she curled up against him, silently begging for his arms around her, but he found it easier than he thought it would be to concentrate on emotional rather than physical needs. He wondered how many married couples shared nights like this.

He had to leave her in the morning so they could both go to work, but he called her three times during the day. He didn't dream up excuses for his calls; instead, he simply listened while she talked. She said she felt as if she were coming down with something; probably just nerves, she admitted. She had no idea what she was going to wear. More importantly, she didn't know what should come after she walked into her parents' home and said hello.

"I'm a basket case," she told him when the receptionist put his call through to her office in the middle of the afternoon. "I haven't had this much trouble reading in years. I've been trying to make notes of things I want to bring up but I'm not getting very far."

"Can you get away? Why don't you come over here? You can watch me try to make sense out of this delivery order," he offered. He could have kept his distance, let her struggle on alone but the thought never entered his mind.

Fifteen minutes later, Lynn was parking her car next to his office trailer. The tentative grin she gave him was both brave and embarrassed. "I feel like such a coward," she admitted after he led her inside so they could have a moment alone.

"I'm just having dinner with my parents. This isn't an IRS audit."

Gabe laughed and pulled her close. He held her until it seemed to him that she'd transferred some of her tension to him. "I've been audited. Be glad it isn't that."

"You have?" Lynn seemed genuinely interested. "How did it turn out?"

"It was long and drawn out, but I survived, I think to the disappointment of the officer holding the audit. Do you really want to hear about that?"

"Anything," Lynn said with a shaky sigh. "Anything to keep my mind off this weekend."

"I don't think it's going to work." Although Gabe would have liked nothing better than to go on holding Lynn indefinitely, he knew her mind would only go to one place. And because of who she was to him, his mind would go there, too. "Okay, lady, you've got another four days before D day. Have you decided what you're going to wear?"

"Clothes." She laughed again from the shelter of his chest. "Definitely clothes."

"That's a start," he admitted before taking her through the mundane but necessary discussion that led to the choice of a skirt and blouse, while he opted for slacks and a dress shirt but no tie. "There! That takes care of that. I don't see as you have anything else to worry about. Your mom has to come up with the menu."

"Poor woman. She never was the world's greatest cook, and now I'm asking her to come up with a meal I probably won't be able to eat."

"You really are out looking for things to worry about, aren't you? So you spend the evening pushing food around on your plate. I'll tell you what. When they aren't looking, you can sneak things onto my plate, and I'll eat them. That's what Brook used to do when my mother served rice."

"Brook doesn't like rice?"

"Hates the stuff. I ate his rice. He took care of my chicken. The only problem with that arrangement was that neither of us would tackle carrots."

This time Lynn's laugh was genuine. "You sound like typical kids," she teased. "Remind me never to serve you chicken or carrots."

Gabe let slide a remark that could point their relationship in a definite direction. Instead, he capitalized on her interest in his childhood to tell her about some of the stunts he and Brook pulled to circumvent his parents' rather rigid standards. Before a yell from his foreman put an end to their privacy, he'd learned there'd been times in Lynn's childhood that were no different from those of other children. She, too, had gone to great lengths to avoid certain vegetables, had stretched her curfew to the limit and had traded nutritious lunches for junk food.

"Are you going to be all right?" he asked before leaving her. "You're not going to want to hear what I'm going to be saying to a certain union bricklayer."

Lynn nodded. She didn't know how much time she'd spent with Gabe, only that she should have come much sooner. He hadn't denied her the right to her apprehension. Instead, he had let her take it out and examine it. Because of that, she was much more ready for the weekend. She'd been right to ask him to join her; he belonged. Maybe in everything that concerned her.

Despite Gabe's warning, a few minutes later Lynn fled the stuffy trailer and found him demanding an explanation of shoddy work from a bull-necked man who had little to say for himself except that his union dues were paid up. Gabe barely glanced at her, but that didn't bother Lynn. She was content to stand back and watch this very special man doing what it was he did to earn a living. He didn't lose his tem-

per with the man; nor did he give an inch in his assertion
that less than perfect work could endanger the safety of
everyone.

Lynn wondered if she could get the judge to come out here
to watch his son at work. Many of Judge Updike's prejud-
ices where his son was concerned, Lynn now realized, came
because the older man honestly didn't know what kind of
man his son had become. The judge was clinging to old ways
and values he understood. That could change in time, but
only if the man was shaken off the treadmill of his life. The
judge might not love her, but he had said he respected her.
It was possible—Lynn might be able to trade on that respect enough to bring the father into the son's world.

That was the thought that took Lynn through the days left
until it was time to leave for her parents' house in Salt Lake
City. She realized that she was, or could be, a new force in
the father/son relationship. Maybe she could become
enough of a force to change that relationship for the better.
She wasn't ready to explain her new calm to Gabe. Instead,
she simply told him that she wasn't fighting her emotions
anymore. "I'll probably say everything wrong, but at least
I'm trying," she told him.

Still, when they were dressed and ready to get into her car,
Lynn handed the keys to Gabe. "You drive. I'll navigate."

When they arrived in Salt Lake City, she'd been ready to
have her sense of direction desert her, but with Gabe's help
they were able to make their way through the city to the
older established tract where her parents had lived for the
past two years. The trees in the front yard were larger than
any at the apartment complex where she lived; the house itself was much smaller than Gabe's. It needed painting, and
she wondered if there were things about her father's health
she should know. When Gabe cut the motor, Lynn closed
her eyes, momentarily losing herself in silence. She and her

parents had pretended too long that certain things had never happened. Dredging them up wasn't going to be easy.

But Gabe was with her. Even if the visit didn't turn out the way she wanted it to, she still had him. Unless too much happened here tonight that he couldn't accept.

Lynn wouldn't allow herself to think about that. She had him tonight.

Lynn's father opened the door. He was wearing a brown sweater that looked a little large on his settling frame and glasses that hadn't been there before. Her mother had always been short and sturdy; now some of that was turning into soft flesh. Lynn could tell that her mother was trying to hold her stomach in. They weren't speaking.

They're as scared as I am, Lynn thought. "Mom, Dad, this is Gabe Updike. I was with him when I called the other day."

"Is he your husband?" her mother asked. "Is that what you wanted to tell us?"

The question was almost more than Lynn could bear. She hadn't known that her father wore glasses, but they didn't know whether or not she was married. "No," she said with what strength she could muster. "Gabe—Gabe and I have been through a lot together."

Lynn's father stepped back with a gesture designed to bring them all inside. Lynn did as the gesture dictated. She felt both nothing and everything, a leaf tossed in so many directions that it might be ripped apart. She was aware that Gabe wasn't touching her, but there wasn't time to think about that. If she did, she might lose control of her emotions. The furniture in the living room wasn't the same as what had been there last Christmas.

"You've been redecorating." she said when she remembered that no one had spoken since they came in. "I'm trying to get Gabe to do something with his place, but neither of us knows much about decorating."

Her mother rattled on for a minute about the weeks she'd spent going to different furniture stores until, accidentally, the two women's eyes met. Helen Tresca's voice trailed off. "Can I get you something to drink? Some wine?"

Wine sounded good, not because Lynn wanted to be numbed but because a glass would give her hands something to do. At a gesture from her father, Lynn sat on the couch opposite the picture window and waited for Gabe to join her. A minute later her mother was handing her a chilled glass. It was a simple gesture, a companionable sort of thing performed hundreds of times every evening in homes across the country, but because Lynn had never had her mother hand her a glass of wine, the moment stayed frozen in her mind.

They weren't mother and child anymore. They were two adults with no knowledge of how to relate to each other. That's why they talked about furniture and the weather and clothing styles.

"I wasn't sure you'd be able to see me on such short notice," Lynn said with courage she didn't know she possessed until she sensed Gabe inches from her.

Rob Tresca blinked behind his glasses. "I don't have to work weekends anymore. I had no idea what a luxury that could be."

Lynn picked up the thread of the conversation. "Tell Gabe that. He's his own boss. He never knows when he's going to have to work. I keep telling him it's easier being a juvenile officer. As long as I don't answer the phone at home, I have my weekends to myself."

"People don't stop having problems at five o'clock, do they?" her father said. "How do you feel about what you're doing?"

"It's exciting," Lynn supplied. She didn't mean to rattle on, but the look in her father's eyes was tearing away at her. *He cared. He cared!* She threw out words about challenge and long hours and successes to keep from thinking about what Rob Tresca's eyes were doing to her. It wasn't until Gabe squeezed her hand that she ran down.

"Dinner's ready. If you're hungry," her mother said.

Lynn couldn't answer. She'd expended everything she had in a discussion of her job. She was grateful when Gabe rose to his feet, pulling her along with him. "Do I smell chicken?" he asked.

"It's a secret recipe my wife's had for years," Rob pointed out. "Actually, it's something she does with a can of mush-room soup."

"Chicken sounds great," Gabe said before Lynn could catch his eye.

Years ago the table in the dining room had been filled with the energy of four children. Last winter twelve people had managed to sit there. Now it seemed strangely empty. Lynn sat across from her mother, trying to find the woman who once asked her nightly how school had gone. Back then, Lynn hadn't wanted to answer. Now she remembered that the questions hadn't come easily, either.

To her relief, Gabe was plunging in, erasing the silence. After a question from her father, Gabe set about clearing up some rumors that existed about aspects of the building trade. Between hearty bites of chicken he outlined the his-tory of the center's development and speculated on its po-tential for even further growth. Lynn concentrated on what he was saying, eating without being aware of the process. He'd told her he didn't know what he would say to her par-ents, but he was doing magnificently.

"That kid Lynn sent over is one of my hardest workers," Gabe was saying. "However, I certainly didn't think so the day Lynn and I met." He turned toward her; the look in his eyes stripped Lynn of every thought except raw love. "She made more of an impression on me than that little thief did."

Lynn knew something was being required of her, but it was several moments before she could put what she was feeling for Gabe at bay and concentrate on the looks from her parents. They would, she decided, have to be blind not to see what was going on.

But then, they'd been blind to so many things where their daughter was concerned. Lynn had accepted the unspoken edict that said they'd talk of ordinary things while they all took a reading of each other, but she no longer felt like a knot of raw nerve endings. Her parents' faces were no longer pinched and wary, the way they'd been when she walked in. It was time, if she had the courage, to touch the past.

"If I have success with delinquents, it's because I understand what they're going through."

"Oh, Lynn." Her mother didn't say any more.

Rob Tresca said the rest. "I wondered when we'd get to that. That's why you wanted to see us, isn't it?"

"I can't help it, Dad." She thought she'd be bitter, but all Lynn felt was emptiness. "Sometimes I wonder if you thought of me as anything except a delinquent."

"Of course we did. You were such a happy baby." Helen's voice was weaker than it had been earlier. "But Lynn, I'd like you to try to think about something now. Because you were a child, I'm sure most of your thoughts were of yourself. That was to be expected. You were too young to put yourself in our place."

"Which was?" Lynn didn't like attacking her mother. Despite the extra pounds, the woman seemed frailer than she remembered her. But there was so much they had to work through, and she didn't know any other way of trying to accomplish it.

Helen turned toward her husband. He put down his fork and leaned forward, glasses sliding lower on his nose. Lynn read no emotion in his eyes. "Which was trying to raise four children, one of whom was so different from the others that we had no idea how to reach her. How to help her."

"Help?" Lynn started trembling. She folded her hands in her lap to hide the fact and didn't allow herself to return the look she knew Gabe was giving her. This was something she had to do on her own.

"I'm sure it didn't look like that to you at the time," her mother was saying. "Lynn, do you remember all the times I pressed you for information about how things were going in school?"

"How could I forget?" For a moment Lynn was a child again, turning away from her mother's probing.

"I already knew the answer." Helen sighed. "I'd already been on the phone to your teachers, to the principal."

"Then why did you ask me?"

"I don't know." When her mother sighed again, there was a shudder in the sound. "Maybe because that was the only communication we had left and I didn't want to lose that."

Lynn didn't want to think about that; it hurt too much. These were her parents. A child doesn't attack her parents. She looked toward Gabe for strength, felt something precious of him reaching out toward her and continued. "I don't think we were communicating at all." She didn't want to hurt her parents, and yet maybe she did. She'd been raw so much of the time as a child. The emotion shouldn't be hers alone.

"Maybe we weren't," Rob Tresca admitted. "You were so different from the others. We didn't have any guidelines for raising you. All that moving around didn't help. We never stayed anywhere long enough for the school to work with you."

"The black sheep."

"Different," her father repeated. "Lynn, we had three bright, enthusiastic children who took to school like a fish takes to water. It didn't seem to bother them that there was a different school every year. Then you came along and started struggling from the first day of kindergarten. You– we knew you weren't retarded."

"You did?" Lynn couldn't remember if they'd ever told her that. Under the table Gabe's hand covered hers.

Her mother nodded. "You walked and started talking at the same age the others did. You were a curious child. So very curious." She laughed at a secret memory. "Believe me, I did enough reading about retardation to realize that wasn't your problem."

"What did you decide it was?" She already knew what the answer was, but a part of her that somehow needed to feel pain asked the question.

"That you were rebelling against us. Against moving around so much."

Lynn knew her face was without expression, but she needed to feel Gabe's fingers intertwined with hers to keep it that way. She had rebelled, but not until later. Until there was nothing left. "Why would I want to defy you? Did you ever ask yourselves that?"

"A thousand times. Unfortunately, we never came up with an answer we could accept. Lynn, we blamed ourselves for the fact that you were always starting over somewhere else. But honey, it wasn't easy raising four children. I could make more money as a dynamite expert than I could doing anything else."

"I know that now," Lynn admitted. "I've been in the world of work a few years."

"Lynn, I hope you can put yourself in our place," her father went on. "Living with you was like living with a time bomb. We knew you were hurting inside. Wanting to explode. Exploding sometimes. But we didn't have any of the answers. No one had told us anything about dyslexia. All we knew was that you weren't mastering a skill the rest of us took for granted."

"And you thought it was my fault." Lynn stopped, letting the words wrap themselves around her. It hadn't been hard to say; it was something she'd accepted years before. It was also the forbidden topic, or had been until now. It came easier because Gabe was bearing some of the load.

"Sometimes." Helen started to reach out for her daughter, but Lynn didn't have the strength to let go of Gabe's hand.

"Not all the time?" Lynn's confidence was shaken. For years she'd hoarded her anger as if it were a necessary emotion. But now that she heard the emotion in their voices, she wasn't sure anymore. She wanted to run, but Gabe was holding her there. His fingers were warning her to stay.

"You started out with all the enthusiasm of any child, but it was stripped away at such an early age," her father said sadly. "When you became a teenager and started rebelling, it was easier to tell ourselves that you were your own worst enemy. That you were doing this to yourself. But we couldn't forget that eager little girl."

Lynn closed her eyes. She didn't want to look at her parents anymore. She wanted to concentrate on Gabe. He was here with her; she could make it as long as he was here. "We had so many fights."

"Too many," her father was saying. "We tried to help you. But the methods that worked with the rest of our children didn't work with you. You didn't want to sit inside with a book in front of you; we insisted you try. That—that's when the arguments started."

"It was a vicious circle, wasn't it?"

Lynn jumped. She hadn't been ready for Gabe's voice. She opened her eyes but could meet his only for a moment. The child her parents were painting wasn't one she was proud of; she was afraid of learning what Gabe thought of that person.

"Lynn was frustrated. We were angry. Sometimes it was the other way around, but the tension was always there. By the time Lynn was a teenager, we knew she had a learning disability, but that sometimes seemed like the least of our problems." Rob Tresca stopped long enough to remove his glasses and rub the bridge of his nose. "Gabe, you know a woman very different from the child we were trying to raise. I don't expect you to understand."

"I think I do."

Something in Gabe's voice rocketed off Lynn's heart. More than anything she needed his support, and yet maybe he was withdrawing it. There wasn't much she'd liked about herself as a child. She couldn't blame Gabe for not liking that person, either. "It would have been so different if we'd known I was dyslexic from the start," she said hollowly. "I wonder what I would have been like if—"

"Speculation isn't going to change what was," Gabe interrupted. "You have to deal with the reality of what you were."

"Don't you think I have?" Lynn spat out. She didn't want to fight with Gabe, not here and not ever, but he was trying to tell her something when she'd lived with that fact all her life. She didn't need it pounded into her by him. Especially not by him.

Gabe's voice was without emotion. "I'm sure you have. What I'm saying is that I don't believe making 'if' part of the conversation is going to do anyone any good."

Lynn couldn't deal with what he was telling her. Not now. She'd come here because it was something she wanted to do for Gabe. Tonight she'd heard her parents voice what had only been feelings years ago, but there was more. That was what had to be dealt with. "Were there any good times?"

Her question hurt. She could tell that by the look on her mother's face, but no matter how much the words cost all of them, they had to be asked. She wondered if Gabe had any idea how close she was to cracking.

"Oh, yes, Lynn. Don't you believe that?" The pain in her mother's voice tore at Lynn's heart. "There was . . . Remember the summer we spent with your father's parents? They had that place by a lake, and you learned to row a boat. You would have been content to spend the rest of your life there."

Lynn had forgotten. It was a good summer, but then summers always were. "I didn't feel any pressure there," she said. "Grandma and Grandpa spoiled all of us. I think—" she laughed softly "—I think the only work I did was to help feed the dogs. What kind did they have?"

"Cocker spaniels. They raised them commercially. You loved the puppies. If you weren't out in the lake, you were with the dogs."

"We had a dog," Lynn went on. She was caught up in the past, unable to let go. "A collie named Buff. What happened to her?"

"Old age," her father explained. "But we have one of her puppies. Lad is—what?—about twelve years old. Buff used to wait for you kids by the sidewalk every afternoon. We felt it was important for you kids to have a dog for a sense of continuity. A sense of belonging."

"I told Buff everything," she whispered. "Brandy kept a diary, but Buff was my confidant. He was better for me than any of those counselors the schools had me see."

Lynn still had no idea what Gabe was thinking. She was barely aware that he was still holding her hand, but when he spoke, his words were for her parents. "Now I understand why my mutt takes to Lynn the way he does. They speak the same language."

Rob Tresca spoke to his daughter. "One of those counselors told us to get rid of Buff so you'd be forced to communicate with people instead of animals."

"But you didn't do that, did you?" Lynn fought to keep emotion out of her voice, but it was there nonetheless.

Her father shook his head. "Call it parents' instinct. We might have made a lot of mistakes raising you, but it didn't make sense to take away the one thing you could confide in." Sorrow crept into his voice. "We were told so many different things by so many people that after a while we didn't know what to believe. Gabe, Lynn threw us for a loop."

"I threw myself for a loop," Lynn managed to say.

Lynn's mother had been staring at the carpet; even when she spoke, her eyes remained downcast. "I hoped I'd never have to tell you this, but when the judge sent you to the youth center, we were relieved."

"You wanted me out of your lives." Lynn was both fascinated and chilled by the sounds of her words vibrating throughout the room. "I was already living in foster homes. Why did you want me locked up?"

"No, no." Helen Tresca repeated. She was shaking her head like a weary fighter. "We weren't thinking about you being locked up. We were...it was the only way we could be sure you wouldn't slip away completely. At least, we told ourselves, at the treatment center you wouldn't run away from your demons."

"Oh." Lynn tried to say more, but her thoughts were still hung up on what her mother had said. They'd been relieved when she was sent away. That wasn't hard to understand. She shouldn't be feeling so alone. At length, she managed to work her way around the emotion. "The center was supposed to accomplish what my parents couldn't. That's what the judge who sentenced me said. It had to be a relief to have me not your responsibility anymore."

"Yes."

Lynn shut her eyes. She'd been expecting that, and yet it hurt. They'd given up on her. That was what she'd come here to hear. She wasn't being denied that.

"Why?"

That was Gabe talking. Lynn tried to open her eyes, but they refused to heed her command. Locked away the way she was, Lynn could do nothing except listen.

"Why were we relieved?" her mother was saying. "A million reasons. And one reason."

One. Lynn opened her eyes and found her mother's face.

"Because we'd failed our daughter so completely."

Chapter Twelve

"Of course you can buy an indoor rose. I mean, why can't you?" Lynn faced Gabe with exaggerated defiance. "A culture that can come up with silk flowers that draw bees has to have developed roses designed to grow inside."

"I didn't say you can't buy an indoor rose," Gabe said around the small nails gripped between his teeth. "What I said was I don't want one."

Lynn planted her hands on her hips. "How am I going to do any decorating around this place if you keep throwing roadblocks in my way?"

"Anything but roses, okay? Roses belong outside. It says that somewhere in the manual."

Lynn didn't bother to point out that that particular manual was a figment of Gabe's imagination. They'd been working at putting up paneling in Gabe's bedroom since early morning, and Gabe was entitled to a touch of insanity. "What does that manual of yours say about feeding the hired help?"

"Who says you were hired? Haven't you ever heard of slave labor?" Gabe drove home the last of the small-headed nails and stepped back to admire his handiwork. "I don't know why I didn't do this a long time ago."

Lynn tiptoed up behind Gabe and snatched away his hammer. "Because you didn't have a slave to do your fetching and carrying. No more, fella. I am not going to be blamed for that oversized wall socket. You're the one who cut the opening too large, not me."

Gabe took a step toward Lynn, his eye on the upraised hammer. "I'm a building contractor. I don't make mistakes."

"Says who?" Lynn ducked out of Gabe's way, backing up until she was stopped by the sawhorses set up near Gabe's bed. "I wonder what your men would think if I told them you can't cut a simple sheet of paneling without making a mistake."

"You wouldn't." Gabe took another menacing step. "Not if you ever want to eat again."

Lynn pretended to be considering her options. "If you'll look at the window in my apartment, I'll drop the blackmail. I'm not going to go through another Denver winter with that thing sticking."

"You don't have to spend the winter there."

Oh, Lynn knew all right. In the week since they'd visited her parents, Lynn had done a lot of thinking about where her life...where their lives were heading. Gabe had been under less pressure than usual at work, which meant they'd be able to spend every evening together. For the first two nights they hadn't talked about their trip to Salt Lake City, but by Wednesday Lynn had been able to open up about it. She and her parents still had a long way to go, she realized, but they'd erased years of silence and strain over dinner in one evening. They could erase even more in the weeks and months to come. She could have them come visit her at her apartment, tell them of the times when, while she was in college, she'd wanted to get on the phone and ask them for advice but pride got in the way.

Or she could invite them to Gabe's place and tell them the same things.

"I've been thinking," Lynn started to say softly. "I think I'd like to learn to ski."

"What does that have to do with what we were talking about?"

"Nothing." Lynn straddled one of the sawhorses and threw back her head to work out the kinks that came from holding paneling in place while Gabe glued and tacked. "Do you know what I was thinking about?" She closed her eyes to help her concentrate, but because her perch was precarious, she had to open them again. "If it had been anyone but you there, I don't think I could have told my parents what I did. Or listened to what they had to say."

"I take it that's a good sign." He wanted her to say it.

"After we left my folks and drove all night to get back home, I kept dozing off. Every time I woke up, you were there beside me."

"Trying to stay awake." Gabe lowered himself onto his bed and absently dusted at his jeans.

"I know." Lynn gave him an apologetic smile. "I should have helped you drive, but I felt as if I'd been through the wringer."

"Been dragged through a knothole backwards was the way you put it."

"I told you that, didn't I?" There was no surprise in Lynn's voice. "I told you a lot of things that night."

"If you're asking if you rattled on, the answer is yes."

"I just hope I made sense with my parents." Lynn ran her hand over the rough edge of the two-by-four she was straddling. "They weren't failures. I'm sorry they went through so many years believing that."

"So much time lost," Gabe whispered. "So damn much time."

"But maybe it's over. Or at least we've started in that direction. I meant it about wanting to have them over for Thanksgiving dinner." Lynn leaned forward slightly. "I hope I can learn how to cook a turkey by then."

"You could practice on me," Gabe offered. "I've eaten some strange concoctions in my years as a bachelor. My stomach can handle just about anything."

"Thanks a lot." Lynn glared at Gabe. "I appreciate your vote of confidence."

"You're the one who brought up the subject of your cooking," Gabe pointed out. "What do you think? Would the judge approve of what we're doing here?" He nodded at the rich oak paneling.

"I'm not sure approval is a realistic goal," Lynn pointed out. "But he may be coming around. The judge had to contact the juvenile department about something earlier this week. He asked for me."

"He did?" Gabe had been studying his handiwork on the far wall, but now he focused on Lynn. "You didn't tell me."

"I wasn't sure how I felt about it then, but I've decided that I'm going to try to develop a new relationship with your father. One not muddied up by the past."

Gabe rose from the bed and held out a hand to help Lynn off the sawhorse. "Do you think that's possible?"

"I won't know until I try, will I? But then, I'm trying a lot of new things these days."

"Like clearing the air with your parents?"

Lynn kept her hand in Gabe's. "Yes, that. And paneling a wall. I still say that one section is upside down."

"It is not! Look at that one knot there. It's a continuation of the one in the section next to it. Sometimes—" Gabe jerked Lynn after him as he stepped forward for a close-up look of the smooth sheets now covering the wall. "Sometimes I think being dyslexic has affected your eyesight."

"My eyesight?" Lynn turned away from Gabe so he couldn't see the upward tugging at the corners of her mouth. "You just won't admit you made a mistake. Anyone who makes the wall socket opening two inches larger than it needs to be can't be trusted to do anything right."

"So?" Gabe blustered. He was still holding on to her hand. "Like you said, an oversized cover will hide that."

"So what are you getting so testy about?" Lynn didn't dare look at Gabe. Male pride! "If you don't tell anyone you goofed, I won't, either."

"I goofed? Who took the measurements for that opening? Hmm? Trust a woman to do one simple thing and she screws up."

"Wait just a minute." Lynn ran her eyes over the project, looking for something else to give him a hard time about. "You're the one wielding the saw. You'd already cut two other openings. I'd think a contractor would know enough to know something was wrong."

"That settles it." Gabe pulled Lynn hard against his side. "The next time we work on a project together, you keep your mouth shut."

"Like fun—" Lynn didn't get the rest out, for Gabe effectively stopped her words with a kiss. Just before she closed her eyes, Lynn caught the mirth in Gabe's eyes.

Lynn could have continued the game, but she didn't. It was easier to concentrate on nothing except the bone-deep satisfaction that came from being in Gabe's arms. They'd been carrying on a mock argument since starting on the project four hours earlier. There were times when it was more than play—twice, actually, when they'd stomped around in frozen silence—but not once had Lynn contemplated leaving him to finish up alone.

She'd learned something that Saturday morning. She could have an argument with Gabe and still want to end up in his arms.

"Actually," Lynn whispered when he let her up for breath, "that isn't a half-bad job for a novice."

"So I'm a novice, am I? We'll see about that." Lynn was standing barefoot in a fine dusting of saw dust, but that didn't seem to bother Gabe. He lifted her in his arms and deposited her on his bed. He undressed her almost without her being aware of it. A minute later she was touching him, feeling the most exquisite tenderness she'd ever experienced in her life. There was nothing about her he didn't know. He'd gone with her to her parents' house. He had seen her raw edges, just as she'd seen his. She wouldn't have had the courage to let him see those edges if she didn't love him.

And known he loved her.

Gabe lowered himself beside her. His hands were like airy feathers on her body. "Do you remember when we went camping?"

"I remember." Lynn slid her legs down along Gabe's and nibbled lightly at his lower lip. "That's something I'll always remember."

"Why?"

Lynn knew why he was asking. She wasn't afraid of the answer. "Because that's when I told you I loved you. When you said you felt the same."

"Where does it go from here, Lynn?" he asked, but there was no answer until much later. Their lovemaking took her a world away from reality. She couldn't smell the glue used on the paneling, couldn't hear the sound of a motor being tuned up next door. There was nothing except Gabe Updike and the magic he was capable of performing. She lost herself in his strength and goodness, found herself in his tenderness and humanity. They'd been spending most of the past week together at his house. She couldn't remember going back to her place for more than a change of clothes. During that time together, they'd talked, phoned Brook, even sent her parents a picture of the construction site. They went their separate ways during the day, but at night they were together. In Gabe's bed.

A long time later Gabe asked, "Do you want to flip for it? One of us can clean up this mess while the other finds something to eat."

"You cook." Lynn had slipped back into her underwear but had no idea where she'd left her shoes. "I'll get the shop vac."

"Modern women," Gabe grumbled as he headed for the kitchen. "Can't keep them barefoot and pregnant anymore." He turned around, a grin on his face. "At least not pregnant."

Lynn made a motion as if to throw Gabe's hammer at him. "You're a better cook than I am, anyway," she pointed out. "Are you sure about the rose?"

"No rose. What about one of those things they hang from the ceiling that look like a bunch of fuzzy caterpillars?"

For a moment Lynn's mind was a blank. "Do you mean a fern?"

"Yeah." Gabe smiled. "A fern would look good near the paneling, wouldn't it?"

Lynn agreed that it would. "But I think they need attention. They have to be misted, or something."

"Then that's your job. Don't bother me with those details, woman. I have a meal to cook." Gabe exited with a flourish that would have done a Shakespearean actor proud.

Lynn put on the rest of her clothes but gave up on trying to find her shoes. First she swept up most of the sawdust and then finished with the battered shop vac Gabe had supplied. She shook the bedspread and gathered up the tools.

She was heading for the garage with them when she heard Gabe whistling in the kitchen.

Lynn dropped the tools on the nearest chair and crept closer. Gabe had turned the kitchen into more of a mess than necessary for a Thanksgiving dinner, but he obviously enjoyed what he was doing. It was incredible, Lynn thought. Since getting up that morning, they'd had two serious disagreements about how to panel over a rough-finished wall, and yet Gabe was whistling, and her eyes were misting from watching him.

Where do we go from here? he'd asked.

"Gabe? Do you really know how to cook a turkey? I was thinking. Maybe my sister and her husband could come, too."

There was something white, flour or baking mix, dusting his beard. Lynn almost laughed when she first saw it, but when he started to speak, she forgot about it. "Yeah, I know how to cook a turkey. But I'm not going to come over to your apartment and play guest chef."

"That's not what I'm asking." She took a deep breath. The step she was about to take was the biggest she'd ever contemplated. "I'd like to have it here."

"So you can play guest chef's helper?"

"No." It was said. If he picked up on that, everything would be out in the open.

Gabe dropped the spoon he'd been holding and came toward her. "Then what?"

Lynn didn't speak until she was safely in Gabe's arms. "I want to move in with you."

Gabe's reply was a long, shaky sigh. "You mean it?" he asked a minute later.

"It's been a strange week." Lynn knew she was starting somewhere in the middle, but she didn't know how else to do it. "I had so many reasons for living on my own. It was something that had been built into me. At least I thought it had. But Gabe, we fought this morning, and I still wanted to be here.''

''It won't be our last fight. And I can't promise you that it'll always be like this.'' He held her even tighter.

''Do you think I don't know that? We've got the rest of this house to work on.''

''We.''

''Yes, we. A little while ago you asked where we were headed. I'm trying to answer you.''

''You're shaking.'' Gabe ran his lips over Lynn's forehead.

''I always shake when I ask a man to let me move in with him.''

''No second thoughts?'' Gabe pushed her back and stared down at her, giving her nowhere to look but up at him. ''You know what you're asking?''

Lynn nodded. She didn't try to break eye contact. ''We're both the black sheep of our families. We belong together. You asked me what I remembered of our camping trip. There's something else I remember. I felt safe with you there with me. Nothing's ever going to change that feeling.''

''You don't need your own space? I'm sorry, Lynn, but I have to hear your answer.'' Gabe was shaking a little himself, but Lynn chose to ignore that. ''I believe in a lot of sharing.''

''Sharing.'' Lynn sent the word back to Gabe in a mist of breath. ''Take me back to that ghost town, please. There are so many things I want to do with you.''

''Not so fast.'' Gabe's lips were tight, but Lynn detected something dancing in his eyes. ''I'm not going to be a kitchen slave unless there's a payoff for me.''

''A payoff?''

"Yes. You're going to have to make an honest man out of me."

"As in—marriage?"

"As in marriage." Now they were both trembling.

Lynn had her answer. She gave it with her arms, her lips, her heart beating in time with his. "When?" she asked when they finally broke free.

"Tonight. Is that soon enough?"

Laughing, Lynn buried her fingers in Gabe's beard and pulled him down toward her. "Tomorrow. We're going to be busy tonight."

And they were.

Chapter Thirteen

Gabe is never going to believe this, Lynn thought.

Because she'd had to sit outside the judge's chambers for more than half an hour, she was a little irritated when she walked in, but now it was all she could do to keep from breaking out in a silly grin.

"You say it's a pilot program?" Lynn was asking the three men assembled in judge Updike's richly paneled office. "How long a period of time will the funding cover?"

Robert Lonac, the assistant school-system administrator, answered without having to refer to his notes. "Two years. We're fortunate in that respect, since most projects of this type are usually funded for no more than a year, but we've been aware for some time that education for youngsters in detention has been piecemeal at best."

Lynn nodded in agreement. "Particularly for those who will be in a structured situation for a long time. I think it's a marvelous idea, but I'm still not sure how I can help."

"Because you've been there," Judge Updike supplied. He nodded in the direction of Richard Wheeless. "Dick here has been pushing for a tailor-made program for delinquents for years, but in addition to having to secure the necessary funds, we were also looking for input from someone who had the life experience to let us know if we were on the right track."

Lynn still couldn't believe all this was happening. The presence of the director of the county detention facility, in addition to the judge and an educator, couldn't be a figment of her imagination, but that Judge Updike would recommend her was a little too much to fathom. "I'm not a teacher," Lynn pointed out. "I wouldn't be able to give much input into which techniques work and which don't."

"I disagree," Dick Wheeless said. "Lynn, you and I have worked together long enough that we know how each other thinks. I just wish you'd told me about your being dyslexic before."

"I wish I had, too," Lynn could now admit. "But I didn't know you were contemplating changing the focus of the school at the center so it would be geared toward those with learning disabilities."

"Which is the majority of our 'guests.' And even those who don't have learning disabilities aren't going to be harmed by being assimilated into the specialized programs we'll be using."

Lynn stifled a grin. Dick had been speaking social-work jargon for so many years that it was second nature to him now. She turned toward Robert Lonac. "You said your office will be supplying most of the educational material. If you have that, why do you need me?"

"Because we actually have access to more material than we need," Robert explained. "There is more than one strategy being utilized when it comes to educating those with a learning disability. It's the latest bandwagon; everyone seems to be jumping on it. However, not all of the programs are equally effective. We'd like to tap your personal experience. Get it from the horse's mouth, so to speak.

Which approach or approaches do you believe are going to give us the best result?''

Again, Lynn had to shake off the feeling that she was the only one in the room who hadn't forgotten how to speak simple English. But she was being presented with the opportunity of a lifetime—because Judge Updike had recommended her. There was only one answer. ''I'd be delighted to help in any way I can. In fact, what I think I'd like to do is take time to study the material you have and write up my reactions. Ah, what kind of time frame are we looking at?''

When Dick Wheeless reassured her that the program wouldn't get under way for a couple of months, Lynn relaxed. Somehow she'd find time to work certain essential personal matters in with the additional work load. Lynn rose to her feet and shook hands with the men. She deliberately went to the judge last. ''I hope you aren't too busy Saturday night, because you and your wife are invited over for dinner.'' She left before having to explain to the other men why she had a personal relationship with Judge Updike. She'd let him do that.

Since it was already late afternoon, Lynn didn't bother going back to her desk. Instead, she turned in her state car and then drove over to a grocery store. She bought what she'd need for the shrimp casserole she'd been wanting to try and hurried to Gabe's house—their house—to get started on dinner. She'd kicked off her shoes and was elbow deep in sautéed onions when Gabe arrived.

''If that isn't domestic,'' Gabe observed from where he stood at the entrance to the kitchen. ''The little woman cooking dinner.''

Lynn snorted in mock indignation, but that was only a smokescreen for what she was feeling. The man had no right to look so damn sexy. True, his T-shirt looked like a refugee from the ragbag, and grease from some source she didn't want to know about had turned his jeans into a lost cause, but the man inside the clothes was everything she'd ever wanted. "This little woman has some serious talking to do," she said. She walked over to him and reached up for a welcoming kiss. "You smell like a locker room."

Gabe gripped her shoulders and demonstrated the finer points of a real kiss. "My brother smells like a locker room," he pointed out a long minute later. "I smell like a diesel engine."

"It'll never sell." Lynn was thankful that Gabe hadn't released her. How one man's kiss could strip her legs of all their muscle was beyond her, but she wasn't complaining. "Dinner's going to take a little while."

"It wouldn't if you'd spent the day in the kitchen the way you're supposed to." Gabe guided her back to the counter so he could take a closer look at what she was creating. "What do you mean, you have some serious talking to do?"

"We do." Lynn reached for the recipe but didn't attempt to read it. "We have to talk. When are we going to get married?"

"I told you. Tomorrow." Gabe made a grab for a shrimp, but Lynn slapped his hand away.

"That's what you said last week," she pointed out. "But we haven't set a date."

"As I recall, you were waiting to hear what your sister's plans are. Have you talked to her yet?"

Lynn nodded. "I called her after you left this morning. I'm supposed to get back to her this evening. It looks as if it's going to be a toss-up which one of us gets married first."

"Then all we have to do is find a date that doesn't conflict with her plans." This time Gabe succeeded in popping a shrimp into his mouth. "As long as we get this wedding out of the way before the Superbowl, any time is okay by me."

Lynn turned toward Gabe so she could watch his reaction. "There's one more consideration. I'm going to be pretty busy at work for a while."

"Yeah?" Gabe looked confused. "You being promoted or something?"

"Don't I wish. No, but I will be working on a special project that involves your father."

Gabe had been reaching for her, but his hands remained frozen in space. "My father?"

"You know—gray-haired man, wears black robes a lot."

"Don't get cute with me, Lynn Tresca. He isn't working with juvenile cases anymore. What does he have to do with what you're doing?"

Lynn took Gabe's hand and placed it on her shoulder. She could have helped him close his mouth but rather enjoyed seeing the look of disbelief in his face. "Apparently your father is involved in more than I gave him credit for." Briefly she related her meeting in the judge's office. "Gabe?" She didn't try to stop the enthusiasm from rising in her voice. "I've wanted to do something like this for so long. I didn't think I had anything to offer the educational program at the detention center, but when I think of focusing on teens with learning disabilities—Gabe, that's going to reach so many kids."

"You are excited, aren't you?"

"Of course I am." Lynn buried her head against Gabe's chest and wrapped her arms around him. Having a role in what was going to happen was a thrill in itself, but it meant even more because she had someone to share her excitement with. "I wonder—maybe they'll let me sit in on some of the classes."

"You could come in as a guest speaker. You know, exhood makes good."

"Thanks for nothing, fella." Lynn didn't take offense. Because she was secure in Gabe's love, she knew he was happy for her. "It's the chance of a lifetime. I just wish it wasn't happening right now."

Gabe lifted her chin so that she was looking at him. "No, you don't wish that. When something like this comes along you have to jump at it."

"I know. But I really wanted this time to be for us."

"We'll have our time, honey." Gabe's kiss left no doubt in Lynn's mind that he believed what he was saying. "Lynn, we have the rest of our lives together. Besides, maybe you can bring some of that material home and show it to me. I'd like to know what it's all about."

God, she loved him! "You're a good man, Gabe Updike."

"I know. And now, woman, what about dinner?"

While Gabe showered and changed into clean clothes, Lynn finished putting the casserole together and placed it in the oven. She was in the living room, thumbing through the evening paper, when he came up behind her and shook his wet head over her. "Anything exciting in the paper?" he asked.

"There's a good price on dog food. I think I'll pick up a couple of bags for Ranger." Lynn waited until Gabe was sitting beside her and then rested her head against his shoulder. "Have you talked to him about my becoming a part of the scene?"

"I think he's already figured that out. Look, I don't think there's going to be time to move the rest of your things over here until the weekend. Is there anything left at the apartment that you can't live without?"

Lynn had everything she could ever imagine needing in the strength and warmth of the man sitting next to her. She closed her eyes and let the newspaper drop to her lap. During the day she seldom had time to stop and think about the man who'd become so essential to her. When they were together, it was as if she were discovering him all over again every time. Although he would have preferred to slip away somewhere to get married, he understood her need to have their wedding be more than that. Once they'd agreed on that, they'd made the joint decision that Brook should be the one to stand up with Gabe. She wondered if there'd ever be a time when they didn't understand what was going on in each other's head. "Your towels are a disgrace, but I can survive," she finally managed to say.

Gabe groaned. "I can see it coming now. Feminine touches all over the place. The next time I get together here with my foremen, you'll probably serve petits fours and tea."

"Not me." Lynn wrinkled her nose in disgust. "I'm not going to play hostess to any of you characters. That's something else I've been thinking about . . ."

Gabe thought he saw it coming. He knew that his place was masculine with a capital *M*. He didn't blame Lynn for wanting to add a few touches that said a woman now lived here, too, but he wanted her to understand how he felt. "You were thinking about how a living room is no place to conduct business," he answered to ward off having to hear it from her.

"Is that what you thought I was going to say?"

Gabe wasn't fooled. There wasn't anything casual about the way she'd presented her question. "Yes," he answered. "Living rooms are for couches and drapes and coffee tables, not for spreading out a blueprint. That's what you were going to say."

"Wrong." Lynn was still leaning against him, but he could sense the tension in her body. "Gabe, I don't care if this place makes the cover of a decorating magazine. What's important is that it reflects what we are. What I was going to say is do you think you could hire some of your men to come in one day and put in a lawn?''

"You want a lawn?" Gabe had never given that a moment's thought.

"Not all over," Lynn hurried on to say. "But I was looking at the yard the other day. We could organize things so there was an area reserved for the equipment you need, and we could still have a lawn."

A lawn. What she wanted was such a simple thing. Something he wanted to give her. "How about a border next to the house for flowers?" For someone who'd never given his property more than a cursory glance, things were easily falling into place. "It's zoned so I can put up a large garage behind the house. That'd get a lot out of the way."

Lynn jabbed him lightly in the ribs. "Let's not get too carried away. The neighbors wouldn't know what to make of you."

"It might give them the idea to do a little cleaning up of their own." Lynn's elbow was sharp against his side, but he didn't mind. "How long is dinner going to take? I'm starved."

"About a half hour."

"Long enough. I'm not that starved."

"Oh?" Her tone was teasing. "What do you have in mind for killing a half hour?"

"We could step off the boundaries for the lawn." Gabe rose to his feet and pulled Lynn up beside him. "Put in stakes so we could get an idea of how much of a flower garden you need." He reached down and lifted her up in his arms. "Make a list of things like peat moss and grass seed." He started to carry her toward the bedroom. "Get started on a blueprint for the garage." With his foot he kicked the bedroom door closed behind them. He lowered her onto the bed, feeling blessed beyond words. The woman reaching for him was the source of so much happiness, so much that was good. He didn't have the words to tell her that. All he had was his love freely given.

It was given in return.

Lynn was halfway between the real world and the one created on the trail of their lovemaking when the oven timer went off. She took a moment to nuzzle a path from Gabe's beard to his chest and then pushed his heavy arms off her. "This meal has to be eaten right out of the oven or it falls or something." She reached for a lightweight bathrobe, wrapped it around her and picked up her pillow. "Are you going to get up?"

Gabe propped his hands under his head and stared up at the woman he was going to marry. Her hair was pushed off to one side, her cheeks rosy from brushing against his beard. The bathrobe did nothing except stir his desire to see her without it. "Nope."

"Then—" Lynn lifted the pillow over head in a menacing gesture "—you're in for it, fella." Before he could ward off the blow, Lynn brought the pillow down on Gabe's head, hard.

He bellowed and yanked the pillow out of her hands, but by the time he'd pulled it off his face, Lynn was on her way out the door. Gabe pulled on jeans and walked barefoot into the kitchen, where Lynn was removing the dish from the oven. It smelled fantastic. "There may be hope for you yet," he observed as he brought his nose near the rising steam. "We might not have to spend our entire married life in a restaurant."

Over shrimp they settled on a wedding date in three weeks and an alternate date in case Brandy couldn't make the first one. While Gabe cleaned up the kitchen, Lynn dialed her sister's number.

"What are you doing on the twenty-sixth?" Lynn asked.

"I take it I'm coming to your wedding," Brandy said in a businesslike tone that disappeared after the first sentence. "So you really are serious, are you? And with the judge's son yet. Ironic, isn't it?"

"I don't know if ironic's the right word or not, but we're going to invite Gabe's parents, too." Lynn shot a glance in Gabe's direction, but if he heard, he gave no indication. "You're sure you'll be able to make that date? It won't interfere with certain plans of your own?"

"No. Greg's over here now," Brandy explained. "We won't be tying the knot until about two weeks after you. That's what happens when you fall in love with an international businessman. They're always being sent to Europe or some darn place when they're needed to put a ring on a woman's finger." Lynn waited until Brandy was done giggling. "But I've nailed his foot to the floor," Brandy went on. "How about if you and what's-his-name come here to make sure we do this wedding business right. You'd be experienced by then."

Lynn deliberately projected her voice. "What's-his-name and I would love to come to your wedding. I happen to know that putting on monkey suits and standing around all day eating petits fours are among his favorite things to do." When Gabe glared at her, she stuck out her tongue and continued. "I wonder what the folks are going to say when they learn we're both getting married?"

"Have you told them yet?" Brandy's voice was back to being serious.

"No...but I think they've kind of figured out what's going on."

"Tell them. Now," Brandy pressed. "They deserve to know."

Lynn agreed. What she didn't try to explain to her sister
was that she wanted the moment to be special. Their reaction was more important than she was willing to admit. She
cleared up a few points with Brandy and then hung up. Her
smile was a little tentative when she turned toward Gabe.

"Now it's your turn." She handed him the receiver.

"My turn for what?"

"For calling your parents. You *are* going to tell them that
you let some woman trap you, aren't you?"

"Yeah." Gabe wiped his hands on a dish towel before
taking the receiver. "You didn't say anything to the judge
when you saw him today, did you?"

"I told him they were invited over for dinner this weekend, but I didn't tell him we were getting married." Although Lynn was watching Gabe closely, she was unable to
gauge what he was thinking.

"The judge isn't going to want to eat here," Gabe pointed
out.

"He didn't say no."

"He didn't?" Gabe looked genuinely confused. "What
did he say?"

"Nothing. If I remember, I made it more of an order than
an invitation."

Gabe laughed. "You might be the only person in his life
who can get away with that approach. Why don't you call
them?"

Lynn moved around so she could take over the task of
cleaning up the kitchen. "Because it's your turn."

Her logic apparently satisfied Gabe. Although Lynn's
hands were in soapy water, she was concentrating on what
she could hear of the conversation. Gabe started by telling
the judge that he'd heard about the program aimed at
reaching delinquents with learning disabilities. For a moment after that the conversation seemed to bog down. "You

don't have any other plans for Saturday night, do you?'' she heard him ask. "We really would like to have you over for dinner. That's—there's something we need to discuss.''

Gabe glanced over at Lynn. Although she was smiling encouragement at him, it was the other emotion he found in her eyes that propelled him on. What he'd done to deserve love like that, he didn't know. "Lynn and I are getting married the end of the month. It's going to be a small wedding. We'd like to have you there.''

"I wondered if it might be something like that,'' the judge was saying. Gabe heard a small sigh in the background and realized that his mother had been on the extension.

"She's a beautiful person, Gabe,'' his mother was saying. "You're a lucky man.''

"I know I am. You'll come?''

For maybe the first time in years, his mother answered first. "We wouldn't miss it for the world, Gabe. It's what I've always wanted for you.''

Gabe had to speak around something that had lodged itself in his throat. "You're a sentimentalist, Mom.''

"No, I'm not, Gabe. And I'm not a dreamer, either, but your happiness has always been important to me.''

For a moment Gabe railed against the order that ruled in his family, but he wasn't calling to see if a lifetime pattern could be changed. Lynn wanted his parents at their wedding, and because she did, he did, too. "It won't be anything fancy. I'm not even sure where we'll have it.''

"Anywhere as long as it isn't at that house of yours,'' the judge broke in.

Gabe could laugh now. A year ago, even a month ago, he couldn't, but Lynn Tresca had mellowed him in ways he didn't fully understand. "It won't be here,'' he replied "Ranger doesn't like crowds.''

"Me, either," the judge said. "I don't know how Brook can concentrate with all those people staring at him. Did I tell you? We got a letter from Brook last week. He's moving out of that playboy mansion he was in. He's buying a house."

"You don't suppose that means the kid is growing up, do you?" Gabe was, he realized, looking forward to Saturday night. He'd mix the judge a drink and show him the new paneling in the bedroom. If it felt right, he might even tell him about the reason for the oversized wall socket. "Look, why don't you bring the letter when you come? I'm still not convinced that he can write."

"Is Brook coming to the wedding?" his mother asked.

"I hope so," Gabe replied. "I've been trying to reach him for the past couple of days, but if he's moving, that's probably why I haven't been able to get him. We want to put him to work as my best man." As Lynn slid close to him, he wrapped his free arm around her and brushed his lips over the top of her head. "Mom? Do you still have that recipe for chocolate cake? The one with mayonnaise in it? I'm trying to teach Lynn how to cook." He winced as Lynn ground her bare heel into his foot.

"We'll bring it," the judge said. "And why don't you tell Lynn that if she wants to see it, I'll have a copy of the grant proposal made for her. She might like to have some of the background."

"I'm sure she'd be interested," Gabe supplied. "You really think she'll be able to help?"

"Of course. That young woman is nobody's fool, Gabe. She'll know what material will reach those delinquents and what will turn them off. I know we surprised her this afternoon, but as I told her, she's been down in the trenches. The rest of us haven't."

No, we haven't, Gabe thought. He held Lynn tight against him, wondering if he'd always feel this alive around her. The answer came when she slipped her arms around his waist and her breath disturbed the hairs on his chest. "Saturday night, then. Dad, I'll tell Ranger you're coming, and make sure he's on his best behavior."

Lynn took a shaky breath. "Did you hear what you just said?" she whispered.

Because Gabe was concentrating on the feminine warmth blending with his, she had to repeat it before he looked at her. "You called him Dad. I don't think you've ever done that before."

"Not for a long, long time." There was a core there, something Gabe had never felt before, but he needed more than saying the word once. Understanding might come easier after Saturday night. He handed the phone over to Lynn.

She had to look up her parents' phone number. She was double-checking to make sure she'd dialed correctly when her mother picked up the receiver. "It's your daughter," Lynn said. "The one who can never remember your phone number."

"Lynn. Oh, darn, your father is at a meeting. I wish he were home."

"That's all right." Lynn tried to ignore Gabe's toes inching along her instep. "I'm not going to make this long, because we're really running up the long-distance bills tonight, but it looks as if your daughters are following in each other's footsteps."

"What? I don't understand."

She hadn't done that well. Lynn tried again. "I take it my very successful sister has told you that she's getting married."

"Yes, to Greg. Oh, Lynn!"

"Yes." Lynn shut her eyes against a wall of emotion that took her breath away. Her mother was happy for her! Lynn dropped her head to Gabe's chest, not caring what he thought of her tears. "I—Gabe and I are going to do the same thing."

"That's wonderful. Congratulations. Oh, no. I'm not supposed to tell the bride congratulations, am I?"

"That's all right." Now that her world was falling back into place, Lynn regretted that she hadn't taken the drive to Salt Lake City to tell her folks in person. But that would have meant waiting, and she wanted her parents to know the news the same night that Gabe's did. "I'm not a bride yet. I won't be for about three more weeks."

"Three weeks? That's awfully fast, isn't it?"

Lynn didn't know if her mother was thinking it, but she wanted to clear everything up. "It's fast because we don't want to wait, not because we have to. Mom, I've never felt this good about anything in my life before. I want you and Dad to be part of it."

"Of course we will. He'll be so happy. We'd love to see where you're living."

"I'm not so sure about that," Lynn said, laughing. "Let's just say that Gabe's been too busy to do much with his place."

"Let's just say I'm a slob," Gabe said into the receiver before turning his attention back to the task of running his toes upward from Lynn's ankle.

"He isn't really a slob," Lynn continued. She didn't pull away from Gabe. "He does have some rough edges, but you know how it is with men."

"The problem is we can't live without them," her mother said with a laugh. "Are you sure you're going to have everything ready in three weeks?"

Lynn explained that the wedding would be limited to family members. She reassured her mother that Brandy had promised to be her attendant, but when her mother asked her what they were going to do about a honeymoon, she drew a blank. "I have no idea," she admitted. "We haven't talked bout it."

"Don't spend it traveling. That's what your father and I did, and it was a mistake. Go somewhere without a telephone and stay there."

Lynn had never thought of her parents as a couple of newlyweds starting out on their life together, but as the image took life, she was grateful to her mother for saying what she had. "We're open to suggestions. What am I going to wear? You're right. There is a lot to be done, isn't there?"

"We'll get through it, Lynn. Your wedding day is once in a lifetime. We want it to be perfect."

A few minutes later Lynn put down the receiver and buried herself in Gabe's arms. *We*. Her mother had said "we." "I'm so glad they're going to be here," she whispered. "Gabe? What if I hadn't let you talk me into clearing up the past with them?"

"I didn't talk you into anything, honey." Gabe waited until Lynn was looking up at him before continuing. "The time was right for you and your parents. I'm just glad I was there when it happened."

"A wedding." Lynn sighed. "It's really going to happen, isn't it? With our parents and everything."

"Everything." Gabe reached for the receiver. "If I can get a hold of the kid, that is. Why don't you go put on some clothes or something while I call him? Otherwise, I'm going to get distracted, and we'll never get the paper read."

Lynn disappeared into the bedroom. She walked without thinking toward the dresser that was now filled with her things. She picked out a T-shirt but stopped short of slipping it on. She had no interest in reading the paper. She stretched out on the bed and rested her head on the pillow, waiting.

Five minutes later Gabe walked into the room. "What do you think of Los Angeles?"

Lynn didn't open her eyes. "For what?"

"For a honeymoon. Brook wants us to see his place. Something about Rachael having it furnished by then. We're going to pull a swap. He wants to show her Denver while we go stay at his place. We'll be alone. You didn't get dressed."

"You noticed."

Gabe lowered himself onto the bed. "There's one thing you're going to have to get straight, woman." His hands were on the tie holding her robe in place. "When I tell my women to get dressed, I expect them to obey." A gentle tug and Lynn felt cool air on her breasts.

She opened her eyes and reached for him. "That isn't dressed."

"You noticed."

Harlequin American Romance

COMING NEXT MONTH

#165 LE CLUB by Beverly Sommers

Wynn Ransome was Le Club's most eligible male, high praise considering the clientele of the chic Manhattan health spot. Terry Caputo was there to catch a murderer. They met on the exercise bikes, and Wynn made his first move. As duty warred with destiny, Terry feared her stakeout was about to become a date.

#166 THE DEVLIN DARE by Cathy Gillen Thacker

Marine boot camp did strange things to people. Mollie Devlin thought she'd taken leave of her senses. When her bunk buddy dared her to make a conquest of dynamic Dave Talmadge, Mollie set out to win Dave's heart. Unfortunately, she never stopped to consider the dangerous consequences.

#167 AFTER THE STORM by Rebecca Flanders

Every time Kevin breezed into his hometown, he demolished Kate's groceries and ran up her phone bill, proving that tv's ultimate sex symbol was actually the ultimate nuisance. Until one night when the wind began to roar through Victoria Bend, Mississippi, and there was only Kevin to teach Kate a lesson in heroism and once-in-a-lifetime love.

#168 OPPOSITES ATTRACT by Karen Pershing

Could opposites attract? The answer was no. But could opposites get along? For Carrie the answer was the same. She simply didn't want to get involved with a man who wore impeccable three-piece suits. But no matter how hard Carrie tried to convince herself of that, Max tried even harder to create the impossible.

HARLEQUIN HISTORICAL

Explore love with Harlequin in the Middle
Ages, the Renaissance, in the Regency, the
Victorian and other eras.

Relive within these books the endless ages of
romance, set against authentic historical
backgrounds. Two new historical love stories
published each month.

HIST-A-1